AFTER ALL

LATITUDE & LONGING
BOOK THREE

BRYCE OAKLEY

Edited by Heather Flournoy

Cover Design by Bryce Oakley

ALSO BY BRYCE OAKLEY

The Adventurers

Something Far Away and Happy

Against The Grain

Never Mine

Every Version

Latitude & Longing

One Last Run

Shift the Tide

After All

Holiday Romances

Most Wonderful

All Aglow

Ghosted Christmas Past

The Snowy Springs Holiday Romances

Baking Spirits Bright

Rebel Without A Claus

The Kaleidoscope Album

Undone

Bewilder

Midnight

Bloom

Revel

The Kaleidoscope Album Box Set

CONTENTS

For the whole damn group chat.

CHAPTER 1

MAGGIE

THE MIRROR WAS CROOKED AGAIN.

Maggie stepped back, tilted her head, then stepped forward and nudged the brass frame slightly to the left. The sunlight from the front windows caught the beveled edge and flared across the dusty floor of Found & Chosen, turning the whole room momentarily golden.

The shop looked like a curated dreamscape — part vintage showroom, part botanical lounge, part cabinet of curiosities. It smelled like old books and new soil, and looked like a flea market had made out with a greenhouse and then gone to therapy. On any given day, customers could find a Depression-era butter dish beside a hand-painted tarot deck, or a Victorian fainting couch draped with a handwoven blanket. Some customers came for the fiddle-leaf figs, some came for the feeling, as though maybe, just maybe, they were about to stumble across exactly the thing they didn't know they needed.

Old apothecary cabinets lined one wall, filled with antique postcards, brass keys, and ceramic thimbles. Cascading pothos and sleepy monstera plants softened the hard lines of midcentury credenzas and art deco bar carts. The scent of lemon balm and cedar hung in the air, thanks to the incense Colette insisted on burning near the register.

"Just admit defeat," Colette called from the counter, where she was reorganizing a display of hand-thrown mugs glazed in smoky lavender. "That mirror hates you."

Maggie stuck out her tongue. "Or maybe it's just cursed."

Colette raised a brow over her tortoiseshell glasses. She had the kind of effortless cool Maggie had always admired — messy bun, oversized cardigan even in the late Texas summer, dark jeans rolled at the ankle, and red lipstick that somehow never smudged. "Do you think that makes it more or less valuable?"

"Definitely more, are you kidding?" Maggie pushed a lock of blonde hair behind her ear and crossed back toward the display table, adjusting a linen runner that had bunched. Her reflection in the shop's curved windows caught her off guard — she looked so tired. Even her twelve-step skin care routine had lost its magic, apparently. Maybe she should start googling whatever Lindsay had done to her face.

The shop was quiet this Thursday morning, just the hum of the ceiling fans and the occasional creak from the wood-plank floors. Outside, the street traffic was sparse. A couple wandered past, hand in hand.

"Anything good come in from the estate haul?" she asked, folding a stack of vintage tea towels.

Colette perked up. "Couple of hideous lamp bases, a box of untouched wedding china, and one very eccentric swan-shaped dish that I think would be a perfect tampon holder for the bathroom."

Maggie blinked. "A what?"

"You heard me. It's porcelain. Very detailed. I'm naming it Tamp-swan."

"That's horrifying." Maggie shook her head. "Swans are so pretentious."

"Pretentious? They're just so pretty."

"Yeah, and they know it," Maggie insisted. "The worst of the waterfowl by far."

Colette shrugged. "It's going in the bathroom next to the flamingo soap dish. Don't fight me."

Maggie gave a reluctant laugh. "There's a 'Don't Flock in the Bathroom' cross-stitch pattern in our future. My friend Danica could whip it up on her next night shift, if we need."

Colette grinned, then her expression turned thoughtful as she continued to watch Maggie.

A customer walked in, and Maggie quickly turned away, grateful for any excuse to get away from the open invitation in her friend's face.

Maggie shook her head, immediately knowing what that look meant. Colette was her best friend in Austin, and Maggie had begged to help at Found & Chosen when Rosie started preschool last spring. She'd been "volunteering" in her friend's shop ever since, just to get out of the house and feel like she had a purpose again.

It had been about six months since she and Gwen said the word out loud: separated. Not in court. Not even officially. When Gwen was home, she slept in the guest room. The kids accepted it like they accepted all the small weirdnesses of adulthood — with questions that trailed off when the answers got vague. Mommy has her own room now. That was enough for them.

Gwen wasn't home often anymore. Her travel schedule for work had instantly filled up, and Maggie felt a mixture of disappointment and relief whenever she checked their shared calendar and saw another trip booked. Their lives still ran in tandem, like parallel train tracks — close, but not touching.

Now it was late August, and school was back. Jude and Arlo, her seven-year-old twins, had started second grade, while Rosie — five, stubborn, and firmly anti-pants — marched off to kindergarten. Maggie had never been more grateful for the excuse to get out of the house for weird morning hours at the shop. She had purpose again, and that felt good.

And as for Colette being her only friend who knew about the separation... well, most of the time it was fine, but sometimes Colette started giving her those looks. The "I'm here if you need to talk because you're clearly miserable" looks.

Those looks were part of why she told herself she hadn't told her best friends from college yet.

Between Gwen's endless work trips and Maggie's well-timed excuses — bad Wi-Fi, late school pickups, feigned exhaustion — the truth had stayed neatly off-camera. The group was too busy with spreadsheets and engagement rings to notice.

She didn't want to ruin the dynamics. Didn't want to draw attention. Didn't want Danica and Pete's swiftly approaching bachelorette trip and upcoming nuptials to turn into a pity party.

But really?

Saying it out loud made it real.

She still loved Gwen.

And that was the hardest part.

She loved Gwen's crooked smile and the way her short curls always stuck up at weird angles in the morning. She loved her deep voice and quiet humor, the way she built LEGO castles with the boys and let Rosie brush her hair for twenty minutes at night while humming the song from the Rapunzel movie without complaint.

But she also remembered... everything else. The silent way Gwen had dealt with the grief of terminating their pregnancy, then Maggie's mom. Gwen hadn't been there. She'd poured herself into work. Came home late. Said, "What do you need from me?" and probably meant it, but didn't just take action.

The grief hadn't broken Maggie. Loneliness had.

Her phone buzzed. A text from Kiera.

KIERA

Vegas itinerary incoming 💃 Hope you're ready for tequila shots and strippers.

MAGGIE

Hell yes. I've been wanting to see these "pole fitness" moves for a while now.

KIERA

I am not the stripper.

MAGGIE

I'm changing my RSVP to no, then.

KIERA

I'm telling Gwen you're harassing me.

A wave of guilt washed over Maggie, and she locked her phone.

Colette was watching her again.

"Oh, I made a note of it on the whiteboard calendar, but I wanted to just remind you I'll be in Vegas for my friends' bachelorette the weekend after next," Maggie said.

"Yeah, I remember. The friends who don't know about..." Colette gestured vaguely.

"Yeah."

"I'm assuming Gwen's not coming to that?" Colette asked.

Maggie smirked. "Gwen hasn't come on a trip yet. I think she's technically out of town that weekend, so I've already set her mom up for childcare. She's not invited or anything."

"It's weird that you go on trips with two couples and you don't get to bring your partner," Colette said.

Maggie shrugged. "Gwen didn't go to college with us. I feel like it would be weirder if she came."

Colette quirked a brow but said nothing.

Maggie hadn't told Kiera and Danica. Or Izzy. Or Pete. Not because she wanted to lie.

Only because she didn't know how to explain what it meant to still love someone who hadn't been there when it counted. Someone who was now just... not present. Like a shadow on the wall. Familiar, but faded.

Colette rounded the counter and leaned against it. "You should tell them."

"Believe me, it wouldn't be the weirdest secret someone has kept in our group," Maggie said with a forced grin. "Besides, who wants the sad divorced lady at their bachelorette party? Isn't that all about—"

"Being single and celebrating it?" Colette said. "Which is why a joint bachelorette party is so weird to me."

"God, you are so straight sometimes," Maggie said, shaking her head.

Colette laughed and gave her a strange look, but again, didn't say anything.

She spent the next few hours rearranging displays, swapping out a set of ochre throw pillows a customer had ordered online and staging a new "eccentric kitchen essentials" shelf featuring a charcuterie board in the shape of a middle finger.

After, she slipped out the back door and into the hot afternoon air, letting it press against her like a warm wall. Her car was waiting in the small lot behind the shop, already baking. She climbed in, started the engine, and turned the AC on full blast. Then she hit the call button. Colette was right. She had to just be honest with her friends.

"Well, hello," came Kiera's cheerful answer. "I know what you're going to ask, and yes, the penis straws have already been ordered."

"Perfect. I'd expect nothing less." Maggie smiled but

didn't respond right away. Her eyes were on the traffic, but her thoughts were somewhere else entirely.

"You okay?" Kiera asked, softer now.

"Yeah," Maggie said, too fast. "Excited for a weekend of debauchery, obviously." The trip was coming up quick — just over a week and a half away.

"Uh-huh." Kiera didn't push, but Maggie could practically hear her raised eyebrow through the phone.

This was it. This was the moment she could tell Kiera. Her mouth went dry, and she drummed her fingers on the steering wheel. "Sorry, I've been swamped with the shop," Maggie added.

"How can you be swamped with a volunteer job in a shop you don't own?" Kiera asked with a laugh.

"I have never half-assed anything," Maggie said.

"Nope. Full-ass Maggie."

"Coincidentally, that was also my nickname in high school."

"You're ridiculous," Kiera said.

Maggie swallowed again. Her courage was fading fast. "Anyway, I'll be there for the trip. Just let me know what you need."

"Expect chaos. Possibly matching jumpsuits."

Maggie winced. "If I end up on TikTok, I'm suing."

"No promises," Kiera said. "Wanna FaceTime later tonight and go over the last of the details?"

"Sure. I miss your gorgeous smile," Maggie said. Maybe she'd be braver tonight. Maybe she'd have a glass of wine and practice what she was going to say in the mirror.

"Sure. Izzy would love that, too. Maybe we can nail down the last of the details. I have a spreadsheet that could rival Danica's."

"Feel free to keep that to yourself," Maggie said. "Okay, talk later?"

"Love you, Mags."

Maggie hesitated, then said, "Love you too."

She hung up and let her hand linger on the phone. Then she turned onto the access road toward the kids' school and let herself slip comfortably back into mom mode.

CHAPTER 2

THE RENDERING TOOK UP MOST OF THE WALL. TWENTY-THREE acres of glossy, full-color ambition — glass towers, rooftop gardens, sun-drenched promenades where a neighborhood used to be. Gwen studied it from across the room, arms crossed, teeth worrying the inside of her cheek.

Her Denver office was a disaster and not the creative kind. Drafting tools and take-out containers shared space with a half-finished coffee she didn't remember ordering. She stepped closer to the wall display, tapping at her tablet, adjusting the angle of a shaded overhang by exactly one degree.

Still wrong.

She zoomed in on the drone overlay beneath the rendering — grainy and real. The neighborhood didn't look like much from above, but Gwen had taken a liking to it immediately. Trees that didn't line up, buildings too stubborn to crumble in a pretty way. Kids standing outside the laundromat that smelled like lavender detergent. The taqueria with a mural of a girl with wings and a busted halo. She'd taken a picture and posted it to her Instagram story earlier that day.

Now it was a dotted parcel on a map. A zone to be cleared. A checkbox between her and the title she'd been chasing for five years.

Principal Architect.

A role that meant prestige. Stability. A stake in the future of the firm. She'd done everything right — nailed timelines, delivered elegant solutions, managed teams without stepping on egos. She was known for clean design, quiet precision. Vision.

But vision didn't always close the deal. Not like the bold ones did. The architects who schmoozed, who pitched big even when they didn't have the details. The ones who didn't flinch at compromise if it meant the numbers looked right.

Gwen didn't schmooze. She didn't charm her way into contracts or smooth over city council resistance with glad-handing and thin promises. She cared too much. About history. About context. About the story a place told before she ever touched it.

"Jesus, Gwen," Melinda said from the door. "Blink twice if the rendering's holding you hostage."

Gwen startled slightly, spinning around. "Just refining the ingress flow on the south pedestrian axis."

Melinda raised an eyebrow. "You've got ingress coming out your ears."

Melinda, with her glossy waves and sharp blazers, always looked like she'd stepped out of a style editorial. She had a polished charm, quiet but commanding, and a smile that made people agree with her even before she said anything. As the firm's Design Director, she was both mentor and gate-keeper, the person whose praise meant something, and whose silence meant more.

"I'm fine," Gwen said, brushing past her to grab a

different stylus from the cup on her desk. She hated when her voice sounded that clipped.

"I know it's hard to be out of the Austin office for so long, but you skipped lunch again?"

"I wasn't hungry." Gwen tapped her pen against the edge of her tablet, adjusting the site flow again, even though it didn't need it.

"Is it the pitch? Or the politics?" Melinda's tone softened. "Because if it's the project, you should say something. No one wants this to wreck you."

"It's not wrecking me," Gwen said, too fast.

Melinda stepped inside now, crossing the office with her usual quiet confidence. She had that uncanny ability to read people like specs — systematically, patiently, until something gave way.

"You've been here every morning before seven. I don't think I've seen you take a full lunch break all week. You answered a client email at two a.m."

"No, I didn't." Damn. She thought she'd scheduled that for seven.

Melinda raised her eyebrows. "Gwen."

Gwen exhaled, looking down at her tablet. "I just want it to be good."

"It is good. That's not the issue. The issue is whether you're going to run yourself absolutely ragged and then be of no use to me," Melinda said, though her expression carried warmth.

Gwen's phone buzzed, distracting her. A text popped up from Izzy.

IZZY

Hey, are you in town?! I just saw your IG story.

Gwen nearly flinched.

Another message appeared before she could swipe it away.

IZZY

Come meet us at happy hour this afternoon!

Melinda's eyebrows rose. "I'm firing you."

Gwen's entire body went stock-still. "Wh-what?"

"Just for the afternoon. Go away. Get out of my sight," Melinda said. "Go to happy hour with your friends."

"Oh, they're actually just my wife's friends," Gwen said, cheeks heating with relief and embarrassment.

"Go. Or I really will fire you," Melinda said, pushing Gwen's phone toward her with perfectly manicured nails. "And I want a picture for proof or I'm putting you on a PIP."

Gwen rolled her eyes. "You can't do that. That's a workplace lawsuit waiting to happen."

Melinda quirked an eyebrow. "I can, and I will."

And judging by Melinda's tone, Gwen didn't want to push further.

GWEN PULLED up to the brewery wearing the wrong outfit — tailored trousers, a button-up, and the wrong shoes for gravel. The late-afternoon sun was still warm despite the crispness in the air. Denver in late summer: blue skies, brown grass, and a patio full of people sweating in flannel while pretending to enjoy IPAs.

She spotted them immediately at a long picnic table under a yellow umbrella. Izzy waved, already halfway through a pint, her laptop still open next to Pete's. Kiera sipped something in a plastic cup and looked pleasantly exhausted, hair pulled into a loose bun and a lanyard still around her neck. Danica arrived just after Gwen, still in scrubs, pulling her hospital badge off her top.

The group seemed already mid-conversation, laptops pushed aside for now. Gwen gave a nervous wave.

"Look what the wind blew in," Izzy said, standing to give Gwen a one-armed hug. "You clean up nice."

"I came from work."

"What a nice surprise," Kiera said, next in line for a hug.

Izzy smirked. "Your aura is very 'competent lesbian in charge of zoning laws.'"

"Close enough," Gwen said, sitting down at the end of the bench. Her back tensed automatically — these weren't really her people. They were Maggie's.

Danica leaned in to give her shoulder a squeeze. "I'm so happy we stalked you victoriously."

"Want a beer?" Pete asked, standing from the table.

"I'll take anything normal," Gwen said with a tight smile.

"Define normal," Danica said.

"Nothing sour, pink, or bitter."

"Wise words to live by," Izzy joked, nodding. "Grab her the honey wheat."

"Sounds perfect," Gwen confirmed.

"Wait, wait, you can't leave us hanging. *What* was the culprit of the weird smell in your car?" Izzy asked, turning back to Pete.

"A fermented juice box," Pete said with a frown. "I think it must have been Quinn's."

Gwen cringed. "One time I found Rosie's bottle of milk under the front seat way too late. I swear it was sentient and begging for death."

Kiera shook her head. "That is a smell that really stays with you."

Pete and Danica took everyone's beer orders and went inside.

Kiera leaned forward, resting her chin on her hand. "Okay. We need to talk bachelorette plans."

Izzy groaned. "Can we not do this sober?"

"You're on your second beer," Kiera pointed out.

"Exactly."

Gwen shrugged, feeling instantly awkward. Maggie had mentioned the trip, but Gwen knew Maggie had been keeping their separation quiet from the group while Pete and Danica were wedding planning.

"I'm sure you'll all find increasingly hilarious ways to torture Pete and Danica," Gwen said with a forced smile. She just had to make it through one beer and then she could leave. She wondered how long was a polite amount of time before she could ask the group for a selfie to send to Melinda.

Izzy tilted her head. "Why do you say that like you're not coming?"

Gwen blinked. She opened her mouth, then closed it, not sure what to say.

"We explicitly told Maggie you were coming this time," Kiera said, her tone sliding into her authoritative teacher voice.

Gwen's pulse lurched, adrenaline spiking like she'd missed a step on a staircase. She kept her face carefully blank, but her fingers curled around the edge of the bench. Heat bloomed behind her ears, spreading down her neck in a slow flush. She stared at the condensation on Izzy's glass, weighing her options. Lie? Deflect? Laugh it off? The silence stretched a beat too long. The hum of the patio and the clink of glasses grew unbearably loud.

"I'm so sorry, not this time. Someone's got to wrangle the Terror Trio at home," she finally said, shrugging.

Izzy's eyebrows knit as she studied Gwen's face.

"Maggie mentioned your mom was watching the kids?" Kiera asked. "Do you want me to call her?"

Gwen's panic flickered visibly before Kiera smiled sweetly.

"I'm kidding," Kiera said. "Mostly. But really, I will call her."

"Who are we calling?" Danica asked, sitting back down beside Kiera. Pete took the seat next to Gwen, passing her a very normal-looking beer.

"Gwen can't come to the bach party," Kiera said.

Four sets of eyes locked on Gwen. Especially Izzy's — sharp, unblinking. Gwen had always avoided being on the receiving end of that stare. Now she felt sweat prickle at her hairline. "I'm so sorry," she repeated. "Kids, you know?"

Izzy gasped. "No, no. You *have* to come. You're half the reason we even believe in love."

Danica added, "Seriously, we'll figure out childcare. Or bring them, I don't care. I'll make a spreadsheet. Please say yes."

Pete leaned in, eyes gleaming. "Gwen. Come on. You're the most stable person we know. This party needs grounding energy."

Gwen hesitated, heart thudding. They didn't know. About the separation. About Maggie.

And Maggie didn't know she was at this happy hour.

Pete cleared her throat. "I think we'd better get the boss on the case," she said, already pulling out her phone.

Gwen panicked. "Wait, who is—"

An old picture of a silly, nineteen-year-old Maggie popped up on the screen, eyeliner smudged and wrapped in a blanket scarf. It must have been a college photo. Gwen's chest squeezed at the image, at the memory of what Maggie had been like at twenty-three, when they'd met in grad school. So vibrant, like the sun glowed directly out of her skin.

When Maggie answered the video call, her expression was distracted, like she'd picked up without checking who was calling. Her eyes flicked over the screen and landed on Gwen — then widened slightly.

She looked completely different. Pale, drained, tired. Still stunning, just *different* now. Her lips parted in surprise. Gwen wasn't supposed to be here. Not like this.

"Maggie," Pete crowed. "Guess who just agreed to come to Vegas?"

Maggie blinked. "I — what?"

"I did not say that," Gwen said, holding up her hands like she was under siege.

"She's in," Kiera said triumphantly.

"Oh. Great," Maggie said, her voice catching before she smiled too quickly. "That's great."

Gwen's cheeks burned. "Guys. No. I have to watch—"

"Maggie, who's watching the kids while you're both in Vegas with us?" Danica asked the phone screen, shooting a mischievous grin toward Gwen.

Izzy's gaze never wavered. Gwen resisted the urge to kick her under the table.

"Uh, I don't know. Gwen, your... mom, I assume?" Maggie asked, and Pete turned the screen toward Gwen in time for her to see Maggie take a massive gulp of wine.

Gwen's eyes widened in a desperate plea for understanding, but Maggie kept a forced smile. "I want it on the record that this was not—"

Pete whipped the phone back toward herself. "I'm so excited to have both of you at our bachelorette party. It really means so much to have you there, given you're our favorite married couple and we really look up to your relationship."

Maggie stuttered, and Gwen glared down into her drink. Pete was laying it on thick, and Gwen's cheeks burned with frustration and shame.

Maggie made a quick excuse to end the call, and as soon as Pete hit the red button, she and Danica high-fived.

"You're coming," Pete announced triumphantly. "Confirmed!"

"I knew we'd figure out a way," Danica said, practically bouncing. "We need a room with a hot tub."

"We need three rooms in the suite. And matching silk

robes. And Gwen, you're doing pole dancing lessons with us. Nonnegotiable," Kiera added.

"Gwen, what's your karaoke song?" Danica asked.

"Y'all," Gwen said weakly, trying to interrupt the tidal wave of enthusiasm. "I still haven't said yes."

"You didn't say no," Izzy replied, voice sharp with amusement.

Gwen's mouth opened and closed. She glanced down at her drink like the beer might offer an escape hatch. All of them were smiling. All of them wanted her there.

She didn't know if she wanted to go. She didn't know if she could.

But watching their joy — seeing Maggie's tired face on the video screen, listening to the way they already counted her in the plans — something cracked open in her chest.

"Okay," she said. "I'll try to figure out things with my mom, but I make absolutely no promises."

There was still a way to backtrack, to change her mind quietly before flights were booked and deposits locked in. She hadn't actually committed. Not really. She could still find an excuse, she told herself. Something believable. Something that wouldn't make Maggie hate her.

But even as she thought it, she knew the damage had already been done.

CHAPTER 3

MAGGIE

To say Maggie was upset was an understatement.

Maggie. Was. Pissed.

She'd spent the better part of the past fifteen hours fuming, positively enraged that Gwen had put them in such an awkward position. Why had Gwen even met up with her friends at all? Why hadn't she just said she couldn't come? Why did she have the audacity to look so gorgeous sitting at a brewery picnic table, her top two shirt buttons undone and her hair tousled?

Wait, no. She was getting sidetracked.

Maggie was furious, and she was going to flip a table in the only place where she let her guard down anymore: their couples therapist's office.

Virtually, of course, given that Gwen was still in Denver. Dr. Elowen had given them the option of telehealth appointments early on, and they were useful for when Gwen was traveling — which was always — or when Maggie couldn't stand the idea of sitting in the same quiet room together — which was growing more often.

The video call window blinked to life on Maggie's laptop, and there she was: Dr. Elowen's serene office, all soft sage and warm lamplight. Even over Zoom, it still managed to look like the set of a very gentle television show about feelings, not a room where Maggie had cried dozens of times over the past six months, both virtually and on that stupidly soft greige couch.

Maggie sat rigidly in her chair, arms crossed so tightly they were starting to go numb. Her mouth was tight. Her jaw ached. Her camera was slightly tilted, casting shadows across her face, but she didn't fix it. She didn't want to look polished. Not today.

Gwen's square popped into place a few seconds later. She looked freshly showered, hair still damp and pushed back, the silvery strands at her temple highlighted against her dark locks. Ugh, Gwen even made aging look good.

No. Focus. Stay mad, she told herself.

Pete's voice at the brewery still echoed in Maggie's ears. *"Guess who just agreed to come to Vegas?"*

And there it was. The rage.

Dr. Elowen gave her usual soft greeting. "Good morning, Maggie. Gwen. I'm glad you both made time this morning."

Gwen nodded. "Good morning."

Maggie didn't say anything.

"Maggie," Dr. Elowen said, not unkindly, "you look like something's sitting heavy. Want to start today by sharing what's there?"

She let out a short breath. "Gwen is crashing my friends' bachelorette party. She said yes. To the bachelorette party. Last night, on a call with everyone. Didn't even hesitate."

Gwen shifted in her square. "I didn't want to be the one to tell them the truth about us. I didn't want to make a scene."

Maggie turned, eyes sharp. "You *were* the scene."

Dr. Elowen's eyebrows raised. "All right, let's unpack this from the beginning. Gwen, would you like to start?"

As Gwen recounted being invited to the brewery, then peer-pressured into agreeing, Maggie couldn't help rolling her eyes.

Dr. Elowen's pen paused mid-note. "Gwen, tell me what motivated that decision."

"I panicked. I didn't want to derail the whole group. They all started in about how we're their favorite married couple, and I just felt so complicit in this lie. I didn't want to be the one to break it open."

Maggie let out a bitter laugh. "There were plenty of other choices here, and you skipped straight toward the most difficult one."

"Isn't that what you've been doing?" Gwen's voice was quiet but steady.

Maggie's jaw dropped, and Gwen held her stare even through the screen. "Wh—"

Dr. Elowen held up a hand. "Let's pause and recenter. Maggie, what was it about Gwen's choice that felt so upsetting?"

Maggie blinked fast, like that might slow the heat rising behind her eyes. "Because I was blindsided."

Dr. Elowen nodded. "So there's anger in being surprised from both sides. Justified, I think. And underneath it, maybe hurt?"

Maggie didn't answer, but her throat tightened. Angry tears welled in the corners of her eyes.

Dr. Elowen shifted. "Maggie, what did it feel like when Gwen said you made her complicit in a lie?"

Maggie exhaled slowly. She briefly considered crossing her arms and not answering at all. Instead, she twisted the edge of her shirt in her hands. "I don't know. I'm still considering that."

Dr. Elowen looked between them. "You're both holding a lot of silence right now. But silence has its own weight. What would it mean to be honest with the people around you? With your friends?"

Maggie's heart thudded. "I haven't told them because if I do, it'll take over everything, Danica's and Pete's wedding planning, Izzy and Kiera just got engaged. I was going to tell them, eventually. I just don't want to be the sad subplot in their big weekend."

Dr. Elowen made a sound of acknowledgment. "You're worried about inconveniencing your friends, yes, but also their perception of you. What do you think is your friends' real perception of you?"

"You heard Gwen. They were all talking about how they look up to us as their favorite married couple." Tears streamed down Maggie's cheeks in earnest now.

"I hear you saying you think your friends see your marriage as perfect, and you're not ready to let that facade go just yet?" Dr. Elowen's voice had taken on a soft, coaxing sound.

Gwen was quiet, but her expression crumpled slightly at that.

Dr. Elowen paused, then looked thoughtful. "Telling your friends the truth doesn't have to feel like admitting failure. It could mean admitting that you're in a season of change. That you're trying to do something hard. That honesty doesn't have to be a final chapter. It can just be the next page. None of that is a weakness, Maggie."

Maggie looked away, toward the sliver of backyard visible through the window. The crepe myrtle bloomed stubbornly in the heat. "I don't know how to do that. Without breaking something."

"What isn't broken already?" Gwen asked quietly.

The words sat between them like a shard of glass.

Dr. Elowen let the silence stretch. Then: "So. Do you continue the lie? Or do you make space for a more complicated truth? One that might hurt but might also let you breathe again?"

Maggie hated how much she wanted that. The breathing. The clarity. The relief of saying, out loud, what she said in her head every night: *This isn't working. We're not okay. I don't know if we'll make it.*

Dr. Elowen's voice came soft but steady. "You don't have to make a decision about your marriage today. But you can decide whether you want to keep pretending. Or whether it's time to let people see where you really are. Secrets are so heavy to carry alone."

Maggie swallowed. "What if where we are is just... lost?"

Dr. Elowen smiled faintly. "Then maybe the next step is making a decision."

Maggie stared at the screen. At Gwen. At herself, that tiny square of herself. And for the first time in a long time, she felt something shift.

Not fixed. Not healed. But maybe ready to try.

"Okay," she said softly. "I'll think about telling them. About starting with the truth."

Dr. Elowen nodded. "That's all I ask. The next honest step."

WHAT SEEMED simple in therapy rarely had a way of remaining simple. *Just tell your friends*, Dr. Elowen had said. How hard could it be to just be honest?

The conversation with Dr. Elowen had left her feeling like she'd been emotionally sandblasted. Too much rawness, not enough buffer. All this talk about choices — decisions, action. Maggie made decisions all day long. For the shop. For the kids. For Gwen, more than half the time. Her life was a one-woman circus act of to-do lists, quick pivots, and keeping fragile things from breaking.

She wasn't indecisive. She was just tired.

She got through the rest of the day spinning ways the conversation could go in her head. She'd call Kiera. FaceTime her. No, call. It'd be better not to see her face. Or should it be Izzy? Something about the earnest, calm way Izzy looked at her, held her through her grief... had done so twice now. Maybe she'd better tell Kiera and Izzy at the same time. She texted them while folding laundry after dinner, asking if they were around and free for a chat.

"Mama, bath time!" Rosie cannonballed into her legs, squealing as Jude chased after her, while Arlo buzzed down the hallway in sock feet, yelling something about an alien sighting in the laundry room.

"Do you think you got more avocado in your mouth or your hair tonight?" Maggie teased.

Rosie lifted a hand to her hair, then wrinkled her nose in a mischievous smile. "Maybe my hair."

"Let's take a bath in Mama's bathroom, far away from those pesky alien invaders in the laundry room," Maggie suggested, reaching to corral the boys upstairs with her.

After a particularly chaotic bath time where Jude showed off his newfound passion for singing the chorus of "Yellow Submarine" thirty-seven times, she let the boys pick out pajamas while she brushed Rosie's hair, leaning in to press her nose against the gentle scent of watermelon shampoo.

Most days, she didn't feel like she was good enough at anything, but here? She never had to question that this was exactly where she belonged.

They all crammed into Rosie's bed to read a chapter of *Fantastic Mr. Fox*, then both boys separated into their own bedrooms. She wished everyone good night and had that familiar, bittersweet squeeze in her chest of feeling simultaneously grateful for the break and missing her kids already.

She opened the door to her office, which had become more of a kid's storage room for now, to track down a button that she had to sew back onto Jude's pants. Once, she'd spent hours in this room, making art with abandon. Going to grad school for art history and criticism had sucked a lot of the joy out of creating for the sake of creating, and having less time to be by herself meant having the actual energy for projects was rare. She'd never tell Gwen that she was jealous of Gwen's hours every day to think only of her own projects — when was the last time Maggie had that kind of freedom? The privilege to stay home with the kids was just that — a privilege — and she recognized that she was lucky to be able to do so, but it came with its own trade-offs in self-actualization. One reason she'd been stalling the divorce was that she selfishly couldn't envision *not* being home with the kids, and how did she and Gwen reconcile that?

Dozens of half-finished projects sat around the room, mostly for the kids' sensory bins or costumes or random ideas she'd hyperfixated on. She opened a drawer and found the button she was looking for, then walked out of the room without looking back.

She escaped to the back patio with her phone. She didn't bother with a drink. Just needed air, a few minutes of quiet, and the illusion that her life was something she could still control. The summer heat clung to her skin even after sunset, the air thick with humidity and the scent of crepe myrtles and grilling meat from a neighbor's yard. Cicadas screamed from the live oaks overhead, and the patio chair creaked as she sat, letting the warmth of the cushion seep into her legs. Somewhere in the distance, a dog barked and a screen door slammed. The night had that distinct Austin texture — soft and slow and sticky.

She dialed Kiera, hoping this conversation wouldn't feel as awkward as their last.

"The penis straws are delayed in transit, but I think we'll still be okay," Kiera said as soon as her face popped onto the screen.

"Well, hello to you, too. What's the glitter cannon status?" Maggie asked, stalling uneasily.

"Oh, we're saving that for the last night. In case Danica tries to bail. Or Pete does. We're an equal-opportunity disaster prevention unit."

Izzy's face popped into frame. "Disaster? Did someone say my name?"

Maggie laughed. "Hey, Izzy."

"And guess who else is here?" Kiera tilted the camera.

Danica and Pete appeared on screen, lounging on a couch with identical wineglasses and a chaotic energy that screamed sleepover from hell — in the best way.

"Hey," Maggie said, her broad smile slipping firmly into place like a mask. "Do y'all just hang out, like, all the time now?"

"We watch an episode of *Outlander* every Friday night," Danica explained. "We're finally in Season Three."

Maggie rolled her eyes. "Nerds."

Kiera launched into planning mode. "Okay, so, next Friday night is the big cocktail night. Sequins or leather. No exceptions."

"Sequins," Izzy said immediately. "More spill friendly."

"Saturday's pool cabana and dinner."

"When are pole dancing lessons?"

"Well, I looked around but could only find intermediate, and I don't know if any of you are ready for that yet," Kiera said with a grimace.

"There are levels?" Maggie asked, baffled.

"There are always levels," Izzy said ominously.

Danica appeared next to Pete. "I expected at least one of us to pull something. I just hoped it wasn't me."

"It was always going to be me," Maggie groaned. "Broken arm. Broken nose. Broken vagina."

The group was mid-cackle when the patio door opened.

Maggie startled, not expecting to see Gwen back until tomorrow morning.

Gwen stuck her head out. "Hey, did you move the — oh." Her eyes landed on the screen. "Hey again, everyone."

"Gwen," Kiera squealed like they were old friends.

Pete raised her glass. "GWYNETH, my favorite karaoke duet partner."

"That's not her name," Maggie said automatically, feeling strangely jealous, though she didn't exactly know of whom. "And she doesn't do karaoke."

Izzy leaned forward. "What is Gwen short for?"

"You'll never know," Gwen said, raising one brow.

Danica snorted. "Quiet menace. I want her on my team."

Maggie's lips pressed into a tight line. "Actually—"

Gwen hesitated for half a beat. Her eyes shifted toward Maggie, just long enough for Maggie to realize she was waiting for her to say something. Maggie frowned, looking away.

Pete stole the phone from Kiera, her face far too close to the camera. "Did you get the childcare sorted?"

Gwen glanced toward Maggie, letting her take the reins.

Maggie's whole body tensed. "Uh… yeah, about that."

The group erupted with cheers before anyone could hear Maggie add something after the word *yeah*. Someone said something about matching outfits. Izzy started chanting, "Group trip! Group trip!"

Gwen ducked back inside. The camera panned to a giddy Danica.

Maggie smiled. She laughed. She nodded along. And when she hung up, her hands were trembling.

Inside, Gwen was rinsing a cup at the sink, water running in a slow stream like nothing had happened. The kitchen gleamed with the kind of thoughtful elegance that only an architect like Gwen could pull off — custom cabinetry, quartzite counters, matte brass hardware. The pendant lights over the island cast a warm glow over the wide-plank oak floors. Maggie had picked the tile behind the stove, a Moroccan-style pattern in smoky blues and grays. They'd argued about it for a week, then spent an afternoon installing it together, laughing when Gwen got grout on her nose. That memory lived here, embedded in the walls, even if neither of them ever talked about it. Now Gwen moved through the space like it was neutral ground, like she hadn't just detonated a social bomb in the group chat.

Gwen's sleeve slipped up as she reached for a cup, revealing the edge of her tattoo. Maggie had almost forgotten about it — the sharp Gothic arched window framed in vines. The lines were clean, deliberate, the kind of precision Gwen brought to everything.

It used to fascinate her, that balance of structure and wildness. Now it just made her ache a little. The vines had crept further than she remembered, curling around the empty space like they were trying to fill it.

She caught herself rubbing her own arm, thumb brushing the petals of her old peony tattoo. The ink had faded a little— too many summers, too much sunscreen forgotten—but she still loved it. Hers was softer, looser, like it hadn't known what it wanted to be when she'd gotten it.

Gwen's was all intent. Maggie's was all impulse. Somehow, that had once worked. Now? The stark difference was all she could see.

"I was going to tell them," Maggie said, her voice sharper than she intended. "And then you popped in and they lost their minds. *Gwyneth*?"

Gwen didn't turn around. "Going along with it seems easier for everyone."

"Easier?" Maggie echoed, incredulous. "Not for me it isn't."

"What do you want, Maggie?" Gwen asked, finally turning to face her. Her tone was infuriatingly calm. "You want to be separated but not divorced. You want me to sleep in the guest room, but you won't tell your friends. I don't make decisions anymore because no matter what, it's always wrong."

"That's not fair."

"No? Because it sounds an awful lot like you're mad I went along with yet another decision you didn't want to deal with."

Maggie blinked. "I've been dealing with everything. The kids. The house. Pretending we're fine—"

"No one asked you to pretend," Gwen snapped. "You're the one who didn't want to tell them."

"I was trying to keep things from getting messy with them," Maggie hissed. "I can tell everyone after the bachelorette party. Or the wedding."

"They're already messy. You just don't want to be the one who gets blamed for making it official."

"That's not fair."

"Neither is living in limbo because you won't pick a direction."

Maggie took a step forward. "You think this is easy for me? That I'm sitting here loving the uncertainty?"

Gwen crossed her arms. "You say you're tired of making all the choices, but you won't let anyone else make them either."

The words hit hard, because they weren't wrong. And Maggie hated that Gwen had the upper hand in this — hated that she could sound so reasonable while Maggie felt like she was spinning out.

"So yes, I'm going along with your plan. We can just pretend we're a happily married couple for the weekend and you can tell them when you're ready," Gwen said. "Unless you'd rather be the one to explain why I'm not there." She slowly set the rinsed cup into the drying rack and walked out of the kitchen.

Maggie stared after her, the silence loud enough to drown in. Her stomach twisted. She was flushed, breath tight, heart hammering like it wanted to climb out of her chest. Her brain flooded with a thousand exit strategies — anything that might feel less awful than this.

She could disappear. Change her name. Start a candle shop in Portugal. Or maybe one of those weird bookstores in a town with no stoplights. Somewhere Gwen would never think to look.

Instead, she just stood there, still clutching her phone, as if it could offer her a way out.

Sapphics on the Strip

DANICA

Okay okay okay LOOK WHO'S OFFICIALLY IN THE CHAT?!?

PETE

 our favorite reclusive architect 🤍

KIERA

Welcome to the chaos, Gwyneth!! You can't leave now, this chat is blood-bound. 🧛

MAGGIE

Again, her full name is not Gwyneth.

DANICA

Sorry, I don't make the rules. Gwyneth until proven otherwise.

GWEN

...Hi 

IZZY

Don't worry, we mostly just send memes and argue about who's bringing what to the next potluck.

DANICA

I've been trying to rein in the chaos of this group for years and no one listens to me. Gwyneth, be my ally.

PETE

lies. she's secretly the most chaotic among us.

GWEN

I'll do my best. Thanks for letting me in 

KIERA NAMED THE CONVERSATION "GWYNETH'S GOBLINS".

MAGGIE

Do not make me send a picture of her birth certificate!

CHAPTER 4

GWEN

GWEN WAS EARLY TO THE OFFICE, EVEN BY HER OWN STANDARDS.
She parked in the side lot, slipped in through the alley entrance, and bypassed the espresso machine entirely. Her desk light was the only one on, a soft triangle of gold in a sea of darkened offices. She liked it that way. Quiet. Controlled. Predictable.

She always missed her Austin office when Melinda had her travel somewhere else. Although having Melinda in Denver last week had been a welcome sense of home, Gwen very much preferred not to be anywhere but in Austin, near her family.

Her inbox was already flooded with feedback on the renderings she'd cranked out in a midnight rush, sprawled in the rock-hard guest bed. The comments were mostly minor nitpicks. A few questions about materials. Nothing she couldn't handle. She made a few notes, toggled between CAD files, then closed it all with a sigh. Her eyes drifted to the calendar app in the corner of her screen. Her mom had confirmed she'd still love to watch the kids for the weekend, and Gwen had submitted the PTO request last night. The Vegas trip was blocked in green.

She still hadn't figured out why she'd said yes. It had been a reflex more than a decision — everyone was already cheering, Maggie had frozen, and Gwen had just... gone with it all. Now, it sat inside her like a pebble in a shoe, small and persistent. Part of her regretted it. Part of her didn't. There was a strange thrum of anticipation beneath the unease, like she was waiting for something to shift. Maybe it would be a disaster. Maybe it would help. Maybe, for once, she was allowed not to know.

Melinda knocked once and leaned in. She looked as polished as ever, in high-waisted trousers and a cream blouse that should've been too formal for Austin but somehow looked effortlessly chic on her. Her dark hair was twisted up and clipped, stray curls escaping along her temples.

"You're here early."

"Couldn't sleep," Gwen said, forcing a half smile.

"What's this new PTO request I'm seeing? I didn't know you even knew how to submit PTO," Melinda teased.

Gwen hesitated. "Maggie's college friends are having a bachelorette weekend in Vegas."

Melinda raised an eyebrow. "The ones from Denver that I forced you to see last week?"

Gwen nodded.

"You're willingly attending a bachelorette party?" Melinda gave her a blank look, like she was trying to envision it.

"It's a queer bachelorette party. There will be spreadsheets. And backup snacks. Possibly helmet rentals. It's not that kind of party."

"Uh-huh." Melinda slid her hands into her pockets. "Just make sure someone else covers the rezoning call Monday. You going to need more days off before or after?"

"No," Gwen said. "Just this weekend."

Melinda studied her a moment longer, then gave a short nod. "You look like someone who could use it."

Once she was gone, Gwen stood, stretched, and grabbed her phone. Her brother, Logan, had called twice yesterday. She owed him a conversation.

She stepped outside, letting the glass door thump shut behind her, and wandered to the edge of the plaza across the street. The sun was already hot, casting sharp shadows along the pavement. The firm's building was sleek, modern, glassy… and completely lacking warmth.

Across the street, the old red-brick church stood stubborn and lovely, its steeple a jagged silhouette against the sky. Gwen had once biked past it nearly every day during under-grad and then her early years at the firm. She hadn't even realized she'd missed that until now.

Her phone buzzed.

"There she is," Logan said, voice wry. "You finally remem-bered how phones work."

"Hi," Gwen said. "Sorry. It's been a week."

"It's Monday morning at 7:32 a.m."

"Exactly."

Gwen started pacing slowly, heel to toe along the concrete planter. "I did something."

"Oh god. Did you murder someone at work? Do I need to google how to hide a body on a burner phone or something? Where do you even buy a burner phone?"

"The internet?" Gwen guessed. "Or, I don't know, you live in Manhattan, I'm sure there's a back alley with a guy in a trench coat lined with burner phones *somewhere* near you."

"I am not googling 'where to buy burner phone NYC' on my personal device immediately before you're arrested for murdering a coworker," Logan said dramatically.

Gwen grinned, rolling her eyes. "Okay, it's worse than murder. It may possibly result in my own murder."

"Worse than murder... Did you finally say yes to Jude wanting white-kid dreadlocks?" Logan asked.

Gwen laughed. "God, no. No, I mean, I said yes to going with Maggie's friends on a bachelorette weekend in Vegas."

There was a pause.

"And... Maggie is also going? The friends you've complained about not knowing you're separated?" Logan clarified slowly.

Gwen made a noise of affirmation.

"Gwen..." Logan said softly, like he was waiting for more.

"Everyone assumed I was coming. Maggie didn't correct them. I just... went along with it."

Logan snorted. "That's incredible. Honestly. Think of it this way, a destination weekend surrounded by people disgustingly in love... It's a recipe for making Maggie fall right back into your arms if you play it right."

Gwen groaned. "That wasn't my plan."

"Oh, please. It's genius. Vacation brain plus nostalgia plus alcohol? All you need is one heartfelt slow dance or near-death gambling experience, and she'll be halfway to proposing again."

Gwen laughed, a short, tired sound. "You're ridiculous."

Logan sighed. "You're still in love with your wife. Just own it. Have fun. Look good. Be competent. Don't get heat-stroke. Maybe wear a tank top. You'll be fine."

Gwen let her eyes wander back to the church steeple. "She doesn't want to talk about anything real. Every time we get close, even in therapy, she just shuts the door."

"That's why you're going where real life doesn't exist, so you might actually get somewhere."

Gwen kicked at a loose pebble. "I don't want to manipu-late her."

"You're not. You're just showing her a different way. Big difference."

"When did you start therapy?" Gwen teased.

"I watch a lot of TV," Logan said. "And I'm very wise. But really, you don't have to manipulate her into realizing that you're meant to be together. You just have to remind her why she chose you in the first place."

Gwen wasn't sure she agreed. But the part of her that wanted Maggie to say something, do something — anything — was louder than the part that wanted to take the high road.

She glanced up at the firm's building again. Its sterile exterior glared back at her.

"Okay," she said. "Then I guess I'm going to Vegas."

"Damn right you are," Logan said, catching her up on his day and recent drama with his own work. The familiarity of hearing about something completely apart from her felt nice. Then, suddenly, he gasped. "I think I just saw a pigeon pickpocket someone."

"Stay vigilant," Gwen joked. "Okay, I've got to go back in." They said their quick goodbyes and Gwen hung up, still smiling, and headed back toward the revolving glass door.

Maybe Logan was onto something. Not with pickpocketing pigeons, but with Vegas being a new chance to prove to Maggie that their marriage was still a gamble worth taking.

CHAPTER 5

MAGGIE

THE SUITCASE LAY OPEN ON THE BED, HALF-FULL AND judgmental. Maggie stood at its edge with a suit vest in one hand and a pair of jeans in the other, neither feeling like the right choice. Vegas felt too loud for linen, too synthetic for cotton. Or maybe she just didn't want to go now.

Rosie burst in, a whirlwind in mismatched pajamas. "Can I have a snack that isn't a snack but is still a treat?"

Maggie squinted. "So… dessert?"

"No," Rosie said solemnly. "Something crunchy and special."

"We could have popcorn?" Maggie offered, remembering the bag of Smartfood she'd bought yesterday. "There's some in the pantry."

Rosie lit up. "Popcorn! Yes!"

Maggie watched her bounce back down the hall, then looked at her phone. 3:08 p.m. The afternoon sun streamed through the blinds, lighting up the dust she hadn't had the energy to care about. She sat on the edge of the bed, ignoring the accusatory huff of the suitcase.

When Rosie had first asked why Mommy didn't sleep in Maggie's bed anymore, Maggie had said something about snoring. Rosie nodded solemnly, as though she understood. The boys shrugged it off. Kids accepted things adults choked on.

She reached into her dresser and pulled out an old Rice University hoodie. The hem was fraying, one sleeve scarred by a mysterious bleach mark, but it still smelled faintly of detergent and stress. She'd gone to grad school intending to be on the research side of things rather than the teaching side. Grad school had been a blur of gallery lectures and Claude Cahun research, coffee-fueled nights, and Gwen appearing like an architectural thesis come to life.

Gwen had been all sharp lines and quiet ambition. They'd met at a party thrown by one of Maggie's seminar friends. Maggie spilled cheap red wine, and Gwen wordlessly handed her a napkin. That was the whole meet-cute. Not fireworks. Just a steady hand and a look that said, "I can help."

She threw the sweatshirt into the suitcase, then pulled it back out again. This was Vegas in September. Why would she need a sweatshirt held together by sentimentality?

Her phone buzzed. A text from Danica.

DANICA

How many pairs of shoes are too many pairs of shoes to pack?

Maggie hesitated. She'd told herself it would be easier to be honest, to finally say what she should've said weeks ago: that she and Gwen were separated, figuring out divorce. That it wasn't some temporary funk she could be talked out of. But even as her thumb hovered over the reply, her pulse quickened and her stomach turned over in knots.

Just say it, she told herself. Say it and let it be real. Stop dragging it around like a ghost.

With the kind of impulsiveness that had defined much of

her twenties — and, evidently, still plagued her thirties — she hit *Call* instead of replying.

She could do this. She could rip off the Band-Aid. She could just be honest with her friends. Hell, if Danica told Pete, Maggie wouldn't have to worry about telling Kiera or Izzy, since Pete would inevitably relay the information at warp speed.

"Maggie," Danica answered, her voice already fizzy with excitement. She sounded mid-bachelorette-planning-mode, which, knowing Danica, she absolutely was.

"Hey, babe. Good news, there is no limit to the shoes. They should have their own suitcase, honestly," Maggie joked.

Danica exhaled in what sounded a lot like relief. "Okay, I've made a spreadsheet for outfits, but the shoes were really throwing me. I figured texting my stylist was the only answer."

Classic Danica. Maggie smiled. She heard a few hushed words between Danica and someone else, but she cleared her throat and soldiered on. "Listen, I wanted to tell you—"

"Oh, wait, Pete wants me to put you on speaker. Say hi." Danica laughed. Of course she was laughing. She was engaged, carefree, and about to go to a bachelorette party with her best friends.

"Hi, Mags," came Pete's voice, followed by the distinct *clink clink clink* of a cocktail shaker. "We're taste-testing a second round of grapefruit margs, for science. We need to make sure they're strong enough at the wedding to make Gwyneth dance and weak enough that no one loses a tooth."

"Seriously," Danica chimed in, practically bouncing through the phone. "I can't believe she said yes. Gwen never comes on our trips. It's such a treat to get to know her better and watch how adorable you two are together."

"I've already made a playlist that includes her guilty pleasures," Pete added. "And Kiera printed custom temporary tattoos with our faces on them. We're going full chaos. Gwyneth's not ready."

Danica laughed. "But I am. I'm so ready. I swear if she doesn't end up in a hot tub or a karaoke booth at some point, we've failed. This is going to be epic."

Well, *fuck.*

Maggie opened her mouth. Closed it. Opened it again.

"Yeah," she said instead, her voice barely keeping pace with the thud of her heartbeat. "It should be... so, so fun. Listen—"

"We were just saying how it'll be even better than Telluride or San Diego because Gwyneth's coming. Now we don't have to worry about you being the fifth wheel," Pete said, slurping what Maggie could only assume was said grapefruit margarita.

Danica laughed. "And maybe this time Gwen will actually let loose. Who knows, right?"

She stared at the ceiling, trying to will her pulse back to normal. She really had meant to tell Danica the truth. She *was* going to tell her. But then Pete had started raving about margaritas and Gwen dancing and tattoos with their faces on them, and suddenly Maggie felt like a piñata being asked to hold her own bat.

If they were this excited about Gwen coming, how could she ruin it? How could she deflate their joy with her messy reality — the silence in their house, the absence of Gwen on endless work trips, the separate beds, the half-hearted therapy sessions that ended in more questions than answers?

Now she definitely couldn't tell them. Not without feeling like she was setting off a glitter bomb of disappointment. She could already hear Pete's "Wait, what?" and see Danica's face fall in confusion. It wasn't that they'd be mad, not really. They'd just be... sad, which was so much worse. Then the questions would start. And suddenly their happy, blissful weekend would be about her, and they'd have those pitying looks. Maggie didn't want to be the one to bring sadness to a weekend meant for fun.

So, once again, she swallowed it. She laughed along. She said, "Totally," shortly after, blamed a fictional child-related emergency, and dropped her phone face down on the bed.

She wished she could call her mom. Her mom would laugh until she cried at the mess Maggie was in, then scoop up the chaos and help Maggie through it, like she always did.

The worst part of grief wasn't regret. It was just wishing she could hear her mom laugh one more time.

She blinked back tears, still staring at the ceiling, her eyes tracing the beams she and Gwen had designed together. She didn't believe in God, necessarily, or any kind of religion, but she did feel a bit of comfort imagining her mom watching over her somehow. "What do I do?" she whispered in some kind of prayer, closing her eyes. She stayed like that for a long time, waiting for some kind of sign.

A warmth flooded her body, and she was briefly comforted and in awe before realizing that no, something was *very*, very warm and smelling like... wait. She opened her eyes to see Rosie standing over her, eyes wide as burnt popcorn spilled from a bowl all over Maggie's legs.

"What is this?" Maggie scrambled to brush the popcorn off her legs and onto the floor.

"Mama, Arlo helped me make popcorn but this tastes bad," Rosie said, her eyes welling with tears. "Help."

Maggie took a deep breath, willing herself back from the edge of losing her patience. She put a hand on Rosie's shoulder. "It's okay, honey. I'll help you get some popcorn. First step, let's get the vacuum."

THE AIR INSIDE FOUND & Chosen was cool, pine-scented, and threaded with Motown. Maggie had meant to sneak in to drop off the tags she'd just picked up at the printer near the kids' school, but Colette caught her lurking by a tulip-shaped hanging lamp.

"Tell me you're not such a loser without a life that you have to hang out here for fun," Colette said, walking out from the beaded curtain to the back room.

Maggie gave her a thin smile. "It's less chaotic than home."

Colette, tall and cat-eyed in a vintage silk robe over wide-leg jeans, slid a pair of sunglasses on top of her head. "Okay, so what's with the energy? You look like someone put your self-esteem through a pasta roller."

Maggie leaned on the counter. "Nothing. Rosie and Arlo tried to burn down the house yesterday with popcorn, but crisis averted. Do you think daytime sequins still fly in Vegas, or has it gotten too boring?"

Colette gave her a long, assessing stare. "Vegas isn't real life. But sometimes, stepping out of real life for a minute shows you what matters most when you come back."

"Did we get some psilocybin in the latest shipment or what? When did you become so..." Maggie gestured. "Zen? Wise? Quotable? About sequins."

Colette tapped her temple. "Just tapping into my higher self."

"Does that require a cult oath to a fake guru, or can you do that all on your own?" Maggie teased.

"Maybe you should come with me to one of my meditation retreats. Silence might do you good," Colette said, shrugging.

Maggie snorted. "Being alone with my thoughts sounds like hell, not a reprieve."

Colette smirked. "See? That's exactly why you need it. To learn the difference between intentional quiet and internal panic."

Maggie rolled her eyes. "Or maybe I just need cocktails and sequins."

"Sequins are a form of meditation," Colette said smoothly, but Maggie could see a mischievous glint in her friend's eye. "Each one reflects its own light, each one a tiny mantra."

"God, you're insufferable," Maggie said, but she was laughing now, tension loosening in her shoulders.

"I feel like I'd be a really good cult leader," Colette replied. She leaned across the counter. "Seriously, Maggie, you okay? You've got a pre-Vegas spiral look."

"I'll survive." Maggie rubbed her temple. "I just... don't know what I'm doing. And I hate packing."

"Packing is just editing your life down to the things you want to be seen in," Colette said. "No wonder it's stressful."

Maggie barked a laugh. "Okay, you're terrifyingly good at this. Anything else, cult leader?"

Colette smirked. "Yeah. Take the sequins. Always take the sequins."

Maggie took a deep breath, as if steeling herself for the weekend ahead. "I'll see you when I get back?"

"You can always call if you need, okay?" Colette said, giving her hand a squeeze.

Maggie saluted casually, the barest hint of a smile tugging at her lips. But as she stepped into the bright Texas sun, the humidity hugging her skin like a too-warm blanket, her heart gave a quiet lurch. She didn't know what she was doing — still. Only that she was about to board a plane with her almost-ex-wife and a suitcase full of half-truths. And if clarity didn't come soon, she wasn't sure how much longer she could keep pretending that she wasn't unraveling.

When Maggie got home, the kitchen smelled faintly of grilled cheese and the air was full of the chaotic hum of the kids' voices. Gwen was at the table with Jude, orchestrating an elaborate marble run that zigzagged across books and overturned mixing bowls while Arlo tried to crash a monster truck into the structure. Rosie lay on her stomach nearby, coloring and softly singing.

Maggie bent down, kissed each kid on the forehead, and headed upstairs to finish packing.

"Listen," Gwen said from the doorway a moment later, leaning against the frame in that maddeningly casual way she had. "I'll back out of the Vegas trip if you really want."

Colette's words floated up in Maggie's memory — about stepping out of real life for a while. "No. I'm still a fucking coward, and I didn't tell Danica. And they're so excited to see you," she admitted, rubbing at her eyes.

"I'll be the bad guy," Gwen offered, hands slipping into her pockets. "I'll tell them I have a work thing."

"No. Come to Vegas. It'll be a fun trip, and… we could just pretend to be okay for the weekend, if you're good with that." The feelings in Maggie's chest were a mess of anticipation, hope, and deep, humiliating dread.

Gwen's brows lifted. "Okay, so… we're doing this?"

Maggie shoved another stack of clothes into her suitcase. "I guess so."

A grin flickered across Gwen's face — quick, mischievous — and for a heartbeat Maggie thought she saw actual excitement there. Then Jude yelled something about Arlo creating a marble disaster, and Gwen winked at her before disappearing back downstairs to save the game.

CHAPTER 6

GWEN

THE THERMOSTAT IN DR. ELOWEN'S OFFICE WAS ALWAYS SET TO what Gwen would call "unseasonably cozy" for the month of September. It made her blazer feel like a weighted blanket she hadn't agreed to. Maggie sat across from her, curled into the corner of the couch like she might disappear into the upholstery if she tried hard enough.

Dr. Elowen looked between them, pen balanced on the edge of her notebook. "So."

"We're going on the trip," Gwen said. She sat up straighter, smoothing her slacks with a deliberate palm. "Together."

Dr. Elowen gave a slow nod. "That's a big decision."

"We agreed," Gwen said. "I was all in for taking the fall, but we decided together." She added it like a badge of honor, hoping Maggie noticed.

She knew Maggie was upset. Gwen could read it in her clipped tone over the past few days, the carefully blank expression. But she also couldn't pretend this choice hadn't lifted something off her. For the first time in months, she felt a strange kind of relief — a flicker of freedom, maybe. Not from responsibility or consequence, but from the limbo that had slowly calcified around them. She wasn't expecting a miracle. She wasn't even expecting forgiveness. But the idea of being in Maggie's orbit again, even briefly, somewhere outside the weight of their shared house and history — that felt like something she hadn't let herself want before now.

Maggie did notice. Gwen could tell from the way her lips pressed together, her expression flickering between impressed and bracing.

"Have you talked about how you'll handle this shared lie... this, uh, shared story in front of your friends?" Dr. Elowen asked, crossing and uncrossing her legs.

Gwen's eyebrows rose and Maggie caught her eye, her matching surprised expression telling Gwen they were on the same page about Dr. Elowen being so straightforward.

"Let me put it this way. How will you handle accommodations?" Dr. Elowen added. "I think it's best if you plan for what you're about to encounter to reduce anxiety and conflict in the moment."

Maggie shrugged. "They booked a suite at some fancy hotel. I'm not sure what the exacts are. I just sent over our share of the cost and let someone else handle the details."

"A suite? I thought we'd all have our own rooms," Gwen said, a nervous flutter in her stomach.

Maggie shrugged. "I think every couple has separate rooms within the suite, but I haven't asked the specifics or researched the floor plan."

"Do not tempt me with floor plan research," Gwen joked.

Maggie actually laughed. A short one, but real. "You'd probably ask the hotel concierge for a fire exit map and then reorganize the furniture for optimal flow."

"I *do* care about safety and aesthetics," Gwen insisted.

Maggie held up her hands in a gesture of appeasement. "I never thought otherwise."

Dr. Elowen smiled gently, setting her pen down. "So this really is something you're doing together. Is it a reset? A trial run? An experiment?"

Gwen looked at Maggie, but she wasn't sure either of them had the answer.

Dr. Elowen glanced toward Maggie. "Why am I feeling a negative energy coming from your side of the couch?"

Maggie shrugged. "I'm having a lot of conflicted feelings."

Dr. Elowen raised her eyebrows. "Want to share any of them?"

Maggie's shoulders lifted again.

Dr. Elowen never gave up that easily. "Has this decision affected any other major decisions about your separation?"

"No," Maggie said, like it was easy for her to admit.

Gwen flinched.

Dr. Elowen glanced between the two of them. "It seems to me like Gwen is stepping up and being there for you when you need her to be."

Ah, this recurring theme. Gwen had Maggie's caustic words of their very first session six months ago memorized, like they'd burned the inside of Gwen's brain upon hearing them.

"You weren't there. Not when my mom died. Not when I needed you. You buried yourself in work and asked me what I needed like I was going to hand you a list. I didn't want a list, Gwen. I wanted you."

Those words had haunted her, mostly because they'd been true. And she'd spent almost every day since in a tangle of trying to judge whether Maggie wanted her to step up and be there now, or wanted her to stay away, to let her deal with her suffocating grief alone.

"Let me ask you this, Maggie. How are you feeling about her joining? About the choice to not tell your friends?" Dr. Elowen added, yanking Gwen back to the present.

Maggie clenched her jaw. "I..." She trailed off, taking a

deep breath through her nose. "I initially felt like Gwen was punishing me for delaying telling my friends, and now I'm caught in this big lie, and my friend group is not exactly... fantastic when it comes to honesty, so I'm just feeling... Well, I'm feeling frustrated, to be honest."

Dr. Elowen nodded, then glanced toward Gwen. "How does it make you feel to know she's frustrated about this?"

Before Gwen could answer, Maggie began again. "On the other hand, I'm grateful to Gwen for rolling with this absolutely ridiculous plan. My friends are happy and engaged, and I don't want to be the one divorced sad lady drunkenly slurring that love is a lie the whole weekend."

The very specific mental image was not difficult for Gwen to conjure: Danica and Pete cozied up together, Izzy and Kiera comfortably holding hands, and Maggie, all by herself. She grimaced.

Maggie looked toward the ceiling. "So really I'm feeling conflicted, is what it comes down to. Gwen saved me from an awkward and uncomfortable situation by, in turn, creating a new awkward and uncomfortable situation. Except this time, only *we're* uncomfortable, not everyone else, you know?"

A crease formed between Dr. Elowen's eyebrows, and she seemed nervous. That made Gwen feel nervous, too, like watching a surgeon pause mid-incision to check the manual.

Gwen turned toward Maggie. "I wasn't trying to pressure you into telling them."

Maggie glanced her way, the weight of her bright blue eyes shining wholly on Gwen in a way that felt both familiar and surprising.

For the first time in what felt like ages, Gwen felt like they were standing side by side instead of across a chasm. She didn't know what that meant yet. Some silent accord passed between them — an unspoken agreement that maybe they could do this. Maybe not forever. Maybe not even well. But together, for now.

"I'm going to respect Maggie's boundaries, and it's only a weekend," Gwen said. "As for everything else after… I don't know."

There was a pause. The hum of the AC kicked in overhead. Dr. Elowen looked thoughtful. "It's okay not to have the whole story written yet. But going on this trip might offer you both some clarity about what's next."

Gwen wasn't sure if she wanted clarity or just a few days where nothing needed deciding. Still, she'd made the choice to go, and for now, that was enough.

As they rose, Dr. Elowen glanced toward the door. "Maggie, can I speak to you alone?"

Maggie glanced nervously toward Gwen, but then nodded. "Of course."

Gwen slipped out the door and back into the easy routine of giving Maggie her space.

W HEN THEY RETURNED HOME from therapy, the kids were in bed and her mom was sitting on the couch. Maggie gave her a short wave and murmured acknowledgment and thanks — she hadn't seen Maggie hug her mom since her own mom had passed. She wanted to ask Maggie what Dr. Elowen had wanted to talk to her about in private but was torn about wanting to let Maggie have her privacy. Maggie didn't seem like she wanted to share, anyway, as she hurried up the stairs and into the primary bedroom they once shared.

Gwen flopped down onto the couch beside her mom. "Thanks for watching the kiddos this evening. And this weekend. And for everything," Gwen said.

"You know I'm always happy to hang out with my grandbabies. Lord knows Logan will never give me any," her mom said with an eye roll. Her graying curls were clipped back, and she had a mug of chamomile tea in one hand, the kind of serene air Gwen had always associated with her. "You okay, honey?"

Gwen smiled weakly, her voice dropping to a whisper. "I'm going on a bachelorette trip with my almost-ex-wife where we have to pretend everything is fine. Define okay."

Her mom leaned forward to set her tea down with a *clink*. "Are you hoping to rekindle something? Or are you just going for the group games and cucumber water?"

Gwen hesitated. "Did you talk to Logan? Because he was so Team Rekindle, I was surprised."

Her mom's smile softened. "He might have mentioned something."

Gwen bit her lip, considering. "I don't know. Honestly, I'm hoping something — anything — will shake us loose. We've been... stalled. This in-between space is starting to feel permanent."

"That sounds challenging," her mom affirmed.

"Challenging like trying to breathe through plastic." Gwen let out a short laugh. "Sure, let's throw me into a weekend full of spa treatments and couple-y friends. Maybe the awkwardness will kill me before the ennui does."

Her mom studied her face for a moment. "You used to lean into challenge. Take risks. Even the hard ones. You chose a field that's ninety percent rejection and ten percent ego. You rode a bike everywhere, for god's sake."

"Yeah, when I was twenty-four and immortal," Gwen muttered.

"Maybe," her mom said. "But you were brave. I think you still are. This trip might not fix anything. But if it gives you a better sense of what's left, then maybe it's worth it."

Gwen sighed. Her chest still felt tight, but she nodded. "I just want to stop feeling like we're waiting for something that's never going to happen," she admitted.

"Then maybe stop waiting," her mom said as though it

were obvious. "Take a risk. Get back on the bike. Maybe with a helmet and a reflective vest."

Gwen blinked, not sure whether to cry or laugh.

Her mom leaned toward her, pressing a kiss to Gwen's forehead. "You're doing okay. Better than you think."

Gwen's chest squeezed with affection, and she hugged her mom. "Do you want the guest bed?" she asked. They'd be leaving early enough in the morning that her mom would be a great help with getting the kids off to school and Maggie and Gwen into an Uber to the airport roughly around the same time.

"No, I hate that bed. I'll sleep here on the couch," her mom said with a knowing smile.

The night outside thrummed with cicadas, their steady chorus folding into the syrupy warmth of an early Texas fall. A faint breeze carried the scent of cut grass and something faintly sweet, like memory trying to sneak in. Inside, the house was still, as if the walls themselves were holding their breath. She stood there in that quiet, feeling the pause between heartbeats, suspended in a moment that could tip either way.

Kiera named the conversation "The Final Countdown".

KIERA

okayyyyyy my loves, happy Bachelorette Day!!!!

PETE

IT'S HAPPENING ✈

IZZY

I've been up since 5, I'm basically feral now.

KIERA

Please save that energy for the actual party.

DANICA

Maggie?? Gwyneth?? Are you packing your most chaotic selves??

MAGGIE

My suitcase is 40% sequins, 60% sunscreen.

GWEN

My offering will be a Costco jar of ibuprofen.

IZZY

Thanks, Dad.

PETE

vegas should pay US for the show we're about to put on.

KIERA

Reminder: cocktail bar reservations are at 8 tonight, so no one pass out before then.

PETE

can't wait to see all your faces. love you degenerates.

DANICA

Group pic tonight or it doesn't count. Last fling before the ring, people.

PETE

can someone please tell my beautiful fiancée she does not need to bring a sparkly cowboy hat??

MAGGIE

Can someone please tell Pete's beautiful fiancée that I'm not getting on this plane if she doesn't bring a sparkly cowboy hat?

CHAPTER 7

MAGGIE

THE AUSTIN-BERGSTROM AIRPORT WAS ALREADY HUMMING, THE low-grade chaos of people dragging wheeled bags and scanning departure boards like they were waiting for divine intervention. The smell of burnt espresso from the coffee kiosk hung in the air, mixing with the faint tang of jet fuel drifting in from the gates.

Maggie stood in the security line beside Gwen, who looked like she'd dressed for a board meeting instead of a bachelorette weekend — crisp white button-up, navy slacks, leather shoes polished enough to catch the fluorescent glare. Her carry-on was zipped tight, squared off like it had been measured with a ruler.

"Okay," Maggie said, shifting her bag higher on her shoulder. "Ground rules for the weekend. What's our stance on PDA?"

Gwen arched an eyebrow. "I didn't realize we had a stance."

"Of course we have a stance. We can't exactly be holding hands or making heart eyes in front of everyone. Not unless you want the conversation to spiral into 'why didn't you tell us you separated' before we've even had our first overpriced cocktail."

"So… subtle?" Gwen asked.

"Subtle," Maggie confirmed. "Like we tolerate each other's presence but not in a 'wow, they hate each other' way. More in a 'been married so long we barely notice the other person's there' way."

"That sounds romantic," Gwen said dryly.

"It's not supposed to be romantic. It's supposed to be believable."

The line inched forward. Gwen leaned just close enough for her shoulder to brush Maggie's — on purpose, Maggie was sure — and she ignored the urge to step away.

By the time they cleared security and found a pair of seats at their gate, the overhead announcement was calling final boarding for a flight to Denver. Gwen sat across from her instead of beside her, which Maggie appreciated, and pulled out her phone.

Maggie was digging through her tote for a granola bar when she noticed the typing. Not the lazy, single-thumb scroll of someone killing time, but the clipped, fast pace of someone firing off a work email.

"Are you seriously working right now?" she asked.

"It'll take two minutes," Gwen said, eyes still on her screen.

"Classic Gwen. You're already buried in work before we've even taken off for vacation," Maggie snapped. "How much work are you planning on doing this weekend?"

Gwen's eyes flicked up, annoyance apparent in her expression. "If I don't send this now, it'll hang over me the whole flight. This is the last email, I promise."

"God forbid you let something hang over you for a few hours," Maggie muttered.

That made Gwen look up, her eyes cool but steady. "You think I like that my brain works this way?"

"I think you don't try very hard to make it work differently." Maggie rolled her eyes.

The boarding call for their flight echoed over the PA. Gwen slipped her phone into her bag without another word. When they stood, Maggie caught the faintest crease between Gwen's brows — the one she got when she was choosing to bite back whatever she wanted to say.

They filed onto the plane in silence like strangers.

Half an hour later, the seat belt light was off and Maggie was flicking through her Kindle library offerings when Gwen shifted beside her.

The heat of their argument had cooled. They'd always been quick to resolve fights before… well, before the last few years had made everything feel so much more complicated. Maggie dared look up at Gwen, seeing Gwen's calm and open expression.

"Should we practice?" Gwen asked.

Maggie blinked. "Practice what?"

"Holding hands." Gwen's expression was casual, like she was suggesting they split a bag of pretzels.

Maggie narrowed her eyes. "You're ridiculous."

"Better to look natural when we have to do it in front of everyone later."

"This is stupid," Maggie muttered.

Against her better judgment, Maggie let Gwen's warm, steady palm slide into hers. The heat of it seeped up her arm, settling somewhere in her chest. It felt achingly familiar, like muscle memory — like something her body had been waiting for without her permission. Her thumb twitched, a ghost of the way she used to stroke Gwen's knuckles. She tried to tell herself it was nothing, that she was just playing along. But the quiet press of Gwen's hand in hers made her wonder what exactly she was trying to protect herself from. Her eyes found

Gwen's, dark with meaning and intent. When was the last time they'd held hands like this? It was such an innocent gesture, and yet Maggie felt like she was being stripped bare.

"Anything to drink?" the flight attendant asked, making Maggie jolt and pull her hand free, fingers tingling from the loss of warmth.

"A ginger ale for me and a Diet Coke for her," Gwen said, smiling up at the attendant. "And can we get an extra couple of cookies? My wife can't resist them."

Maggie couldn't decide if being so known was annoying or sweet. Perhaps both. She glanced back down at their hands and forced a casual smile, leaning back like it hadn't meant anything.

"And should we try kissing? Just to make sure we can sell it?" Gwen's tone was quiet, though the quirk of her mouth held a hint of mischief.

Maggie rolled her eyes, leaning farther away. "Don't push your luck."

"Ah, you're right. Gotta save some of that for Vegas," Gwen said, turning to face out the window. Maggie could have sworn she saw the barest hint of a smile on Gwen's face in the reflection.

The lobby of the hotel was a sensory overload — chandeliers dripping crystals, the sharp scent of cologne and floral arrangements, the clatter of wheeled suitcases across marble. Maggie spotted the group clustered near the check-in desk, and before she knew it she was dashing toward them. They collided in a tangle of arms and squeals, the kind of reunion that turned heads. Everyone was talking at once, laughter ricocheting off the marble walls.

Gwen hung back, her steps deliberately slow. Pete suddenly noticed her across the lobby and bellowed, "GWYNETH!"

The entire group turned, grinning, waving her over like she'd been missing for years. Maggie's heart gave a strange skip as Gwen finally crossed the distance, her calm presence sliding into the storm of affection and noise like it belonged there all along.

An elevator ride and an argument over hotel key tapping techniques later, the hotel suite door flew open. The suite was somehow both massive and wildly inconvenient. Two sunken living areas — one complete with a circular couch — a kitchenette, a dining nook, but only two bedrooms. Maggie surveyed the pullout couch before her. Kiera stood in the middle of it all, blinking like she'd been personally betrayed.

"It said it slept eight," Kiera exclaimed, waving her phone in the air like it might offer a better explanation.

"Technically, it does," Izzy said, gesturing toward the pullout couch. "It just doesn't sleep eight in any way that won't make our friendships weird."

"How do two bedrooms equal eight sleeping arrangements?" Maggie asked. "Is there some kind of bed in the pantry? A secret annex we haven't found?" She hoped desperately for a secret sleeping nook situation.

The alternative? A bed in a public room shared with the woman she hadn't shared a bed with in months.

"Do we think I should call down to the front desk?" Kiera asked, still naively hopeful. "Get it changed?"

"No need." Gwen sat down on the sofa, patting the cushion. "Mags and I can take the pullout."

Maggie's head snapped toward her. "Can we?"

"We're the boring married couple," Gwen said with a smile, though Maggie recognized the strain beneath it. "We won't need a door like all you new-relationship honeymooners."

Izzy looked like she was going to argue, but then her eyes cut toward Danica and Pete — already setting their suitcases down in the bedroom farthest from the suite entrance — and nodded. "Let's definitely keep that far room for the bachelorettes. Obviously."

Kiera sighed, shuffling her suitcase toward the other private room. "That's very kind."

Maggie busied herself with finding the extra sheets in a closet, trying to keep her face neutral. She could feel Gwen's presence behind her like a heat source. What would it be like to be in the same bed with Gwen again? Would Gwen need to be reminded this was all pretend, all just an act to save her friends from the heartbreak of her own heartbreak?

"You didn't have to be such a chivalrous martyr," Maggie muttered.

"Yeah, well, I kind of did." Gwen was already taking the decorative pillows off the couch. "Unless you'd rather share a room with Izzy and Kiera."

Maggie raised an eyebrow. "Sounds cozy."

Gwen smirked. "What was it you told me about how Kiera flosses in bed? Or was it toenail trimming?" She raised her voice toward Kiera and Izzy's open door.

"I do not trim my toenails in bed," Kiera yelled. "It was in the bathroom like a perfectly regular person."

The corner of Maggie's mouth twitched. Damn it.

They moved in parallel, setting up the pullout with the efficiency only long-married — or recently separated — people could manage. Maggie tried not to notice how Gwen's shirt clung to her toned back when she leaned down to tuck the sheet. Good lord, would she need to be the one reminded of boundaries? She shook her head and focused on the task.

"It's like sleeping on a ravioli," Maggie said, pressing the large lump in the middle of the mattress.

"We've weathered worse," Gwen replied. "Remember that cabin in Santa Fe?"

"You mean the one with the wasps in the walls on our honeymoon?"

"They were bees."

"Listen, I understand their importance and I will still

never forgive their species for the childhood trauma of *My Girl.*"

There was a beat. Then Gwen asked quietly, "This is fine, right?"

Maggie smoothed a wrinkle from the top sheet, then stepped back. "It's fine. It's temporary," she whispered, not daring to look Gwen in the eye as she said the words.

CHAPTER 8

THE SUITE WAS PURE CHAOS. MUSIC WAS PLAYING FROM TWO different speakers — Izzy's phone in the kitchenette competing with Kiera's on the vanity counter in the nearest bedroom — while blow dryers roared and curling irons clicked shut like some kind of synchronized metallic insect. The air smelled faintly of hair spray, perfume, and the citrusy gin from the half-drunk cocktails abandoned on every flat surface.

Gwen leaned against the doorframe of the living room, drink in hand, watching Maggie get her eyeliner perfect in the reflection of the darkened TV. Pete was perched beside her on the circular couch, teasing her about wearing "mom shoes" to the club until Maggie threatened to hurl a throw pillow at her.

She wasn't used to this kind of pregame energy — the shouting across rooms, the sudden bursts of laughter, the way people slipped in and out of conversations without them ever really ending. But Maggie was in her element. She moved between her friends like they were different rooms in a house she'd lived in forever — checking on Danica's dress zipper, refilling Izzy's glass without being asked, tossing Kiera a tube of lipstick from across the room.

It hit Gwen then, sudden and heavy: Even if they went through with the divorce, Maggie would be fine. She'd have this — this noisy, loyal, ridiculous crew who loved her without conditions. The thought was a comfort and a knife at the same time.

Maggie helped Danica with her earring, standing in the middle of the living area in a sleek, short black dress that showed off her long legs. The floral tattoo on Maggie's arm had always looked alive to her. The lines weren't perfect — too fluid, too much motion — but that was the point. It reminded Gwen of how Maggie moved through life: messy, impulsive, so different from her. She took another sip of her drink, looking away before Maggie caught her staring.

The suite door swung open, letting in a gust of hallway air and the sound of the casino floor somewhere far below. Izzy and Kiera walked in like they'd pulled off a heist, grinning so hard it looked painful.

"Okay, okay, don't freak out," Izzy said, which was, of course, the cue for everyone to freak out.

A woman followed them in. Tall, with sun-warmed skin, an easy smile, and hair the exact shade of expensive whiskey. She wore jeans that fit like they'd been sewn directly onto her and a black tank top that left her arms — strong, sculpted arms — completely bare.

"This," Kiera announced, throwing her hands up like she was unveiling a prize on a game show, "is Pete's sister, Lillian. Surprise!"

There was a beat of collective squealing and clapping. Pete leapt up from the couch to hug her, Danica already moving in for her own.

Gwen straightened automatically, forcing her mouth into a polite smile as Lillian made her way around the room, greeting each person in turn. Her handshake was firm and warm, and she held Gwen's eyes just a beat too long before moving on. Exactly Gwen's type, damn it.

And Maggie saw it. Gwen caught the flicker in her wife's — ex-wife's? — eyes from across the room. Not quite jealousy, not quite curiosity, but something sharp enough to register before Maggie smoothed it over with another laugh and turned back to Pete.

"She's only here for two nights," Izzy was saying, "but she's in her own room, so she's not part of the Great Bed Shortage of 2025."

"Bless you for that," Gwen said, earning a laugh from Kiera.

The chaos picked right back up, but Gwen kept stealing glances at Maggie, wondering what exactly she'd seen in that look — and why she wanted to see it again.

The group spilled out of the suite in a noisy, glittering wave, heels clicking against the carpet, Gwen trailing near the back with Lillian as the others chattered about drink menus and which clubs had the "least gross" bathrooms. The elevator ride was a crush of perfume and laughter, Pete making an exaggerated show of fanning herself when Danica whispered something in her ear.

The hotel's cocktail bar was tucked behind a set of brass-trimmed glass doors, the kind of place that seemed designed to make you forget the casino was just down the hall. Low lighting, soft jazz drifting under the hum of conversation, and curved velvet couches arranged in little pockets of intimacy. Everything gleamed — marble tabletops, cut crystal glasses, the gold-flecked mural behind the bar. Even the cocktail list read like a novella: smoked rosemary, elderflower foam, artisanal bitters you could never find outside a zip code with a trust fund.

Maggie was immediately claimed by Pete and Izzy, who had spread themselves across one of the deep couches like they'd been saving the space for her. Gwen hesitated only a moment before sliding onto the couch opposite — next to Lillian.

"Thought we lost you there," Lillian said with a grin, leaning back like she owned the space. Her arm brushed Gwen's as she picked up the menu. "What's your poison?"

Gwen glanced across the low table at Maggie, who was laughing at something Pete said, her head tipped back just enough to make Gwen remember exactly how her throat felt under her mouth. She forced her gaze back to the menu. "Depends what you recommend."

Lillian's smile widened, slow and sure. "Dangerous answer."

Across the table, Maggie's laugh faltered, just barely, before she reached for her own menu. Gwen caught the flicker again — that quick, contained reaction that made her wonder if maybe she wasn't the only one feeling off-balance tonight.

The server arrived to take orders, and the table filled with talk about garnishes and glassware. But under it all, Gwen felt the hum of awareness — of Lillian beside her, of Maggie watching.

THE FIRST ROUND of drinks had barely hit the table before Pete was waving down a server with a conspiratorial grin. "Special occasion," she stage-whispered, jerking a thumb toward herself and Danica. "We want bottle service."

Gwen raised a brow, but in Vegas, the words didn't sound quite as absurd as they would in Austin.

Ten minutes later, the bottle girl arrived in a glittering corset top, heels that defied physics, and a grin brighter than the sparkler blazing from the top of a frosted champagne bucket. She held up a bottle of vodka and a bottle of champagne like she was presenting crown jewels, the sparkler spitting silver light over the table while the group whooped and clapped. Maggie joined in, laughing as the bottle girl popped the champagne with a messy flourish that made Danica shriek.

Somewhere between pouring the first round and mixing the second, the bar's low hum shifted into a pulsing bass. The crowd thickened, the lights dimmed, and conversation became something you had to lean into. Gwen felt Lillian's shoulder brush hers as they ducked their heads together, a mutual concession to the noise.

"So," Lillian said, voice warm in Gwen's ear. "How did they rope you into this circus?"

Gwen could feel Maggie's gaze before she even glanced up — sure enough, across the table, Maggie's eyes were fixed on them, her fingers idly circling the rim of her glass. Gwen kept her own expression neutral, even easy, but she let her shoulder rest a beat longer against Lillian's before leaning back.

"Same way they get everyone else," Gwen replied. "A mix of emotional blackmail and alcohol."

Lillian laughed, tipping her glass toward Gwen's. "And here I thought you were just here for the champagne."

Gwen clinked her glass lightly against Lillian's, then let her eyes slide back to Maggie — just for a moment. Not enough to say anything. Just enough to let her notice.

No flirting. Nothing she could be called out on. Just a quiet reminder that Gwen could still get someone's attention... and maybe, just maybe, still wanted Maggie to care.

Lillian shifted, angling herself toward Gwen so they could hear each other without shouting. "You here for all three nights?" she asked.

"Apparently," Gwen said, sipping her champagne. "I've been informed it's a marathon, not a sprint."

Lillian's mouth curved in a way that made it hard to tell if she was amused or sympathetic. "I live here, so I'm more of a day-trip sprinter myself. Two nights on the Strip would probably kill me."

Gwen blinked. "Wait, you live here? In Vegas?"

"Technically," Lillian said, rolling her wrist. "Henderson. Suburbs. I avoid this part of town unless I'm dragged out for a birthday or some sort of family obligation." She glanced toward Pete, who was now arm in arm with Danica on the couch. "This counts as both."

"What do you do?" Gwen asked, curiosity outweighing her usual guardedness.

Lillian's expression warmed. "I'm a tortoise biologist."

Gwen tilted her head. "That's… not an answer I get often."

"Probably not. I work with a conservation group that monitors and relocates desert tortoises during construction projects. Mostly pipeline oversight — making sure nobody steamrolls through a habitat without noticing."

Gwen took another slow sip, considering her. "That sounds… important. And a little like being the tortoise police."

"Pretty much," Lillian said with a laugh. "Only slower."

Gwen chuckled, but her eyes flicked up, drawn again to Maggie across the table. She was still talking to Izzy, but her gaze kept darting back, sharp and unreadable.

If Gwen had wanted to play it safe, she'd turn away, keep the conversation light. Instead, she leaned in just enough to catch Lillian's next words, her hand resting casually on the back of the couch, close enough to imply an ease she didn't actually feel.

From this angle, she could see both of them — Lillian's open, easy smile and Maggie's subtle, restless watching.

And Gwen… Well, she let herself enjoy both.

She took her time with the next sip of champagne, letting the fizz pop against her tongue.

"So how long have you been doing that?" Gwen asked.

"About eight years," Lillian replied. "It's not glamorous, but I like knowing I'm actually helping protect something that can't speak for itself—"

"Sorry, what was that?"

Maggie's voice cut in, smooth but edged, and suddenly she was there, sliding onto the low couch across from them. Her knees brushed Gwen's before she leaned toward Lillian. "I couldn't hear over the music."

Lillian turned to her with an easy smile. "I was saying I work with desert tortoises — mostly relocation during pipeline projects."

"That's... very specific," Maggie said, eyes glinting. "And noble."

Gwen tipped her glass to her mouth, hiding the curve of her smile behind it. She didn't dare let it show — how much she recognized that look in Maggie's eyes, how much she secretly liked being the reason for it.

Lillian launched into a story about tagging juveniles in the Mojave, and Maggie stayed perched forward, nodding politely but keeping one hand resting on Gwen's knee.

Gwen left it there.

And she kept her smile to herself.

THE BASS of the song faded out, replaced by the glittery synth hook of a song Gwen hadn't heard since college. "Oops!... I Did It Again" poured through the speakers, and the mood in the room shifted instantly.

"Oh my god," Danica gasped, already shoving her drink into Pete's hand. "We have to dance."

"This isn't really a dancing place," Izzy called out, looking around.

"Everywhere's a dancing place if you just start dancing." Kiera was laughing, grabbing Danica's wrist and dragging her toward the open space between two sets of couches.

Pete, grinning like she'd been waiting for this exact moment, turned to Lillian. "You're coming too."

Lillian laughed, a little reluctant, but let herself be hauled away.

That left Maggie and Gwen on the couch, the music pulsing around them.

Maggie's gaze caught hers, a wordless invitation in it. Gwen gave a small wave toward the impromptu dance floor and gestured with her nearly empty glass. "You go. I'm getting a refill."

Maggie's mouth tilted like she might argue, but she just nodded and disappeared into the crowd.

As Gwen started to rise, Izzy dropped into the seat beside her, cheeks flushed from the music and the champagne, a faint shimmer of champagne on her smile.

"Hey," Izzy said, glancing at her phone. "So… Kiera's mom just texted to ask if we've set a date yet. What is with moms and wedding planning? They all lose their minds."

Gwen laughed, easing back into her chair. "Already? You've been engaged, what, three months?"

"Two and a half," Izzy corrected, mock-serious. "Apparently that's long enough for everyone over fifty to start panicking about venue availability."

"Ah, yes," Gwen said dryly. "The sacred wedding timeline."

Izzy grinned. "Exactly. Like if we don't lock down a caterer tomorrow, our love will just… expire."

They both laughed, the music thumping softly in the background.

"So," Gwen said after a moment, "do you have plans? Or are you two just enjoying being engaged?"

Izzy tilted her head, her smile softening. "I mean, when I'm not freaking out about Kiera waking up one day and realizing she was wrong when she said yes? Mostly that second one. I think we're just… basking. You know? Getting used to saying fiancée without sounding like we're quoting someone else."

"That's a good stage," Gwen said. "You only get it once."

Her fingers curled around her glass, and before she could stop herself, she was back in that moment years ago — on a weekend getaway in Texas Hill Country. They'd been sitting on a weathered porch swing at a B&B, cicadas buzzing in the twilight, the air thick with the scent of wildflowers and mesquite. Maggie had her bare feet tucked under her, glass of wine in hand, cheeks flushed from a day spent swimming in the river. Gwen had pulled out a small leather ring box, her hands trembling just enough to make Maggie's eyes go wide. She'd asked her then and there, no big crowd, just the two of them and a sky turning gold.

Maggie's yes had been quiet but certain, and she'd leaned in with a smile that felt like the start of forever.

It had been simple. Perfect.

"You okay?" Izzy asked, tilting her head.

Gwen shook herself back to the present, forcing a small smile. "Yeah. Just remembering what that feels like."

Izzy studied her for a second longer than was polite, then softened it with a sip of her drink. "And what about you two?" she asked, casual in the way people are when they're absolutely not being casual.

Gwen tried to keep her face neutral. "Us?"

"Yeah, you and Maggie." Izzy's shrug was practiced nonchalance. "Everything good? I know when we were all there after Maggie's mom died, things felt a little tense."

For a beat, Gwen could only smooth her thumb along the rim of her glass, like there might be an answer hiding there. Their group of friends had attracted more dancers to their crowd. Maggie was dancing, hair sticking to her temples, scream-singing the lyrics to a song — badly, too, like she'd forgotten every beat of rhythm she'd ever had. She'd thrown an arm around Danica, belting out the chorus, eyes shut and grin wide.

Something in Gwen's chest pulled tight. Nostalgia? Ache? Both.

"Of course," she said finally, her tone steady but not quite convincing even to herself. "Yeah, we're good."

Izzy didn't push, but Gwen caught the faint tilt of her brows, the way her gaze flicked between Gwen and the mess of Maggie on the dance floor. Izzy leaned back in her chair, letting the music swallow the moment. "Well," she said, a hint of wry amusement threading her voice. "I'm glad."

Gwen's throat worked. She looked back to Maggie — her wife, still, technically. The sight was magnetic.

And the worst part? It always had been.

CHAPTER 9

MAGGIE

MAGGIE NURSED A LUKEWARM GLASS OF WATER ON THE BALCONY, the city glittering below like it had been waiting all day to show off. Inside, Gwen was already asleep — curled on the pullout like she had something to prove about not needing comfort. Maggie had hovered for a minute, watching her breathe, before retreating out here where the air didn't taste quite so thick.

She should have been tired. She was tired. But her brain had other ideas. Top priority among those thoughts seemed to be: Gwen at the bar earlier, talking to Lillian. She'd met Lillian before, back in college, and had even liked her back then. Back when she was kind of awkward and nerdy. Now she was gorgeous, desert-biologist Lillian, who wore her confidence easily. Maggie had only caught bits of the conversation, the easy tilt of Gwen's smile, but it had been enough to make something sharp flare under her ribs.

Jealousy. God, she hated it. She wasn't supposed to feel that anymore. They were separated — technically free. She had no right to bristle over whoever Gwen did or didn't talk to, no matter how perfect their bone structure.

And yet.

Maybe Gwen would do better with someone like Lillian. Someone cool and contained, who didn't leave laundry in damp clumps on the bathroom floor or cry at sappy commercials. Someone who wouldn't fall apart when things got hard.

The thought made Maggie wince. She took another sip of water, forcing it down like penance.

The balcony door slid open with a soft scrape, and Danica stepped out, equally rumpled, carrying her own glass. "Couldn't sleep?"

Maggie huffed. "Still dehydrated from all the tequila we pretended wasn't tequila."

Danica chuckled, lowering herself into the chair beside hers. "God, I'm drunk enough to feel this tomorrow."

"Me too." Maggie grinned despite herself. "We're not as young as we used to be, huh?"

"Speak for yourself," Danica said primly, and they both snorted into their water.

Silence stretched for a beat, not uncomfortable, just the kind that knew how to breathe. The Strip's neon pulse filled the space between them.

"I'm glad you're here," Danica said finally, quiet but certain.

Maggie's chest pinched. Guilt, sharp as always. She was glad too, but being here meant pretending, meant smiling at Gwen when her heart was a mess of contradictions. Still, she found herself nodding, voice rough. "Yeah. Me too."

Danica shifted, side-eyeing her. "So. Are you going to tell me more about your life? Or do I have to drag it out of you like always?"

Maggie raised an eyebrow. "Isn't this your trip? Shouldn't we be talking wedding plans or something?"

Danica grimaced. "Dear god, no. Please don't even

mention a wedding to me right now. Wedding planning is the worst."

Maggie nodded in understanding.

"So, you know how Pete had that Bulgarian fort in mind for the ceremony?"

Maggie nodded. Pete had told everyone to wait on buying flights or hotels but had at least given them a destination to start planning for. Maggie figured it'd be somewhere strange and wonderful. The good thing about a small wedding was Pete and Danica's ability to be a little chaotic about the cemented plans. She'd expect nothing less from Pete, but she was sure Danica was panicking internally.

"No, wait, I just said I wasn't going to talk about this," Danica paused.

Maggie raised a brow. "What's up with the fort?"

"They suddenly want this hysterically large rental fee, like five times the amount we'd agreed on," Danica said. "I don't know. Pete is crushed. She had her sights set on this stupid fort—"

"What do you want?" Maggie asked, sipping her water.

"I don't care where we get married. I just care that my best friends and my family are there. It could be in my parents' backyard for all I care," Danica said. "Hence why I've let Pete decide that part. I don't know if you know this, but she tends to have strong opinions."

"Ah, yes, she hides it well." Maggie snorted. "Wherever you get married, we will all be there, and it will be wonderful. I promise."

Danica offered her a small smile, then sniffled and took a deep breath like she was clearing her head. "Okay, now your turn." She nodded. "Catch me up."

Maggie groaned, tipping her head back. "How much are you willing to bribe me with greasy breakfast food tomorrow in exchange for my life story?"

Danica laughed, bumping her shoulder lightly against Maggie's. "Unlimited hash browns. Now talk."

Maggie swirled the last of her water, watching the ice melt into nothing. "Okay, fine. Life updates. Let's see…" She ticked them off on her fingers. "Still helping part-time at the shop. Kids are healthy, occasionally feral. Gwen's mom comes over and helps with the kids sometimes, which is nice."

"That does sound nice. You like her, right?"

Maggie shrugged. "She's always been very kind to me."

Danica reached across the space between their chairs and squeezed Maggie's hand. The unsaid phrase hung in the air: You like her, but she's not your mom.

Maggie squeezed Danica's hand back. "So, yep, that's the highlight reel."

Danica smiled into her glass. "Not to make this weird, but your hair looks amazing right now."

Maggie snorted. "It's just the lack of humidity, I bet. My hairspray doesn't melt off before it can set here."

For a while they just sat, the Strip buzzing like a different planet below them. It was almost easy, falling into the kind of friendship rhythm they used to have before everything got complicated.

"How are things with Gwen? When we were there after…" Danica paused, as if she wasn't sure she should remind Maggie about her mother's funeral. Like it wasn't always in Maggie's mind. "Well, when we were there last time, I was worried about you."

Maggie's mind flicked through everything she could unload — the shouting match where she'd said she was done, the uneasy quiet that followed, the not-quite resolution of the guest room arrangement. All of it sitting just under her tongue, waiting, but too heavy to hand over tonight.

Maggie shrugged again. "It's fine." It wasn't a lie. Things were fine. She was fine. She was dealing with everything just fine.

Danica gave her a long look. "I'm always here if you want to talk."

"I pay someone a lot of money to hear about all that, don't worry," Maggie said. Her mind flashed to Dr. Elowen pulling her aside after their last session, suggesting she consider a personal therapist to work through her grief. She'd handed Maggie a list of colleagues. Maggie had tucked it into her nightstand, telling herself she'd revisit it after Vegas.

"I am always here. Not as an objective listener, but as a Team Maggie listener," Danica added.

"I know." Maggie nodded, pressing her lips together. "Tell me something good. How's work?"

Danica's expression softened in that way it always did when someone mentioned her job. "Quiet, for once. But it's actually bad luck to say that. If you say the Q word, it never lasts long. You know how it is — one week I'm getting a full three or four hours of sleep, and the next it's every isolette full, alarms going off down every hallway."

"Jesus," Maggie muttered. "And you just… handle that."

Danica gave a little shrug, almost embarrassed. "It's what I signed up for." Then, after a beat, "Sometimes it's a lot. But I love it."

"Of course you do." Maggie smirked, shaking her head. "You're like the calmest person under pressure I've ever met."

Danica laughed, bumping her knee against Maggie's. "Hardly. You should've seen me lose it at the coffee machine last week when someone left an empty pot. I wrote a strongly worded Post-it."

Maggie barked a laugh loud enough to echo against the glass railing. "Wow, slow down, you absolute lunatic."

And for a second, it was simple again — the two of them, tipsy and honest, the night stretched wide open around them.

By the time she slipped back inside, Danica had gone to bed, and the suite was quiet except for the hum of the AC. The pullout couch looked almost inviting in its awkwardness, sheets rumpled, Gwen cocooned in them like she'd negotiated a truce with the hotel bedding.

Maggie set down her empty water glass, then crawled carefully onto the mattress beside Gwen. The frame squeaked a little, and Gwen shifted but didn't wake. Typical. She could sleep through fire alarms.

Maggie lay there on her side, staring. Which was stupid. Creepy, even. But her chest ached with it — the soft line of Gwen's jaw, the strands of hair fallen across her forehead, the shape of her breathing, steady and unbothered. It was like muscle memory, that pull toward her.

A massive pang of longing crashed over her, so sharp it left her breathless. All she wanted was to tuck herself into that curve, slide her arm around Gwen's waist, pretend none of the last year had happened.

But then — on cue — her brain marched out the litany. Gwen the workaholic, gone more nights than not. Gwen, sitting stiff and silent when Maggie needed her most, like when they'd chosen to have an abortion. Like when her mom died and Maggie was the only one with her.

She'd shoved that afternoon into the basement of her memory — the blur of paramedics in the hallway, the metallic smell of oxygen tanks, her body shaking so badly she could barely hold her mother's hand. And the guilt lingered, sticky and insistent: that in her mom's final moments, she hadn't been the calm, soothing daughter she thought she should be. She hadn't been graceful or strong. She had been terrified, begging her mom not to leave her, and she still carried the shame of it like a hidden scar.

Gwen had never known that. Maggie had never let her. She'd never felt more alone in that moment, and all she'd wanted was Gwen to be there.

But Gwen wasn't there. She'd been halfway across the world at a conference in Lisbon and hadn't answered her phone for two hours.

Izzy had been on the first flight to Austin. Izzy was there, and then Kiera. Gwen hadn't gotten home until the next day.

Deep down, she knew that expecting Gwen to somehow bend the laws of time and space to get home faster was impossible. She knew that her mother's unexpected heart attack wasn't something that Gwen had purposefully planned on missing.

And yet. Maggie's resentment burned hot and familiar. They just had different priorities. Maggie would never come first to Gwen. They just didn't mesh. Not anymore.

Still, when Gwen shifted in her sleep and murmured something soft — something Maggie couldn't quite catch — Maggie felt the tether snap taut again, no matter how she tried to sever it.

She rolled onto her back, staring at the ceiling like it had answers. It didn't.

She told herself to close her eyes, to just sleep. But of course her body had other ideas, keyed up and restless, hyperaware of the slow rhythm of Gwen's breathing a foot away.

Longing was a stupid word, but that's what it was — coiled low in her belly, hot and insistent, demanding attention. The kind of ache she'd once mistaken for inevitability.

She studied Gwen the way you study something you're trying to memorize: the curve of her cheek, the faint frown line even in sleep, the hand curled loosely on the pillow like she was holding on to something unseen. It was ridiculous how badly Maggie wanted to reach out, to smooth Gwen's hair back, to trace the line of her shoulder with a fingertip.

How badly she just wanted their marriage to be something it wasn't.

And then came the counterweight, heavy and deliberate. She remembered Gwen's laptop open on the kitchen counter, glowing at midnight while Maggie sat in the dark, aching and raw. Remembered how Gwen's phone would buzz during dinners, during movies, during everything, and she'd always answer, always prioritize. Remembered sitting alone in the surgery clinic waiting room after the termination, wishing for something more than Gwen's quiet, strained smile after the fact. Thought of the hollow, dark space that had cracked open inside of her when her mother died, and how Gwen's comfort was well-meaning but too clinical, too careful — like she was afraid to feel it with her.

All those absences added up. Maggie reminded herself of that. Forced herself, really. Because otherwise she'd just get pulled under again, the way she always had.

She forced herself to focus, to catalog each reminder like a nail being hammered in: *This is why. This is why.*

They didn't work. They hadn't worked for a long time. The chemistry was still there, sure — but chemistry didn't cook a meal or sit through grief or remember anniversaries. Chemistry didn't keep you from feeling abandoned.

Gwen murmured again, shifting onto her side, her back now to Maggie. And the pang that went through her was humiliatingly sharp.

She clenched her jaw, staring at the ceiling. *This is why*, she repeated silently. *This is why we're divorcing. This is why.*

But the ache didn't care about logic. It just stayed, stubborn and alive, right there under her skin.

MAGGIE SURFACED SLOWLY, head pounding, mouth cotton-dry. The room was still dim, blackout curtains doing their best impression of midnight, but voices tugged her awake.

Whispered voices.

She cracked an eye. Gwen sat on the edge of the pullout, hair perfectly coiffed like she hadn't been face-planted in a pillow all night. Izzy was perched beside her, both of them hunched conspiratorially, mugs of hotel coffee steaming between them.

"I'm just nervous," Izzy was saying, voice low but too awake for this hour. "Like — what if I'm not enough for all of it? Not just Kiera, but the girls. It's not just one person I'm marrying. It's a whole family. And what if I mess that up?"

Maggie blinked, her stomach lurching before her brain caught up. She pushed herself upright, blanket tangling around her legs. "What?"

Both their heads whipped toward her, looking as guilty as teenagers caught smoking behind the gym.

"Izzy," Maggie rasped. "Why are you nervous about marrying Kiera? You two are disgustingly in love. You're like domestic lesbians with matching lunchboxes."

Izzy laughed weakly. "I know. But I'm serious. She's got the girls, she's got her routines — teaching, school drop-offs, bedtime, all of it. I love them, but sometimes I feel like I'm sneaking into a life that already worked fine without me. What if I don't fit?"

Maggie groaned. "I mean, love is chaos, right? It's also work, and guilt, and compromise, and sometimes... sometimes it just stops working, no matter how much you want it to."

The words came out too fast, too sharp.

Izzy frowned, glancing between her and Gwen. "Wow. Thanks for the pep talk."

"I didn't mean it like that," Maggie said, rubbing her temples. "I just mean... love doesn't fix everything. Sometimes it hurts more than it helps."

"Or," Izzy said carefully, "maybe sometimes it's worth the risk anyway."

Maggie looked at her and felt the heat rise in her face. "Sure. If you're brave enough to keep believing in it."

Gwen cleared her throat, giving Maggie a look that clearly communicated: *you might want to stop talking.*

Izzy reached out, squeezed Maggie's ankle gently over the blanket. "You know we love you, right? Even when you're a hungover asshole who goes full doom prophet before breakfast."

That earned a weak laugh out of her. "I'm a delight in the mornings."

Gwen huffed a small sound that might've been a laugh. "Sure you are."

Before Maggie could say anything back, the suite door swung open so hard it hit the stopper. Pete burst in like a storm, wearing sunglasses the size of serving platters and clutching a Liquor Barn bag like it contained the cure for hangovers.

"Rise and shine, sweethearts," she rasped, voice shredded. "I come bearing vodka and Gatorade. Don't say I never loved you."

She froze mid-stride, surveying the crime scene: Maggie, bedheaded and blanket-tangled, caught mid-rant; Izzy, guilty as hell with her mug clutched tight; Gwen, the picture of calm composure, which only made her look more suspicious.

Pete tilted her head, wolfish. "Okay... what the hell are you whisper-goblins conspiring about?"

"Nothing," Izzy said instantly, all smooth and glassy, like she'd been practicing.

Gwen crumbled under pressure. "Murder?"

Every head swiveled toward her. Gwen coughed, cheeks pink.

"Murderously hungry. For breakfast," Maggie added. They were doomed.

Pete peeled off her sunglasses slowly, like a detective about to close the case. "You're all acting shady as hell. What's going on?"

Maggie inhaled wrong and choked on her own spit.

"Nothing," Gwen said firmly. "Maggie's hungover and we were trying to whisper for her sake."

Pete squinted at them, then finally tossed the bag onto the

coffee table with a sigh so dramatic it belonged on Broadway. "Yeah, I feel you."

Maggie could practically hear her pulse in her ears. Izzy kept her eyes glued to her mug, draining it. Gwen's lips pressed together in that maddeningly calm way of hers, but Maggie swore she caught the tiniest twitch at the corner — amusement, maybe.

Pete dug out a bottle and lobbed it at her. "Catch, Bedhead."

Maggie fumbled but held on, hugging it to her chest. She cracked the seal on the Gatorade and gulped half of it like a woman who'd just crossed a desert, but the sour churn in her stomach had nothing to do with dehydration.

Izzy. Drawing out the secrets she and Gwen were squeezing too tightly in their hands, afraid to let loose.

And Pete. Jesus. Pete had bought their cover story for now, but Maggie knew her. Pete was basically a truffle pig for drama. She'd sniff out the truth before the weekend was over if Izzy mentioned anything about Maggie's dark comments.

Maggie set the bottle down a little too hard. Gwen gave her a look, one brow arched. Maggie just shook her head, refusing to elaborate.

The silence had just started to settle — Izzy pretending to study her empty mug, Gwen arranging the blanket like it was a diplomatic task, Maggie clutching her Gatorade like a flotation device — when the bedroom door opened again.

Kiera swept out in a giant straw sun hat, bikini straps visible beneath a gauzy cover-up. "Who's ready for pool day?" she asked brightly, hands on her hips like a camp counselor about to blow a whistle.

Maggie blinked at her through bloodshot eyes. "Define ready."

Kiera rolled her eyes good-naturedly. "You look like you need it more than anyone. Cold plunge, sunshine, hair of the dog…" She clapped her hands once. "Trust me, you'll feel better."

Maggie wasn't sure if she wanted to kiss Kiera for her optimism or strangle her with her sun hat.

Izzy, predictably, perked right up at her fiancée's entrance, setting down her mug and sitting taller. "See? That's the spirit."

Beside her, Gwen's hand smoothed down the sheet one last time before she stood, composed and unruffled as ever. "Pool day it is," she said softly.

Maggie flopped back against the pillow, glaring up at the ceiling.

CHAPTER 10

GWEN

GWEN FELT LIKE SHE'D WANDERED INTO A FEVER DREAM. IT wasn't just a pool — it was a full production. A giant Buddha statue loomed at one end, half in shade, haloed by palm trees. The water glittered a perfect turquoise. House music pulsed from gigantic speakers over a raised stage off to one side, vibrating through the space with surprising volume. The air smelled like sunscreen, salt, and prosecco.

It was barely eleven in the morning, but the place was already buzzing. Packs of women in neon bikinis clutching sloshing cocktails, shirtless guys dancing like they'd been at it since dawn, waitresses weaving through with trays of shots balanced in increasingly concerning quantities. Gwen hadn't been to a pool party since... ever. And she was fairly sure none of them had looked like *this*.

They approached the host stand to claim their reserved table, but luck — or perhaps some god chaos — was on their side. A manager in a crisp polo appeared, effusive about an "upgrade" and leading them through the crowd to a private cabana tucked along one side of the pool

The cabana was absurd, complete with a cushioned U-shaped couch, its own plunge pool out front, and a flat-screen TV bolted to the wall even though no one was going to watch it.

And then the bottle service girl arrived, striding in with the confidence that Gwen imagined was necessary to walk in skyscraper heels poolside. She carried a tray of menus and an expression that suggested she'd seen everything.

"Holy shit," Maggie muttered, already collapsing onto the couch. She draped an arm over her eyes, the picture of a fainting Victorian.

The rest of the group, by contrast, came alive. Izzy and Kiera dove into the menus like they were treasure maps, already debating Bloody Mary spice levels. Danica flagged the waitress down with her bright, type-A efficiency, while Pete groaned in gratitude.

"Thank god," Pete announced, plopping onto the couch. "I love the private pool. Because you *know* people are definitely fucking in that one." She jabbed toward the main pool, where two strangers were indeed suspiciously entangled beneath an umbrella

Kiera gagged. Izzy cackled.

Gwen sat down carefully on the edge of the couch across from Maggie, who didn't move. Gwen was trying not to gape at everything, the sensory overload at odds with the strange comfort of sitting this close to her wife, even if Maggie was sprawled dramatically as if she'd already died of Vegas.

Maggie wasn't just lying down. She was sprawled in a full starfish position. One leg bent, the other dangling off the edge of the couch, her cover-up bunched around her thighs, sunglasses askew on her face even though they hadn't been outside long enough for anyone's retinas to fry. She'd draped an arm over her eyes like she was auditioning for a tragic heroine role — Saint of the Pool Hangover.

And Gwen… God help her, Gwen couldn't look away.

In the middle of all this spectacle — the DJ, the women in rhinestoned bikinis, Pete already heckling the waitress about "maximum garnish" on her Bloody Mary — her gaze kept circling back to Maggie. The wild hair, the bare skin, the absolute refusal to sit upright like a normal person. Dramatic, impossible Maggie, radiating heat and exhaustion and a kind of raw presence that had always knocked Gwen a little off-balance.

She told herself to look away, to focus on anything else. The Buddha statue. The champagne buckets sweating onto the table. Izzy, beaming at Kiera.

Maggie let out another sigh — long, theatrical, and completely unnecessary — and Gwen's chest tightened, sharp and uninvited. The urge to touch Maggie flared, ridiculous and dangerous. To push her sunglasses back up her nose, smooth her tangled hair, slide a palm over the sharp line of her shin where the sunlight hit.

Instead, Gwen folded her hands in her lap, posture straight, expression neutral, like she wasn't teetering on the edge of something that hadn't belonged to her in a long time.

The distraction arrived on silver trays — literally. The bottle service woman swept back in with two busboys trailing behind her, each balancing platters piled high with eggs, bacon, fruit, something suspiciously labeled "hangover fries," and an architectural stack of pancakes that looked like it had been engineered for Instagram.

"Praise be," Pete muttered, attempting a completely incorrect and backward sign of the cross before snatching a strip of bacon straight off the platter.

Danica swatted at her hand. "At least wait until the food hits the table—"

"Too late," Pete said, mouth already full.

Izzy leaned over the Bloody Mary cart the waitress rolled in, eyes wide. "Is that... shrimp? There's shrimp on the skewers. And bacon. Oh my god, is that a slider?"

"It's basically lunch in a glass," Kiera said approvingly, plucking a celery stick and crunching into it.

Maggie finally cracked an eye open from her fainting-couch pose. "If one of those comes near me, I'm suing."

Danica, ever the hostess, was divvying up fruit skewers like she was feeding children at summer camp. "Okay, someone please eat some melon before everyone devours nothing but meat and cheese."

"Melon's just crunchy water," Pete argued, piling a plate like she was preparing for the apocalypse. "Why waste valuable stomach space?"

"It's hydration," Danica insisted.

"Gatorade is hydration. This is sadness on a stick."

Gwen found herself laughing before she could stop it, the sound slipping out quieter than the others' but still real. For a moment, surrounded by plates and snark and sunlight pouring through the cabana curtains, the ache in her chest loosened.

Beside her, Maggie let out a soft huff of amusement too — eyes still closed, but a smile tugging at the corner of her mouth like she'd been listening the whole time.

The table turned into a free-for-all within minutes, all hands reaching and plates clinking. Pete began narrating every choice like she was commentating a sporting event. "Danica's going safe with the melon — classic rookie mistake," Pete intoned, spearing three sausage links for herself. "Izzy's building a Bloody Mary tower. Mad respect. And Gwen... what do we have here? Gwen's going balanced, classic defensive play, fruit *and* carbs. She's in it for the long haul."

"Pete," Danica groaned. "Please just eat."

"I *am* eating," Pete said through a mouthful of pancake.

Gwen let their noise wash over her as she fixed a plate — some fruit, a folded pancake, a few of those ridiculous hangover fries piled with cheese and bacon. She slid it onto the low table next to Maggie, who still hadn't budged from her horizontal sprawl.

"Eat something," Gwen murmured, quiet enough that it got swallowed by Pete's next monologue.

Maggie cracked one eye open, suspicious. "Is this... bribery?"

"Just breakfast," Gwen said simply.

For a beat, Maggie just looked at her, then let out a sigh that sounded almost like surrender. She propped herself up on one elbow and snagged a fry from the plate, biting into it with a noise that was entirely inappropriate for polite company.

"God," she muttered. "Okay, fine. Worth living another day for."

BY MIDAFTERNOON, the cabana had emptied itself into the plunge pool. Izzy and Kiera were attempting some half-choreographed twirl routine to whatever EDM remix was pounding through the speakers, Pete was attempting to do handstands, which she had explicitly been banned from doing, and Danica was still trying to keep her hair dry.

Gwen stayed back, perched on the edge of the couch, watching the chaos. She could feel the thump of bass in her ribs, hear Pete yelling, "Ten out of ten, Olympic form" after surfacing again.

Beside her, Maggie had melted deeper into the cushions, sunglasses slipping low, the curve of her shoulder pink from the sun. She looked exhausted and adorable.

Gwen poured a glass of water from the sweating pitcher and nudged it toward her. "Drink," she said softly.

Maggie huffed but took it, tilting it back in slow sips. When she set it down, Gwen couldn't help herself — she reached out, brushing a strand of hair off Maggie's damp forehead, fingers grazing warm skin.

Maggie stilled, then tipped her head just slightly into the touch. And for a moment they just looked at each other, Gwen's hand hovering, Maggie's lips parting like she wanted to say something but couldn't.

"Thanks," Maggie whispered, her voice rough, meant for no one else.

The sound went straight through Gwen, sharp and unsteady.

And then, thanks to the chaos muppets Maggie called friends, the chorus rose from the pool, loud and merciless:

"Kiss! Kiss! Kiss!"

Izzy led the chant, Kiera howling beside her, Pete smacking the water in rhythm like a drum. Even Danica, blushing, had her hands cupped around her mouth, adding her voice to the racket.

Gwen froze, hand still half in Maggie's hair. Maggie's mouth curved — somewhere between a smile and a dare.

And suddenly the whole cabana was vibrating with the sound of their friends, demanding the one thing Gwen had promised herself she wouldn't give.

Gwen lifted her free hand, waving toward the pool like she could shoo them off. "Enough," she called, trying for stern but landing somewhere closer to flustered school-teacher.

Of course, that was when Lillian appeared, cutting through the chaos like a knife. She strode up to the cabana in a sleek black one-piece that made Gwen want to do a double take, golden skin gleaming, sunglasses perched low on her nose.

"Hey," she said, casual as ever, and Gwen dipped her chin in acknowledgment.

The group only got louder. Izzy had abandoned chanting in favor of wolf-whistling. Pete slapped the water again, chanting, "Cowards! Cowards!" in a terrible British accent.

Gwen felt her face flame. She opened her mouth, fumbling

for something — anything — to defuse this mess before Lillian could read too much into it.

And then Maggie's hand was on her cheek.

She turned Gwen's face toward her and pressed her mouth to hers. The kiss was firm, unapologetic, the kind of kiss that left no room for argument.

The cabana erupted in cheering and whooping and Lillian's nearby laugh.

Gwen's heart stuttered. She hadn't tasted Maggie's lips in months, but her body knew exactly how to respond: a sharp pull low in her stomach, the urge to lean in, to let it last.

She didn't. Couldn't.

When Maggie pulled back, Gwen blinked, pulse hammering. Maggie just smirked faintly, as if to say *See? No big deal.*

Across the way, Lillian arched one perfect brow, amusement glinting behind her shades.

Gwen was caught between her wife's mouth, their friends' chaos, and Lillian's cool gaze, feeling like she might actually combust.

Maggie was on her feet before Gwen could even recalibrate from the kiss. She tugged off her cover-up in one impatient sweep, dropped it onto the couch, and snatched a glass of champagne from the table.

"God help us," Gwen muttered, but her voice was lost under the shrieks from the pool.

Maggie raised her glass in mock salute, then sauntered to the edge of the water, hips already swaying to the beat.

Gwen's chest went hot, traitorous. Because of course Maggie looked incandescent with her bare skin gleaming in the sunlight, hair wild, grin loose and easy in a way Gwen hadn't seen in months. She hated how magnetic it was. Hated how impossible it was to look anywhere else.

A commotion of cheers and whistles rose from the cabana next to them, and when Gwen turned, she saw two bottle girls in matching bikinis pop the tops off massive champagne bottles, spraying twin arcs of fizz over the heads of two men who pumped their fists in triumph.

"Oh *hell* yes," Pete said, practically vibrating, already half out of her chair.

Danica pressed a palm to her chest like she could physically hold Pete back. "No. Don't even think about it."

But Pete's eyes had gone glassy with desire, locked on the foamy spray. "That could be me."

"Exactly," Danica said firmly.

Gwen's gaze drifted back to the pool. Maggie was dancing and laughing with her head tilted back, champagne flute lifted in salute to the wild scene next to them. For a moment, Gwen let herself forget the distance between them, the sharp edges of the last year. For a moment, all she saw was the woman she'd married, sunlight burning across her shoulders, joy spilling out of her like it belonged to Gwen too. And god, Gwen missed her. Missed her in a way that was marrow deep. Missed her so much it almost felt like drowning — sitting there, dry and steady, while Maggie was just out of reach.

CHAPTER 11

MAGGIE

THE AFTERNOON HAD STARTED OUT ROWDY IN THE PLUNGE POOL. Danica, Kiera, and Izzy had claimed a corner, knees tucked, drinks balanced on the ledge, and were busy playing a tipsy version of truth or dare. The dares were ridiculous — Izzy had already dared Kiera to swim the width of the plunge pool with her sun hat on, and Danica had been made to try to whistle the Backstreet Boys with a mouth full of ice cubes. Maggie slid in between them, already buzzing, ready to play.

"Truth or dare?" Izzy demanded, wiggling her brows.

"Truth," Danica said, and she ended up confessing that she once kissed her chemistry lab partner just to get the answers for a quiz. Kiera dared Izzy to sip champagne through a snorkel. Maggie dared Kiera to cartwheel on the slick deck, which almost ended in disaster for herself *and* a plate of nachos.

The laughter was constant, shrieks echoing across the water. Gwen, Pete, and Lillian stayed in the cabana, half participating, half doing their own thing. Pete and Lillian had fallen into easy conversation, catching up like no time had passed, while Gwen pretended to be distracted with the drinks menu but kept sneaking glances at the pool.

When it was Maggie's turn, she lifted her chin. "Truth," she said, like it was its own dare.

Izzy's grin went sharp. "What's the wildest place you and Gwen have ever…" She waggled her brows, "You know."

Maggie choked on a laugh. "That is not fair."

"Perfectly fair," Danica insisted. "You chose truth. Them's the rules."

Kiera looked both horrified and delighted. "Oh my god, please don't answer, but also please answer."

Maggie rolled her eyes, cheeks warming. She could feel Gwen's attention from the cabana, and that made it worse. "Fine," she said, dragging the word out. "The rooftop of the parking garage downtown. Happy?"

The plunge pool exploded into shrieks. Kiera covered her face, Danica howled with laughter, Izzy pounded the surface of the water until it splashed.

From the cabana, Pete's head whipped around. "Excuse me?"

"Legendary," Izzy said solemnly, still half laughing.

Lillian raised her brows, smirking into her glass. Gwen had gone perfectly still, her face impassive, but Maggie felt the air between them heat anyway. She pushed it further, turning toward the cabana. "Should I tell them about the library stacks, too?"

From the cabana, Gwen's voice cut through, calm but deliberate: "Why stop there? What about the Ferris wheel?" Her tone was smooth, but the implication was sharp enough to make Maggie flush all over again. The pool crew shrieked even louder, the noise ricocheting off the walls, and Maggie shot Gwen a look that promised revenge. Gwen only raised her glass, unbothered, eyes locked on her.

"A Ferris wheel?" Danica choked. "How does that even work?"

Pete looked like she was considering the physics of the situation.

"We have to up our game," Kiera joked, and Izzy blushed.

Maggie excused herself from the plunge pool with a laugh, muttering something about needing the bathroom. She slipped through the crowd, dripping and flushed, glad for a moment of escape from all the noise.

But when she glanced back, Gwen was following.

Barefoot, steady, cutting through the chaos with that same focus that made the hairs on Maggie's arms lift.

By the time Maggie reached the relative quiet near the bathrooms — still buzzing with music and chatter, but private enough — Gwen was there too, close behind. She caught Maggie's arm before she could duck into the bathroom, firm and unyielding.

And Maggie, chest heaving, had the insane thought that this was what it had always been between them: push, pull, drag, follow.

The air by the bathrooms was cooler, but Gwen's hands were warm. They stopped just inside the shadow of the stucco wall, close enough that the bass from the pool seemed to vibrate straight through Maggie's ribs.

Gwen's voice was low, controlled. "I know what you're doing."

Maggie widened her eyes, playing dumb. "Oh? What am I doing?"

Gwen stepped closer, deliberately closing the gap until Maggie's back met the wall with a muted thud. The stucco was cool against her shoulders, a contrast to Gwen's warmth pressing in. Gwen didn't just enter the space — she commanded it, blocking out the entire world's chatter and the thrum of bass until it felt like there was only the two of them.

Maggie's breath stuttered, chest rising quick and uneven. Gwen leaned in just enough that her shadow swallowed Maggie's, just enough that Maggie could feel the heat of her body without contact. This was how it had always been with Gwen in private — no polite mask, no tidy restraint. Just focus and intensity, radiating so fiercely it made Maggie's pulse kick like she'd been caught doing something deliciously wrong.

Her fingers twitched at her sides, torn between pushing Gwen back and clutching her shirt to pull her closer. The scent of Gwen's cologne — clean, sharp, familiar — hit her hard, and every nerve in her body seemed to fire at once.

Her chest rose against Gwen's, and for a dizzy second she thought this was it — Gwen was finally going to kiss her. Really kiss her. Not for a crowd, but for them. Gwen's gaze flicked down, lingering at her mouth, and Maggie's lips parted, ready, aching.

"Do you need me to remind you who's in control here?" Gwen murmured.

Maggie swore she felt the words low in her spine. Her lips stayed parted, her whole body screaming *yes*.

Gwen's eyes met hers again. The faintest curve touched her mouth as she whispered, "Exactly."

And then she stepped back

Just like that. Gone.

Maggie leaned against the wall, trembling, heart pounding so loud she could barely hear the bass anymore, every nerve raw and furious with need.

By the time she stumbled back toward the cabana, Gwen was already seated, composed, like nothing had happened at all.

Two bottle girls strutted in, heels clicking, bikinis glittering, each with a massive magnum champagne bottle held aloft like Olympic torches. Music swelled as if on cue, and they started shimmying in perfect sync, sparklers blazing from their bottles.

"Compliments of those guys!" one shouted over the

music, gesturing toward the same drunk men that had ordered a champagne spray.

The cabana erupted — Pete whooped, Izzy scrambled for her phone to film it, Danica covered her face with both hands. Maggie slipped inside after Kiera, deliberately choosing a seat far from Gwen. She busied herself with a towel, pretending to fuss with her hair, all the while feeling Gwen's gaze like static across her skin. The laughter swirled around her, but under it was the sharp weight of her own meddling. She couldn't shake the fear that her warnings to Izzy might've planted doubt, or worse — that she'd managed to dim Kiera's joy in the process. For once, she didn't meet Gwen's eyes. It was easier to stare at the bubbles fizzing over and wonder whether her interference had done more harm than good.

CHAPTER 12

AFTER GWEN PULLED HERSELF OUT OF THE SHOWER, THE SUITE felt quieter, calmer. The bass from the pool was a dull throb through the glass, muffled by heavy curtains. Maggie was stretched on the pullout couch in a towel, hair damp, pretending to scroll her phone but mostly looking like she could fall asleep again if left unsupervised. Pete was starfished across the other couch bed in a robe, muttering about "the champagne flu."

Kiera emerged from the bathroom with her hair slicked into a neat bun, eyeliner sharp and lethal, and a determined glint in her eye. The one that usually preceded group projects, chore charts, and field trips nobody wanted but everyone needed.

"Everyone up," Kiera said, clapping her hands once. "We've got a reservation."

Pete groaned into the pillow. "Cancel it."

"Nope." Kiera tugged at the tie of Pete's robe, ignoring her muffled protest. "We didn't come all the way to Vegas to eat sad nachos from room service. This is supposed to be celebratory. We are celebrating."

"Celebrating what?" Danica asked, emerging from the bathroom in a silk top, lips already glossed. Her tone was too innocent.

Gwen found herself smiling despite the heaviness still lodged under her ribs. The nap had dulled her edges, but it hadn't erased the memory of Maggie in the pool — laughing, sparkling, daring her — and it sure as hell hadn't erased what had passed between them in the shadow of the bathrooms. That was still humming in her veins, quiet but insistent.

DINNER WAS MERCIFULLY QUIETER than the pool had been. The restaurant lighting was low, amber spilling over the table, softening everything into gold and shadow. Their group took up half a banquette — plates of pasta and steak and vegan pizza with overpriced sides scattered like trophies.

Pete stood halfway through the meal, one hand braced on the back of her chair, a glass of wine clutched dramatically in the other. "All right," she announced, voice hoarse but strong enough to carry over the room. "I've got something to say."

Danica groaned, already pink. "Pete—"

"Shh," Pete said, putting a hand to her fiancée's cheek. "Let me."

She cleared her throat, then launched into it — equal parts irreverent and sincere. A list of all the things she loved about Danica, half of them jokes about her obsessive calendar management and half of them so earnest Gwen felt her throat tighten. "Wendell, you make me better," Pete said finally, simple and direct. "You make all of us better. And somehow, for reasons I'll never understand, you want to marry me. Which is insane, but I'm not arguing."

The table broke into laughter and applause, glasses clinking. Danica leaned up to kiss her, eyes shining.

The feeling landed in Gwen's stomach — sweet and sharp all at once. That quiet intimacy, so unshowy, so sure. The kind of thing she used to have, once.

She looked back down at her glass before she could help it, pretending the reflection of the candlelight was what had made her chest ache.

Beside her, Maggie laughed at something Pete said, tossing her head back, hair catching in the glow. Gwen didn't look. Not right away. She just took a slow sip of wine, willing herself to stay composed in the middle of so much love.

She told herself not to. She told herself to focus on the wine, on Pete still holding court at the head of the table, on the flicker of candlelight reflecting in polished silverware.

But she looked anyway.

Maggie was across from her, shoulders relaxed for once, laughing at something Kiera had added to Pete's speech. Her cheeks were flushed from the wine, hair still damp at the ends from her shower. She leaned forward on her elbows, listening intently, and when she smiled — open, unguarded…

It was the kind of smile that had once been hers, that had lit up Gwen's worst days, that had carried them through years of chaos and compromise. And god, it made her chest ache to see it now, angled somewhere she couldn't quite reach anymore.

Maggie caught her looking.

Just for a second, their eyes locked across the table, the noise of their friends receding until it felt like the room had gone quiet. Gwen didn't look away. Couldn't. The air between them was too heavy with everything unsaid.

Maggie's lips curved, faint and fleeting, a secret she wasn't about to share with anyone else.

And Gwen, holding her gaze in the soft golden light, felt that old familiar tug somewhere between her ribs — love and ache, wound so tightly together she couldn't tell which was which.

The air between her and Maggie had gone taut, stretched to breaking, when Maggie blinked like she was recovering from a trance. She cleared her throat and stood abruptly, her chair scraping against the tile floor. "All right. My turn."

Maggie had a pasted smile. "Here's to Pete and Danica — the only people brave enough to willingly corral this disaster crew through Vegas. May your marriage survive overnight shifts, bachelorette weekends, Pete's bad jokes, and an obscene amount of champagne."

The group laughed, glasses raised automatically. Pete cheered, "Hell yeah!" Danica reached and squeezed Maggie's hand.

Maggie sat back down, the laughter was still trickling down from her toast when Lillian, poised as ever, lifted her glass. "If I may," she said smoothly, her voice cutting through the chatter. "I'd like to add one more."

The table quieted, all eyes on her. "It's been such a joy," Lillian went on, "to see all of you celebrate love in such… spirited ways." Her smile flicked toward Pete, who was still half standing, trying to get the waiter's attention for another round. "Danica, Pete — you two clearly bring out the best in one another. I wish you a lifetime of more laughter than arguments, more joy than chaos, and at least a little bit of this sparkle every day. It's been such a joy getting to know each of you and to be welcomed into your group."

She tipped her glass, effortless, golden in the candlelight.

The group let out a warm chorus of *cheers*, glasses clinking again. Danica pressed a hand to her heart, touched despite the blush creeping into her cheeks. Pete made a mock swoon face and laid her head on Danica's shoulder.

Maggie ducked her chin toward her glass, shoulders still tense.

And Gwen sat there, glass lifted, watching it all — the way Pete gazed at Danica, the poise of Lillian, the too-bright smile Maggie hadn't dropped yet, the way Izzy leaned into Kiera with a private smile.

THE LAST OF the champagne was being poured when Kiera straightened in her seat, eyes sparkling with the same intensity that had pried everyone out of the room this evening.

"Okay," she said, clapping her hands lightly against her thighs, "I have an announcement."

Pete groaned theatrically. "Not another toast, for the love of—"

"Not a toast," Kiera said, grinning now. "Reservations. At a piano bar. Ten o'clock."

The table erupted — Izzy whooped, Danica clapped, Pete slapped the table like she'd just won a bet.

"You made us a piano bar reservation?" Pete asked, delighted horror in her voice. "You sneaky little minx."

Kiera shrugged, smug in her practicality. "I know you all. If I didn't, you'd be in bed by eleven. This way, we actually do Vegas properly."

Izzy leaned over to kiss her cheek, murmuring something that made Kiera blush under the low lighting.

Maggie groaned, half into her glass. "Pretty sure I'm still dying from the pool. And last night. And all of Vegas."

"Rally," Kiera ordered, with the command of someone who'd wrangled high schoolers for a living. "You can't bail on my itinerary."

Pete laughed so hard she nearly spilled her wine. "Oh my god, *not the itinerary.*"

"She color-coded it," Izzy added proudly.

Danica perked up. "You did? For me?"

"Of course she did," Maggie muttered, though there was a smile tugging at her mouth despite herself. "She sent it my way, but again, I don't open spreadsheets just as a rule."

"And," Kiera said, digging in a tote bag at her side, then

producing two handfuls of sequined items. "I have sashes and tiaras."

Danica grimaced, but Maggie was already reaching to put on a tiara that proudly read *Miss Behaving*. Gwen's offering simply glittered in a curly, feminine font: *MILF*.

Lillian laughed, pointing up at Gwen's tiara. "Classy," she said. Her own read *Sexy & Single*.

Maggie helped Danica with her Bride to Be sash — Pete immediately tied hers around her waist like a cummerbund.

Gwen sat back in her chair, watching the wave of energy build again, feeling the buzz of it under her skin. A bachelorette party. A nightclub. At ten p.m. Vegas wasn't done with them yet.

Fremont Street was its usual neon circus — showgirls with feathered headdresses taking photos with tourists, people stumbling while looking up at the kaleidoscope ceiling, the hum of slot machines leaking out of every doorway. Their group wove through the crush until Kiera led them into an empty mall area and they stopped beneath a retro neon sign in loopy cursive: *Strangers in the Night*.

"Piano bar," she announced, grinning like she'd just revealed the final square on a scavenger hunt.

Pete threw her arms in the air. "*Yes.*"

Inside was dim and rowdy, the kind of place that smelled like spilled whiskey and glittered like sequins. Two grand pianos faced each other on a low stage, and the pianists were hammering out dueling versions of "Great Balls of Fire," harmonizing with total commitment. The crowd — half musical theater nerds, half retirees who hadn't gone home since 1968 — clapped along like this was holy ritual. Gwen got the idea that there were a lot of regulars at this place.

The hostess wedged them into a table so close to the stage Gwen could feel the vibration of the keys in her ribs. Menus were perfunctory, cocktails named after Sinatra hits: "Luck Be a Lady" martinis, "That's Life" Old Fashioneds, "Fly Me to the Moon" glitter shots. Pete ordered a round of "Regrets I've Had a Few," whatever that was.

When the pianists caught sight of their table — tiaras, sashes, Pete waving like she was running for office — one leaned into the mic. "What are we celebrating here at Strangers in the Night?"

"Bachelorettes," Maggie called out, pointing like the sashes and tiaras weren't dead giveaways. "Two of them!"

The place erupted. The pianists launched into "Going to the Chapel," the whole bar joining in. Pete climbed onto her chair to conduct, arms flailing, while Danica tried to yank her down by the wrist, giggling too hard to succeed.

Kiera slipped a twenty into the request jar, whispering to the pianist. A few songs later, the first chords of "My Girl" rang out, and Kiera took the stage. Her voice wobbled on the first line, but by the chorus she relaxed, her clear, warm alto carrying over the piano. The crowd swayed, clapping along, and Kiera — face flushed, eyes shining — kept her gaze locked on Izzy the whole time. Izzy looked like she might burst, clapping and singing harmony from their table.

The entire room was wrapped in that magic, so sweet, earnest, and nakedly romantic Gwen felt that longing pinch behind her ribs again.

Maggie sat back, sipping her glowing "Regrets" cocktail with a smirk, but Gwen didn't miss the softness in her eyes as she watched.

When Kiera finished, the place roared, the pianists bowing like they'd orchestrated it themselves. Izzy pulled her offstage into a kiss that earned whistles from the bar.

Gwen clapped with everyone else, but her chest ached. She glanced at Maggie, already sliding out of her chair to dance when the pianists switched to Britney Spears.

Gwen couldn't help it. She watched unashamedly. Maggie in full tilt was always magnetic, chaos wrapped in charisma.

The waitress returned with rainbow shots "compliments of the house." Pete raised hers like a torch. "To friendship, chaos, and for this bar keeping all our secrets."

They cheered, glasses clinking. Gwen tipped hers back without flinching. Maggie winced at hers, laughed, then steadied herself on Gwen's shoulder as she set the glass down. The touch was casual, but Gwen felt it like a brand.

The pianists slid from Britney into Elton John, pounding the keys so hard the whole bar seemed to pulse with it. Maggie was already on her feet, tugging Pete up by the wrist. "Come on," she shouted, grinning wild, blonde hair tumbling into her face.

Danica resisted for a second, laughing nervously, then let herself be pulled too. Even Kiera, still pink from her stint at the mic, got dragged into the fray, Izzy swooping behind her like backup. Soon half the group was in front of the stage, Maggie leading the charge, Pete shimmying badly, Izzy clapping on the wrong beat, Danica gamely swaying while Maggie spun her by the elbow.

Gwen stayed seated. She told herself it was because she didn't dance, but the truth was, she couldn't trust herself. Not with Maggie glancing back every few seconds like an invitation.

Izzy sat down beside her, flushed and breathless, short hair sticking to her temples. She grabbed a water glass and leaned back. "I'm not saying Kiera's secretly a pop star, but…" She gestured toward the dance floor where Kiera was laughing, her wavy bob going wild with some hair tosses. "That was kind of incredible."

"She did great," Gwen said, meaning it.

Lillian slid gracefully into the empty chair on Gwen's other side, her cocktail glass glowing faintly under the neon. "She looked radiant," she said smoothly, watching Izzy watch

Kiera with a faint smile. "That's what happens when someone adores you out loud."

Izzy's cheeks went pinker, and she ducked her head with a grin. "Yeah. I'm pretty lucky."

Gwen sipped her water. Out on the dance floor, Maggie had Pete by both hands, spinning her until they were both doubled over with laughter. The crowd clapped along, happy to be collateral in their chaos.

Lillian, lounging with her elbow propped on the back of her chair, tilted her head. "So it's new, then?"

Izzy blinked. "What is?"

"You two," Lillian said smoothly, her smile faint but sly. "Getting together. You've got that shine. Honeymoon glow."

Izzy laughed, startled. "Oh, uh yeah, I guess. New-ish. Not brand-new." Her blush deepened as she tugged her napkin into her lap. "We're newly engaged, actually."

Lillian raised her glass in mock salute. "Savor it. I, meanwhile, am *painfully* single. Watching you two is both charming and vaguely insulting."

Izzy ducked her head again, laughing. "Sorry?"

"Don't be." Lillian's eyes slid to Gwen, sharp even in the dim light. "What about you?"

Gwen stilled. "Me?"

Izzy perked up, suddenly quiet, as if she'd been waiting for someone else to broach it.

Gwen's fingers tightened around her cool water glass. Out on the dance floor, Maggie was bent over laughing, hair sticking to her damp forehead, Pete clapping her on the back. She looked incandescent. She looked like everything Gwen both wanted and couldn't have.

Lillian swirled the ice in her glass, eyes still on Gwen. "Yeah, how did you and Maggie meet?"

The question shouldn't have startled her. But it did. Gwen cleared her throat, fingers tracing the condensation ring her water had left on the table.

"Grad school," she said finally. "A party." She could still see it: a cramped apartment with peeling linoleum, someone blasting Beyoncé through tinny speakers, the smell of beer and cheap pizza. Maggie on the couch in ripped jeans, laughing so loud it had pulled Gwen across the room like gravity. Gwen had been there with a napkin when Maggie had spilled something, taking any excuse to talk to her. "I was... drawn to her. Instantly." Gwen gave a small, rueful laugh. "Moth to a flame."

Izzy's lips curved, soft. Lillian's, sharper.

"Clearly you still are," Lillian murmured. "Even if that's a little dangerous for a moth, don't you think?" She didn't wait for an answer, like she didn't expect one. Then she slid from the table with feline grace, disappearing into the press of bodies and chaos.

The noise of the bar seemed to recede, just for a beat. She hated to admit that Lillian did have a point.

Izzy shifted beside her, shoulders brushing. When Gwen finally glanced over, Izzy was watching her with an expression that was equal parts kind and curious.

Izzy cleared her throat. "So, how long have you two been separated?"

The words landed with more gentleness than Gwen expected, but they still knocked the air from her chest.

Gwen kept her gaze on her glass, the rim cold against her fingertips. There was no use denying it. Izzy knew them better than any of their friends, having spent time with them after not one but two tragedies. Of course she'd figured it out. "It's complicated," Gwen said, tone edging toward final. She tried for her calmest expression, the one that had gotten her through meetings with impossible clients and funerals. "We're... figuring things out."

Izzy's eyes softened, but her voice was steady. "Come on, Gwen. I know you two. Be honest with me."

Gwen exhaled, long and shaky. She hadn't planned on

talking about this tonight — not here, not in this ridiculous piano bar with glowing cocktails and sing-a-longs and Maggie out there twirling like she didn't have a care in the world.

Her throat tightened anyway. "Six months," she said finally. "We've been separated six months."

Izzy's lips parted, but she didn't speak right away. Gwen pushed on before she could stop herself.

"I sleep in the guest room. We only talk when we have to — about bills, the kids, schedules. It's like living with a ghost of someone you…" Her voice caught. She pressed her nails into her palm. "Someone you still love. Even when you know you shouldn't."

The words landed heavy between them, muffled by the crowd's off-key singalong of "Sweet Caroline."

Izzy reached across the table, squeezed her hand once, firm and certain. "That sounds like hell."

Gwen swallowed, blinking hard. "It is."

Out on the dance floor, Maggie laughed at something Kiera said, head thrown back, confetti in her hair. Gwen's chest ached like she'd been carved open.

Izzy's thumb brushed over Gwen's knuckles, grounding her in the middle of all the noise. "Hey," she said softly, almost drowned out by the crowd's ragged chorus. "You don't have to beat yourself up for this. Nobody gets marriage exactly right. Nobody. You and Maggie… you're allowed to be messy. You're allowed to still love each other, even if it hurts."

Gwen blinked hard, the sting in her eyes threatening to spill. She turned her hand under Izzy's and gave it a quick squeeze before pulling back, needing the space.

Izzy didn't press. She just leaned back in her chair, giving Gwen the dignity of silence.

Gwen let out a sigh that felt like it came from her bones, then tipped her glass and drained the rest of her drink in one swallow. The ice clinked when she set it down, a soft sound that somehow cut through the din of the room. "I prefer it when you tell me useless facts when I'm upset."

"Did you know Venus is the only planet that spins clockwise?" Izzy asked immediately.

"That's better," Gwen said, her amusement feeling bittersweet. "Just... we aren't really telling anyone, if you don't mind keeping it to yourself."

"About Venus? Yeah, totally," Izzy said, leaning back in her chair.

Onstage, the pianists barreled into another song, the crowd whooping like it had never heard music before. Maggie's laughter floated above it, bright and sharp, and Gwen sat in the amber glow of the table light, feeling both emptied out and too full all at once.

CHAPTER 13

MAGGIE

MAGGIE HADN'T LET HERSELF FEEL THIS LIGHT IN MONTHS. Maybe years. The piano players had rolled through Queen and Pat Benatar and back again, the whole room shouting lyrics like they were gospel, and Maggie was in the middle of it — hair wild, sweat slick, Pete egging her on like they were co-captains of chaos. For once, she wasn't thinking about Gwen watching her, or what tomorrow would feel like. She was just moving, laughing, spilling neon cocktails down her arm and not caring.

Then the pianists shifted gears. One slid into something soft, tender, the keys spilling a melody that hushed the room. Etta James's "At Last."

Pete turned immediately toward Danica. "Come here, wife-to-be."

Danica rolled her eyes, blushing as always, but she stepped straight into Pete's arms, her laugh muffled against Pete's shoulder as they started to sway.

Maggie turned to find Kiera in front of her, holding out

her hand like they were about to waltz in the middle school gym.

Maggie laughed. "Oh, is this happening?"

"Don't leave me stranded," Kiera said, mock-dramatic, glancing around at the couples already pairing off. Her eyes were bright, flushed from dancing but still shy in that Kiera way.

Maggie took her hand. "Fine. But I'm leading."

"Obviously," Kiera said, her arm looping around Maggie's shoulder.

And just like that, they were swaying among the crowd — Pete and Danica twirling nearby, strangers slow-dancing like they'd known each other forever. The whole bar softened around them, neon and noise dissolving into something intimate.

For the first time all weekend, Maggie didn't feel like she was trying to prove anything. Just warmth, music, and the comfort of a friend.

Kiera's hand was steady on her shoulder as she guided them in a small circle as if they'd actually practiced this. Maggie let herself sink into the rhythm, the sway easy, no pressure to perform.

Halfway through the song, Izzy appeared at Maggie's elbow. "May I cut in?" she asked, already sliding a hand onto Kiera's waist.

Kiera pretended to balk, but her smile gave her away. "I guess you may." She leaned into Izzy without hesitation, their foreheads nearly brushing as they found their own sway.

Maggie stepped back, letting her hands fall to her sides. For a second she smiled, genuinely — because god, Izzy looked like she might actually burst with happiness. But then the awkwardness crept in, heavy and familiar. She was suddenly just... spare. An extra in someone else's love story.

She turned toward the bar, scanning for a server, ready to

disappear into another drink. Anything to give her hands something to do besides clench.

And then Gwen was there.

Not suddenly, not dramatically, but close, warm, cutting into Maggie's line of sight like she'd only been waiting her turn. Her mouth was set in that calm line Maggie knew too well.

"Shall we?" Gwen asked, offering a hand.

It was so simple, so Gwen — understated, even with all the heat thrumming underneath.

Maggie's pulse kicked. She should've said no, she knew that. But her hand was already moving, sliding into Gwen's before her brain could catch up.

"You hate dancing," she said, arching a brow as Gwen guided her back into the slow rhythm of the song.

"I hate *bad* dancing," Gwen countered, sliding an arm around her waist with infuriating ease.

Maggie snorted. "Guess I should warn you, I peaked at middle school mixers."

"I remember," Gwen said, a flicker of a smile ghosting across her lips. "You stepped on my foot three times during our first dance."

"That was nerves, not skill," Maggie said, chin tilting up.

Gwen huffed a laugh, quiet but real, and it buzzed in Maggie's chest like victory.

Still, being this close — Gwen's hand firm at her back, the clean scent of her shampoo threading through the whiskey-soaked air — was undoing her more than she wanted to admit. Banter was safer. Banter she could handle.

"So what's this, then?" she asked lightly, letting her tone edge toward teasing. "Some kind of pity dance?"

Gwen's eyes flicked down, briefly, to her mouth. Then back up. "Not pity," she said.

Maggie's throat tightened. She forced a grin, playful, reckless. "Flattery?"

"Saving everyone else from your heels," Gwen murmured. "Since you're still a menace on the dance floor."

Maggie laughed, loud enough to earn a glance from a nearby table. But the laugh didn't chase away the heat rising up her neck, or the way her body leaned, just slightly, treacherously, into Gwen's.

Their steps stayed easy, side to side, like they'd done this a thousand times before — and they had, in kitchens, at weddings, in living rooms with a baby monitor crackling in the corner.

"Practice, huh?" Maggie said, her grin daring, though her voice cracked a little.

Gwen didn't answer right away. Her hand was steady at Maggie's back, fingers spread, the warmth seeping straight through her dress. The kind of hand that could hold her upright or pull her under without effort.

And then Gwen's gaze dropped. Not subtly, not in passing. Straight to Maggie's mouth.

Maggie's lips parted before she could stop herself, her chest tightening. Every nerve in her body tuned to the fact of Gwen's hand — how close it was to the base of her spine, how it guided her with the lightest touch, how it could so easily pull her closer.

"You're staring," Maggie said, trying for light, but it came out softer.

"I know," Gwen murmured.

The words knocked the breath from her. Maggie let out a shaky laugh, covering the sound of her heart hammering. "Dangerous game."

Gwen's eyes flicked up again, steady, unreadable except for the heat that lingered there. Her hand pressed just a fraction firmer at Maggie's back, and Maggie swore she could feel the ghost of every time Gwen had ever touched her layered into that single moment.

The song swelled, other couples swaying around them, but Maggie barely noticed. All she knew was Gwen's eyes, Gwen's mouth, Gwen's hands — everywhere, everywhere, everywhere.

Maggie swallowed hard, her pulse thrumming everywhere Gwen's hand touched. She should've said something flippant, tossed out a joke to puncture the tension. But she couldn't move, couldn't breathe right, not with Gwen looking at her like that.

"Careful," Maggie managed, voice thin. "You keep staring like that and people might think you actually like me."

Gwen's mouth curved, slow, deliberate. Her gaze dipped to Maggie's lips again before rising to meet her eyes.

"I never stopped liking you," she said quietly.

The words hit like a strike to the chest. They were simple, devastating, undeniable.

Maggie's laugh snagged in her throat, half a gasp. She felt her fingers twitch against Gwen's shoulder, wanting to grip, to hold, to *believe*.

And then the song ended.

The last chords rippled off the pianos, the crowd clapping, whooping, breaking the spell. But Maggie and Gwen didn't move. They stayed there, still swaying faintly out of habit, hands locked in place, caught in a bubble of too much history and not nearly enough air.

Someone at the bar shouted for another Sinatra tune, glasses clinked, Pete hollered something obscene — but none of it reached Maggie.

All she knew was that Gwen hadn't let go.

The applause rolled through the bar, people clinking glasses and laughing, but Maggie barely heard it. Gwen's hand was still at her waist — no, not just there. Tighter now. A subtle press, firm enough that Maggie felt her whole body tip toward Gwen like gravity had decided.

Her breath caught.

Gwen didn't step back, didn't break the spell. Her gaze slipped down again, unmistakable this time, landing squarely on Maggie's mouth.

Maggie's lips parted without permission, a reflex as old as muscle memory. She could feel Gwen's thumb flex just slightly against the small of her back, as if steadying herself... or claiming her.

The room around them kept moving. Izzy and Kiera tangled in their own quiet world, Pete shouting requests at the pianist, Danica clutching her drink with her whole body laughing — but Maggie and Gwen were suspended, untouched, balanced on the precarious edge of something they both knew and had no business chasing.

Maggie's heart thundered: *Do it. Don't. Do it. Don't. Do it do it do it.*

And still Gwen's eyes lingered on her mouth, so close Maggie swore she could feel the ghost of the kiss already.

All she could see was Gwen. The hand tight at her waist. The eyes fixed on her mouth. The press of years, memories, everything unsaid tightening the air between them until she couldn't stand it.

So she leaned in.

It wasn't calculated. It wasn't about proving a point, or showing off, or pretending. It was the most reckless kind of instinct, the simple act of closing the half-inch gap, chasing the thing she'd been aching for all night.

But Gwen pulled back.

Not harshly, not with a shove. Just a subtle step away, the grip at her waist loosening, her face unreadable in the low light.

The rejection landed like a cold splash down Maggie's spine.

Her breath stuttered, lips still parted. For a heartbeat, the urge to laugh it off surged. To make a joke, roll her eyes, blame the alcohol. Anything to keep from showing how it cracked her open.

But inside, she was buzzing, split between humiliation and the undeniable truth that she'd wanted Gwen to meet her halfway, and Gwen hadn't.

Of course Gwen had pulled back. Of course Gwen was the predictable, stable, unyielding one.

Maggie shoved a hand through her hair, trying to laugh at herself, but it came out brittle. What the hell had she been thinking? That Gwen — calm, composed, always-in-control Gwen — would just give in to a messy, public kiss in the middle of a Vegas piano bar when they hadn't been performing for an audience? When it had just been them?

She stared hard at the stage, where one of the pianists was pounding out "That's Life," the whole crowd shouting the chorus like it was gospel. The noise roared, but all Maggie could hear was the thud of her own pulse, the painful echo of Gwen's hand letting go.

Humiliation simmered under her skin, sharp enough to make her stomach turn. She'd leaned in like some drunk college kid, like history and heartbreak didn't mean a thing.

Underneath the embarrassment was something worse, the twist of ache. The part of her that still wanted Gwen to close the gap. To take her face in those careful hands and kiss her like they used to, with patience and fire all tangled up together.

Instead, Gwen had stepped back. And Maggie was left standing in the middle of a crowd that suddenly felt too bright, too loud.

She clenched her jaw, swallowed hard, told herself she'd get another drink, dance it off, laugh until it no longer stung. That was her role in this group, wasn't it? The chaos coordinator. The entertainer.

But the truth sat heavy in her chest: She wasn't angry at Gwen for pulling away. She was angry at herself for wanting her not to. For getting swept up in a moment that she'd ultimately regret.

Her eyes burned before she even realized what was happening, hot pressure gathering fast enough to make her blink hard once, twice, pretending it was the thick air in the press of bodies.

It wasn't.

She pushed back from Gwen, from the whole deafening room. Nobody noticed. Pete was requesting a Shania Twain song, Izzy had Kiera pressed close, Danica was wiping tears of laughter from her cheeks. Perfect cover.

Maggie slipped through the crowd and out the door, her chest tight, heart ricocheting against her ribs. The bar was set back from Fremont in an arcade, tucked between a bowling alley and a Denny's.

And there, in the sad orange light of a Denny's sign, finally, the tears broke loose.

It was stupid. She hadn't cried in months. Not really, not since the last time she and Gwen fought about quality time, or work, or silence. And now here she was, mascara smudging, shoulders shaking like a teenager heartbroken at prom.

She pressed her hands to her eyes, trying to choke it back, but the harder she fought, the harder it came.

It wasn't just the kiss Gwen hadn't given her. It was everything that kiss would have meant: that they weren't done, that maybe all the mess and all the distance could still be undone.

But Gwen had pulled away.

And Maggie stood in the dark, letting herself cry where no one could see, hating how much it hurt and hating even more that part of her still wanted Gwen anyway.

The desert night was warm, dry against her damp skin. Maggie pressed her back to the brick wall beside the door, tilting her head up until the lights blurred and streaked through the tears still clinging to her lashes. She dragged the heel of her palm under her eyes, hard enough to sting.

God, she hated crying. Hated how raw it left her, how exposed, and in Vegas of all places — this city that thrived on facades and glitter and spectacle, not the soft, humiliating sound of someone trying not to sob.

She crossed her arms tight over her chest, willing her heartbeat to slow, trying to pull herself together. People streamed past on the street, laughing, shouting, drunk on oversized daiquiris. To them she was just another shadow against the wall.

Maggie closed her eyes. The air smelled like smoke and sugar and asphalt, sharp enough to ground her, but not sharp enough to cut through the ache.

The door creaked open behind her, spilling piano chords and laughter into the night. Maggie tensed, swiping at her face fast, ready to paste on something casual and mask it all with a flippant remark. But it was Gwen who stepped out.

Of course it was.

Maggie turned her face toward the street, toward the blur of neon overhead. "Go back inside, Gwen. I'm fine."

"You're crying." Gwen's voice was steady, too steady.

"I said I'm fine." Maggie shoved a laugh into the words, sharp and hollow. "Just needed some air. Fremont Street heals all wounds, right? I think there's an Elvis song that says that."

But Gwen didn't leave. She moved closer, the scrape of her stupid dress shoes loud against the concrete, until she was right there — so close Maggie could smell the faint thread of her shampoo beneath the cocktail haze.

And then Gwen's hands were on her face, firm, holding her still.

Maggie startled, tried to pull back, but Gwen's grip was gentle and unyielding.

"What do you want?" Gwen asked, low, urgent, every syllable vibrating through Maggie's chest.

Her throat closed. The question was so big, and so, so dangerous. She shook her head, eyes darting away toward the crowd. "I don't know."

"Say it." Gwen's thumbs brushed against her damp cheeks, her gaze relentless. "Say what you want."

The air between them thickened, hot and electric, as if the city itself had paused to listen. Maggie's breath stuttered, her pulse screaming that she *did* know, she always had, but the words tangled, caught in her chest.

And still Gwen held her there, steady and unflinching, until the silence between them felt like it might break them both open.

Maggie's chest heaved, every nerve firing under Gwen's touch. Her thumbs still rested against Maggie's cheeks, warm, steady, holding her in place like Gwen could anchor her through sheer will.

Then Gwen's voice dropped, low enough that it was almost a growl. "Tell me you want me to kiss you."

Maggie's breath hitched.

"Say it out loud."

Her whole body rebelled, her brain screaming *don't*, her heart pounding *please*. She tried to look away, but Gwen's hands tightened, just enough to keep her there, their foreheads almost touching now. The air between them was hot, charged with too many years of not admitting what she needed.

Maggie's lips trembled. "I... I want you to kiss me."

The words came out raw, cracked open, but once they were there, she couldn't stop. Her eyes flicked helplessly to Gwen's mouth, the gravity of it pulling her in.

Gwen's breath caught against her cheek. Her grip softened but didn't fall away.

"Again," Gwen whispered. "Say it again so I know you mean it."

Maggie's throat burned, tears hot at the corners of her

eyes, but she let the words spill anyway. "I want you to kiss me."

And in that moment — standing in the dark mouth of an alley off Fremont Street, surrounded by laughter and lights and the roar of a city that didn't care — Maggie had never meant anything more.

Gwen's face was so close Maggie could feel the warmth of her breath. Her eyes had gone soft but intent, the way she used to look at Maggie when they were young, and everything felt possible.

She leaned in, just enough that their noses brushed, then stopped.

"Are you sure?" Gwen asked, voice rough, almost breaking.

The pause split Maggie wide open, because of course Gwen would ask, even now, when Maggie was already shaking with need. Of course Gwen would give her one last chance to back away, to pretend she hadn't said the words that had been clawing at her chest for months.

But Maggie didn't back away. She couldn't.

Her hand slid up, gripping the front of Gwen's shirt, tugging her in. She closed the gap herself, pressing her mouth to Gwen's in a kiss that was messy and desperate, nothing like the polished way Gwen usually moved through the world.

It was salt and tears and months, *years* of wanting, and Gwen's hands tightening at her jaw like she'd been starving for the taste of her all along.

The noise of Fremont Street roared on around them — signs flashing, strangers laughing, some drunk tourist shouting *Viva Las Vegas!* — but Maggie didn't hear any of it.

All she heard was the thunder of her own heart and the quiet hitching sound Gwen made when she kissed her back.

The first brush of their mouths might've ended as a stunned, fleeting thing, but Gwen didn't pull away.

She kissed her back. Harder this time, with a sound caught low in her throat that Maggie hadn't heard in years but recognized instantly, like an old song coming on a new playlist.

Maggie gasped against her, and Gwen used it, tilting her head and deepening the kiss until Maggie's knees threatened to buckle. Gwen's hands left her face only to find her waist, sliding down, anchoring her with a grip that made Maggie tremble.

And then her back hit the wall.

The warm brick scraped through her thin dress as Gwen pressed her there, not rough but certain, her body solid against Maggie's. Maggie's fingers clutched at Gwen's shirt, pulling her closer, greedy, aching. "God, Gwen," she whispered against her mouth, desperate.

Gwen swallowed the sound, kissing her deeper, teeth catching at her bottom lip before soothing it with her tongue. One hand braced beside Maggie's head, the other still hot at her waist, sliding just a fraction lower, enough to make Maggie shudder.

Maggie arched into her, letting the wall take her weight, clinging like she could crawl inside Gwen and finally be whole again. And for the first time in months, maybe years, she wasn't thinking about why it wouldn't work. She was only thinking: *more.*

The kiss turned greedy fast, the kind of kiss that had no business happening in public. Gwen pressed into her harder, her thigh sliding between Maggie's, pinning her against the brick.

Maggie gasped, the sound again swallowed instantly by Gwen's mouth, and then her own hands were moving without thought — up Gwen's chest, clutching her shoulders, fisting the fabric of her shirt like she could keep her there forever.

It wasn't neat. It wasn't polished. Gwen kissed like she

was starving, like she'd been holding this back so long it hurt. Their teeth knocked once, Gwen muttered something low and guttural against her lips, and Maggie laughed into it — half-crazed, half-ecstatic.

Gwen's hand slid lower, gripping Maggie's hip, her fingers digging in with enough force to make Maggie arch, reckless, every nerve in her body screaming *yes*.

The glow from the street barely reached them, just enough to paint Gwen's jaw in pink and blue as she pulled back for half a breath, eyes dark, lips swollen.

"Still sure?" Gwen rasped.

"Shut up," Maggie said, tugging her back in, kissing her harder, needier, like the years apart had been erased in an instant.

Her back scraped against the brick as Gwen pressed her deeper into it, their mouths clashing, Maggie's fingers sliding into Gwen's damp hair, tugging, pulling. Gwen groaned — god, that sound — and Maggie felt it roll through her like heat, pooling low, making her want more, more, *more*.

More of Gwen's mouth, Gwen's body, the press of her thigh, the taste of her.

"Oh my god, get a room," Kiera's voice cut sharp through the night, higher than usual, the teasing tone undercut by the obvious awkwardness lacing it.

Maggie jolted like she'd been doused with ice water, scrambling to tug her shirt back down where it had ridden up. Gwen stepped back instantly, expression shuttered, as if she'd been caught in something illicit — which, technically, they had.

Kiera stood a few feet away in the alley glow, arms folded but smile plastered on, not quite reaching her eyes. "Hey," she said, overly bright. "Just wanted to give you the heads-up we're about to do a group song. Danica said to get you for the lower harmonies."

Maggie's pulse was still thundering, her breath coming in

uneven bursts. Her mouth tasted like Gwen, her body still humming from the press of her hands. She managed a crooked grin, trying for casual, though her cheeks burned. "Lower harmonies. Got it."

"Yeah." Kiera's gaze flicked between them, lingering a beat too long.

Maggie nodded, pushing her hair off her face. "Be right there."

As Kiera turned and slipped inside, Maggie exhaled hard, pressing her back to the brick. Gwen was still there, inches away, silent.

Her whole body buzzed with want, with humiliation, with the sick thrill of having been caught.

Neither of them moved.

The door had swung shut behind Kiera, leaving them in the dark, but whatever spark had been igniting them seconds ago was gone — snuffed out by the real world crashing back down around them.

Gwen adjusted the cuff of her sleeve, eyes on the ground, her breath still uneven but her expression composed again, maddeningly so. "We should… go in," she said finally, quiet.

She straightened fast, forcing her arms down, her face into something neutral. "Yeah. We should go," she muttered, already stepping toward the door before Gwen could say anything else, before Gwen could *look* at her like that again.

Inside was chaos, yes. But at least it was safe chaos.

Back inside, the air hit Maggie like a wall — smoke machine haze, stale beer, disco ball lights bouncing off mirrored walls. The pianists were already hammering out the opening chords of "Livin' on a Prayer," and the crowd lost its collective mind.

"Maggie!" Pete bellowed, waving her forward like a deranged choir director.

Someone shoved a microphone into Maggie's hand before she could protest. The others surged to the front — Pete clutching Danica's waist as if they were storming a barricade, Izzy practically glowing as she dragged Kiera beside her, Lillian smirking from the sidelines like she'd known this circus would happen all along, and Gwen joining her to stand nearby without a mic.

Maggie leaned in with the others, shouting the lyrics, pointing to the crowd when the chorus rang of being halfway there.

But inside, she was unraveling.

Her chest still buzzed from Gwen's hands on her, from the taste of her mouth, from the look in her eyes when she'd said *Are you sure?* And then the way she'd stepped back, instantly composed the moment Kiera appeared.

What had made her think that was a good idea? What had made her want that taste, knowing it'd become a craving?

Pete thrust her arm around Maggie's shoulder mid-chorus, sloshing beer down both their backs, and Maggie whooped like she was having the time of her life.

On the outside, the room was roaring. On the inside, her heart was splintering, every lyric cutting like a cruel joke.

The last chorus shook the walls — every drunk tourist, every bachelorette party, every one of her friends screaming until the pianists banged out the final chords and threw their hands in the air like preachers finishing a sermon.

The crowd went wild.

Pete collapsed against Danica's shoulder, shrieking with laughter. Izzy pulled Kiera into a kiss that earned a whoop from three tables over. Even Lillian clapped with a faint smile, the picture of composure in a room of chaos.

Maggie bent over her mic stand, hair sticking to her forehead, lungs burning. Her grin was wide, practiced, perfect. Nobody would guess her hands were still trembling.

She shoved the mic back at the pianist, forcing her voice into something bright. "Another round," she hollered, waving at the waitress. "Shots! Rainbow if you've got 'em."

The table erupted again, everyone cheering like Maggie had just won them the jackpot.

She turned back, smiling with them, laughing too loud. And if her chest still ached, if her mascara was smudged, if her heart felt raw and stupid in her rib cage... well. Shots would fix it. Or at least blur the edges.

CHAPTER 14

THE SUITE FELT CAVERNOUS WITHOUT THE WHOLE CREW CRAMMED inside it. Gwen slipped her shoes off the moment the door closed, sighing as her shoulders dropped. She could still hear the ghost of the piano chords in her ears, the crowd roaring along to Bon Jovi like it was scripture.

Maggie, Pete, Danica, and Izzy had peeled off at Fremont, lured toward the flashing lights of the blackjack tables. Gwen, Kiera, and Lillian had shared a cab back, their laughter quieter, a little worn out at the edges.

Now the three of them sat scattered around the living room that wasn't currently moonlighting as Gwen and Maggie's bedroom — Kiera curled up with her legs tucked under her, Gwen in an armchair with a bottle of water, and Lillian perched gracefully on the couch, kicking off sleek sandals.

Kiera was the first to break the silence. "I kind of can't believe I left them out there unsupervised," she said, half grinning. "Pete with money and alcohol is... well. Good luck to Vegas."

"They'll be fine," Gwen said, taking a sip of water. "And we needed the break."

Kiera nodded, leaning her cheek against her knee. "True. I miss my girls, though. I keep checking my phone like something huge is going to happen in the five hours since my mom texted me last." She laughed at herself, soft and tired. "They're probably just asleep after eating weirdly healthy cereal for dinner and watching *K-Pop Demon Hunters* again."

Gwen smiled faintly. "That sounds familiar. The boys are obsessed with that one." She let herself exhale. "Isn't it weird to miss them even when you're enjoying yourself on vacation?"

"So weird," Kiera agreed, the word popping with tired affection.

Lillian tipped her head, her dark hair catching the lamplight. "See, that's what makes me certain I'm not cut out for it. That constant vigilance, that permanent ache when they're not in the room? I know myself too well."

Her tone wasn't sharp, just steady, almost self-aware. She folded her hands in her lap. "I mean, I know Pete probably doesn't talk about it, but growing up in foster care, bouncing around until I was seventeen... It sucks. For a long time, I thought maybe I'd want to give a kid the stability I never had. But the truth is... I don't think I have it in me."

Kiera shifted, her face open, gentle. "And that's perfectly okay."

"More than okay," Gwen added, surprising herself with the conviction in her voice. "Knowing what you want — or don't want — doesn't make you less. It makes you honest."

Lillian's lips curved in a grateful smile, softer than Gwen had seen all night. "Thank you. Most people just give me the 'oh, you'll change your mind' speech."

"Not me," Kiera said firmly, then smirked. "I can't believe I had more than one, most days. I love them, but they do take over your entire life, you know?"

The three of them laughed, easy and tired, and the room felt warmer for it.

Kiera leaned back against the pullout cushions, twisting the cap off her water. "Honestly," she said, "I can't even picture Pete and Danica with kids. Can you imagine?"

Gwen huffed a laugh before she could stop herself. "I can imagine the baby having a surfboard *and* chore chart by the time it's two."

"And Pete teaching it to swear before it can talk," Kiera added, grinning now. "They'd be those parents who bring the toddler to poker night and let it stack the chips."

Lillian's mouth curved, amused. "Or take it to Vegas for its first birthday."

That got Kiera snorting water out of her nose. Gwen couldn't help laughing too, the sound easing something tight in her chest.

"God help us if they ever do it," Kiera said, wiping her face with her sleeve, still smiling. "The world's not ready for a Pete-and-Danica baby."

"Maybe the world needs one," Gwen offered, still chuckling. "Chaos balanced with color-coded spreadsheets. It could be, like, the first President of Earth or something."

They all laughed again, the sound filling the quiet suite, and for the first time since slipping out of the piano bar alley, Gwen felt her shoulders unclench.

The laughter tapered, leaving only the hum of the minibar fridge. Kiera twisted the cap of her water bottle in her hands, her expression softening.

"Can I ask you something?" she said gently.

Gwen looked over, wary but open. "Of course."

"Do you think you and Maggie will ever have more?" Kiera asked, voice careful, like she was stepping barefoot across glass.

For a moment, Gwen couldn't breathe. Her throat worked. It was one of the first times Gwen had talked so openly about babies since they'd lost their last pregnancy. A termination due to a nonviable chromosomal anomaly. She felt her shoulders stiffen under the weight of it — the memory of sterile hallways, monitors beeping, Maggie's hand clutched in hers as the doctor explained there was no safe way forward. The way Maggie had cried, and how Gwen had swallowed her own tears because one of them had to. That was when their marriage had initially gotten so closed off, when Maggie had begun to retreat into herself instead of lean on Gwen. And Gwen had dealt with it all by throwing herself into work, to get through each day without trying to get lost in the loss of something that hadn't even begun.

She shook her head, quick, firm. "No," she said, her voice steady enough that only she could hear the crack in it. "No, that's… not in the cards."

Kiera nodded softly, her eyes kind, not pushing.

Gwen cleared her throat, forcing her tone lighter. "What about you and Izzy? Think you'll have more?"

Kiera shrugged, leaning back into the cushions. "The girls are already a handful. Most days it feels like I'm running a circus with just the two of them." She smiled, faint but warm. "But Izzy… she's going to make a great stepmom. Eliza and Quinn already adore her. So who knows? Maybe two's enough."

Something in her voice — pride, love, maybe even surprise — made Gwen's chest ache in a gentler way this time. She smiled, small and real, and tipped her water bottle toward Kiera's. "They're lucky," she said quietly.

Kiera flushed, ducking her head, but the smile didn't leave her face.

Kiera took a long sip of water, still blushing faintly, and Gwen let the silence rest between them, easy and companionable.

Then Lillian, who'd been quiet for a beat, shifted on the

couch. Her bare feet tucked neatly beneath her, posture softening in a way Gwen hadn't seen much of.

"You know," she said, her voice low but sure, "you're all incredibly lucky." She glanced between them, the lamplight catching the curve of her smile. "To have this. To have each other as family, even when it's messy. Especially when it's messy."

Kiera blinked, surprised, then smiled. "Yeah. We are."

Lillian looked down at her hands, then back up, and her expression carried something rawer than her usual polish. "I'm grateful Izzy — and you, Kiera — made sure I got pulled into the circle, too. I've... never had people like this before, so it's nice to know it's even a possibility."

The words landed softly, but they stayed. Gwen felt them in her chest, the quiet kind of truth that couldn't be brushed aside.

Kiera's smile widened, warm and a little damp at the edges. "You're stuck with us now. No take-backs."

Lillian let out a laugh, light but real, and Gwen found herself smiling too.

For a moment, the chaos of Vegas, the sharp edges of her own thoughts, even the ache Maggie had left buzzing in her veins — it all quieted. Just three women in a hotel suite, tired and full of honesty and grace.

Lillian excused herself first, thanking them both with a small smile before disappearing to return to her private room a few floors below. A few minutes later, Kiera stretched, yawned, and murmured something about checking in with her mom before bed. Gwen hugged her briefly, then watched the door close behind her.

And then it was just Gwen.

She poured herself another glass of water and carried it out onto the balcony. The night air was dry and warm, neon spilling up from the strip like restless lightning. Somewhere below, a busker was murdering "Viva Las Vegas" on an electric violin.

Gwen sat heavily in one of the metal chairs, tucking one leg beneath her, the other stretched out. She took a slow sip of water, then another, as if hydration could calm the thrum in her chest.

But of course her mind went back there. The alley. Maggie's mouth, soft and frantic against hers. The taste of tears and whiskey. The way her body had fit so perfectly against Gwen's it felt like no time had passed at all.

Her fingers found her hair, tugging through the damp strands, pulling hard enough to sting as if pain might ground her. She leaned forward, elbows on her knees, exhaling.

It had been wrong. Hadn't it? They weren't together. They'd said as much — lived as much — day after day in separate rooms, separate lives. And yet, the moment Maggie leaned in, Gwen hadn't thought. She'd only wanted. God, how she'd wanted.

She closed her eyes, the memory replaying anyway. Maggie saying *I want you to kiss me.* The way she'd said it twice, had been so sure.

Gwen scrubbed her face with both hands. Wrong or not, she couldn't shake the truth humming under her skin: That kiss had felt like coming home.

And now she sat alone on a balcony in Vegas, waiting for a woman she wasn't supposed to love anymore, wondering how she'd survive the rest of this weekend without falling apart completely.

It was another hour before the door clattered open, voices spilling in from the hall — Pete and Danica laughing too loud as they stumbled to their room, Izzy's singsong teasing trailing after them. Then quiet again, the suite settling.

Gwen didn't move from the balcony, her half-empty water glass sweating in her hand. She heard Maggie's uneven steps before she saw her — heels clicking, then the soft scrape as she kicked them off.

The sliding door opened, and Maggie stepped out, her hair mussed, her dress wrinkled, her makeup smudged into something softer. She dropped into the chair beside Gwen with a sigh, sprawling, the picture of messy exhaustion.

Without a word, Gwen reached behind her and slid a cold water bottle across the table. Maggie blinked at it, then at Gwen, then twisted the cap off and took a long drink.

For a while, they just sat there. The lights still pulsed below them, a wash of pinks and blues flickering over Maggie's tired profile. The night air smelled faintly of smoke and sugar, the city still alive while the two of them let silence stretch.

Finally, Maggie tipped her head back against the chair and let out a sigh that was half a laugh. "What do you think Dr. Elowen would make of tonight?"

Gwen's mouth curved, though it wasn't quite a smile. Trust Maggie to invoke their couples therapist like an after-hours punchline.

She swirled the water in her glass, watching the condensation bead and drip. "Depends on which part of tonight you mean."

Maggie gave a short laugh, no real humor in it. "Any of it. All of it. Take your pick."

Gwen looked at her then, really looked. At the woman who was still half-wild from the night, still messy, still luminous, still the only person who could make her feel like this.

Her chest ached with the answer.

Gwen let the corner of her mouth lift, the safer edge of a smile. "Well, for starters, she'd probably say we have questionable impulse control."

Maggie snorted into her water bottle. "That's generous." She sat forward, elbows on her knees, the bottle dangling between them. Her hair fell into her face, the bright lights of the strip streaking through the strands, and she glanced at Gwen sidelong. "But come on. You know what I meant."

Gwen's smile faltered. She swirled the last inch of water in her glass, listening to the faint rattle of Fremont below. "Yeah," she said finally. "I know."

The silence stretched again, thicker this time. Maggie's question still hung there, unspoken but heavy.

The silence settled like Austin humidity in summer, thick and unrelenting. Neither of them moved. Neither of them said it.

And maybe that was safer. Maybe Dr. Elowen would call it progress — choosing not to claw at the wound when both of them were still bleeding.

Maggie cleared her throat, the sound rough in the quiet. "We should get to bed."

Gwen nodded, her fingers tightening once around the empty glass before setting it down with too much care. "Yeah."

Maggie stood first, the scrape of her chair loud against the tile. She hesitated just long enough for Gwen to notice, then slipped back inside without looking over her shoulder.

Gwen stayed a moment longer, breathing in the night air and neon and ache, before following her in.

CHAPTER 15

SHOCKINGLY, MAGGIE WOKE UP CLEAR-HEADED. TIRED, SURE, but not drowning in the pounding regret that usually followed a night like last night. Maybe because after the piano bar she'd stuck mostly to water, letting Pete and Danica take over the shots.

Now, standing on the tarmac with the rotor blades whipping the air, Maggie was wide awake and very aware that she might die. "Jesus Christ," she muttered. "This thing looks like it's made out of Legos."

"Technically you mean LEGO bricks." Gwen was standing silently beside her, observing the helicopter with a sense of calm boredom, like it was her most common mode of transportation.

"No, I mean fucking Legos, Gwen." Maggie rolled her eyes. "This is really the pedantic hill you want to die on?"

"Arlo and Jude would agree with me," Gwen said with a shrug.

Beside her, Danica was pale, one hand pressed to her

stomach. "I already feel motion sick and we haven't even lifted off."

Pete threw an arm around Danica's shoulder, grinning like she'd just won the lottery. "Baby, it's going to be *epic*. I've been waiting for this all week."

Danica groaned. "That's not reassuring."

Izzy adjusted her oversized sunglasses and smirked. "We'll live. Probably."

Kiera gave her a look, then squeezed Danica's arm. "It'll be fine. It's short. And if you puke, at least we'll have a good story."

Maggie was clenching her jaw so tight it hurt. The helicopter gleamed under the Nevada sun, its windows curved like a toy capsule, the blades thrumming loud enough to rattle her teeth. "People weren't meant to fly in things this small," she said, mostly to herself.

"Don't worry," Gwen said. "It's like an Uber with wings."

"That's exactly what I'm afraid of," Maggie shot back, but her voice cracked on the last word.

The pilot, cheerful in mirrored aviators, waved them toward the open door. "All right, folks! Adventure of a lifetime. Buckle in and grab your headsets."

Danica whimpered. Maggie considered bolting. Pete, naturally, bounded forward like a kid at Disneyland.

And somehow, caught between terror and the ridiculousness of her friends, Maggie climbed in after her, Gwen tight behind her.

The cabin was smaller than Maggie expected, all narrow seats and Plexiglas curves. The pilot's voice crackled through the headset — cheery, like he didn't realize he was about to fling seven women to their deaths.

Maggie buckled herself in, knuckles white on the straps. Danica sat directly across, eyes squeezed shut like maybe she could fast-forward the whole ordeal. Pete was already leaning over her, narrating the controls like she knew a damn thing about aviation. Lillian sat on Pete's other side, practically glowing, her sunglasses perched like she was starring in a travel commercial.

"This is incredible," Lillian said, voice tinny in the headset. "Best bachelorette idea yet."

"Thank you," Izzy beamed as if she'd personally invented helicopters.

Kiera looked less certain. She gripped her seat belt with both hands, her smile too tight. "It's all going to be fine," she said, but the way she stared at the horizon said otherwise.

Maggie's stomach dropped as the rotors picked up speed. The helicopter lurched, a stutter of movement that had her swearing under her breath. "Nope. Nope, nope — this is a bad idea."

Beside her, Gwen's hand settled gently over hers, steady and grounding. She didn't say anything at first — just left her warm palm there until Maggie unclenched enough to breathe.

Finally, Gwen's voice came through the headset, calm, even. "It's okay. Just look at me."

Maggie did, though her pulse still hammered. Gwen's expression was maddeningly composed and confident, like she was waiting for a meeting to start instead of about to be lifted into the sky in a plastic bubble.

The ground fell away. Maggie's breath caught.

The Strip dropped beneath them, glittering like spilled jewels, then the desert opened up — vast, golden, endless.

"Holy shit!" Pete shouted, pressing her face to the glass. "We're flying to the Grand Canyon!"

The pilot laughed, angling them toward the horizon. "Ten minutes and you'll see it."

Danica groaned, fumbling for the little paper bag tucked into her fanny pack.

Izzy rubbed her back, already laughing. "Don't puke yet, we're not even at the good part."

Maggie forced herself to keep her eyes on Gwen, not the

tilt of the world outside. Gwen gave her hand a squeeze — firm, certain — and the panic in her chest loosened, just slightly.

And when she risked a glance outside, just for a second, the desert stretched out forever, the Colorado River carving a glittering line through the canyon, impossibly vast, impossibly beautiful.

Her breath caught for a different reason this time.

The others were pressed to the windows, oohing and aahing, Pete practically climbing over Lillian to point something out, Izzy laughing as Kiera squeaked when the helicopter tilted. Even Danica, pale and clutching her paper bag, cracked a smile when Pete kissed the top of her head through the headset mic.

Maggie couldn't look. She tried once — caught the flash of the river glinting like a shard of glass far, far below — and her stomach flipped so hard she thought she might join Danica in the barf bag club.

So she anchored herself on Gwen instead.

Her eyes stayed fixed on Gwen's profile: the clean line of her jaw, the calm set of her mouth, the way the headset sat snug against her hair. Gwen didn't fidget, didn't crane to the window, didn't flinch when the cabin dipped. She just sat steady, her hand still over Maggie's like she'd decided this was her only job.

Maggie gripped back shamelessly, nails biting into her palm through Gwen's skin. The rotors thundered overhead, the canyon unfurling around them, but Gwen's touch steadied her through it.

It was infuriating, how composed she was. Infuriating and unbearably comforting.

Maggie felt her chest squeeze, not from fear this time but from the sheer force of memory — every time Gwen had steadied her before. In hospital rooms. In principals' offices.

At funerals. Always with that same maddening calm, as if she could carry Maggie's fear and her own at the same time.

Her throat tightened. She should look out the window, take in the view everyone was gasping over, but she couldn't. She let her eyes drift down Gwen's jaw, her neck, the bare skin of her arm. All things Maggie had memorized over the years, could draw from memory alone. Technically, she'd been the one to draw the first draft of the tattoo on her arm. It suited her. Of course it did.

The window, the symmetry, the way the vines crept up like they were daring the stone to stay still—it was so Gwen. Precision wrapped in wildness. Maggie traced the air above it with her eyes, half expecting her fingertip to catch on a carved edge.

It looked like something sacred and unfinished at the same time. A cathedral mid-restoration. A space that used to reflect the beauty of the world and was learning how to hold light again.

And maybe that was why it undid her a little. Because Gwen didn't need a tattoo to say who she was, but somehow this one did anyway.

"Still okay?" Gwen asked, her voice tinny through the headset but low enough that it felt private.

Maggie swallowed hard and nodded, her voice gone.

Gwen smiled — not big, not showy, just the faintest curve at the corner of her mouth, like she'd heard the answer anyway.

So Maggie kept her gaze there, clinging to it, riding out the roar of the rotors and the sweep of the canyon with only Gwen's steadiness holding her together.

The helicopter tilted slightly, dipping toward the canyon rim, and Maggie squeezed her eyes shut.

Through the headset, Gwen's voice came, a steadiness Maggie could lean on. "I've got you. Take a look, or you'll regret it."

Maggie forced her eyes toward the window, just for a second. The world dropped away into a vast, impossible chasm — layers of red and gold carved by centuries, the river weaving like a snake at the bottom. The sheer scale of it made her stomach lurch.

She sucked in a breath, then immediately buried her face in Gwen's shoulder, shutting it all out. "I'm fine right here," she muttered, her words muffled against the fabric of Gwen's shirt.

Gwen chuckled, low and warm, the sound vibrating through Maggie's cheek. Her hand squeezed Maggie's once, sure and certain.

Maggie let herself stay there, pressed against Gwen, heart hammering too fast to be fear alone.

The rotors droned steadily, the canyon unfurling endlessly below. Maggie kept her face tucked into Gwen's shoulder, breathing shallow, when a rustle caught her ear.

Kiera, sitting across from Danica, was digging in her bottomless tote bag like she was about to produce a full pharmacy. A moment later, she pulled out a little packet and held it out. "Here. Alcohol wipes. You taught me they help with nausea sometimes, so I always carry one for you."

Danica blinked at her, pale and sweaty, then took the packet like it was holy relic. She pressed the wipe to her nose, inhaled, and promptly burst into tears.

"Oh, my god," she sniffled, voice cracking through the headset. "That is... so *nice* of you."

Everyone froze for a beat. Then Pete let out a bark of laughter, clutching her chest. "She's crying because you gave her a wet wipe. This is *incredible*."

"I'm serious," Danica said, her chin wobbling. "That's the sweetest thing anyone's ever done for me in my life."

Kiera looked stricken for half a second, then started laughing too, her shoulders shaking. Izzy pulled her into a side hug, muffling her giggles against Kiera's hair.

Even Lillian laughed — graceful, delighted, tipping her head back. "We should nominate Kiera for sainthood. St. Kiera of the Anti-Nausea Wipes."

Maggie snorted against Gwen's shoulder, and Gwen's chest moved with quiet laughter under her cheek.

The tension cracked. The fear eased. And for the first time since the rotors had lifted them off the ground, the mood inside the little helicopter was light again.

The helicopter shuddered as it set down on a flat plateau rimmed with scrub and low brush, the rotors whining as they powered down. Maggie could've kissed the ground... if Danica hadn't beaten her to it in her own way.

The second the door opened, Danica bolted out, wobbling across the gravel until she found a sad-looking desert plant. She dropped to her knees and promptly threw up into it.

"Oh, Jesus," Maggie muttered, grimacing as she unbuckled.

Pete followed right on her heels, sweeping Danica's hair back in one practiced motion, grinning like this was the best part of the tour. She threw a big thumbs-up over her shoulder. "It's just like Telluride!"

Maggie barked a laugh despite herself, because of course she remembered. Danica, motion sick after a mountain drive, had greeted them by throwing up in Aunt Jade's porch plants on their first college reunion trip.

"Don't remind me," Danica croaked, her voice weak but full of misery.

Kiera, looking stricken but efficient, crouched beside them and pulled a travel toothbrush and a mini bottle of mouth-wash from her bottomless bag. She pressed them gently into Danica's shaking hands. "Here. These help."

Danica stared at them like Kiera had produced a diamond tiara. Her face crumpled again, tears springing fresh. "You're — oh my god — you're *so nice*." She sobbed while Pete poured mouthwash on the toothbrush.

The sight was so ridiculous that Maggie doubled over laughing, clutching her stomach, the sound sharp and helpless. Even Lillian cracked up, elegant but genuine, covering her mouth with one hand.

Danica tried to wave them all off as she rinsed and spat, tears streaming down her face. "You don't understand. I'm *so grateful right now.*"

Pete patted her back affectionately. "My delicate flower," she announced, eyes twinkling. "Vegas tried to break her, but she lives."

Maggie wiped at her eyes, breathless with laughter, and for the first time all morning, the knot in her chest loosened.

Eventually, Danica rallied — face pale but scrubbed fresh, clutching Pete's hand like she might topple again at any second. The guide waved them toward the rim, cheerful and oblivious, and the group shuffled along in a loose pack, still laughing under their breath about Danica's dramatic exit.

Maggie hung back, her legs shaky in that way they got after adrenaline — whether from fear or... other things. Gwen drifted beside her, quiet as always, their shoulders brushing once, then again, like they couldn't quite manage distance.

And then the canyon opened up before them.

Even Maggie — who'd sworn she wouldn't look, who had kept her eyes glued to Gwen's steady profile in the air — couldn't help it. She stopped dead at the edge, breath catching.

It was too much to take in. The sweep of color, red and ochre layered like history itself, shadows shifting with the sun. The river below a silver thread, so far down it looked unreal. Vast didn't even cover it. It was bottomless, endless, alive.

For a long moment, nobody said anything. Even Pete went still, her arm looped around Danica's waist, her usual grin slack with awe.

Maggie glanced sideways. Gwen was standing beside her,

hair pulled back by the wind, eyes fixed on the horizon. The same steadiness as always, but softer here, her expression cracked open just slightly by the view.

Something in Maggie's chest pulled tight. "Okay," she whispered, mostly to herself. "That's... worth it."

Gwen didn't look at her, but Maggie saw the faintest curve of her lips. "Told you you'd regret it if you didn't."

Maggie let out a breath, shaky but lighter. "Don't get smug."

Maggie folded her arms tight, trying to hide the shiver. The wind tugged at her hair, cool against skin that still felt overheated from adrenaline. Her voice came out softer than she meant, carried off by the canyon air. "I feel so small, like nothing matters."

Gwen finally looked at her. Eyes steady, unblinking, as vast and unyielding as the view itself. "Or maybe *everything* matters, Maggie."

The words hit harder than the height, harder than the endless drop below. Maggie turned back to the canyon fast, blinking against the sting in her eyes. The expanse stretched out forever, but it was Gwen's voice echoing in her head — quiet, certain, impossible to shut out.

The wind whipped harder at the rim, tugging Maggie's hair across her face. She kept her eyes fixed on the canyon, on the impossible sprawl of it, because looking at Gwen again felt too dangerous. Gwen's words were still lodged in her chest like a splinter she couldn't pry out.

"It kind of reminds me of Santa Fe," Maggie said. "The colors." She knew it was a gamble to mention their honeymoon — gambling with whose heart, she didn't know — but she wanted to share the realization.

Her fingers itched before she even realized what she was doing. Slowly, like testing the air, she reached sideways and found Gwen's hand. She laced their fingers together and gave a small, quick squeeze. Not much. Barely anything. But enough.

Gwen didn't pull away. She didn't squeeze back either, not exactly. She just let Maggie's hand settle there, warm and steady in hers, as if that was answer enough.

Maggie swallowed hard, blinking against the wind and the sting in her eyes. For the first time all morning, the world tilted not with fear, but with the unbearable sense that maybe she hadn't imagined it — that maybe, even here at the edge of forever, Gwen was still hers in some unspoken way. She wanted to stay in it… just the two of them, the silence, the ache.

"Group photo." Pete's voice shattered the moment, echoing across the rim like a battle cry. Maggie startled, jerking her hand free so fast she almost stumbled.

Pete came bounding over, arm raised with her phone. "Everybody, huddle up. This one's going on the fridge."

Danica groaned, still looking vaguely green. "I do not need evidence of this day."

"Yes, you do," Pete said cheerfully, dragging her forward anyway. "Posterity, babe."

Izzy had already wrangled Kiera into place, Kiera dutifully brushing hair out of her face and trying not to laugh at the way Pete was corralling them like cattle. Lillian strolled up last, sunglasses on, radiant as always, like this was her magazine cover shoot.

"Come on!" Pete barked. "Maggie, Gwen, stop brooding over the abyss and get in here."

Maggie rolled her eyes hard, but her cheeks were hot, and she didn't dare look at Gwen. She shuffled into place, Pete looping an arm around her neck, pulling her in tight.

"On three," Izzy said, her grin already wide. "One, two—"

"Grand Canyon sluts!" Maggie shouted, and the whole group cracked up, even Danica, and the sound rose bright against the endless canyon air, laughter echoing like it belonged there, as the camera shutter clicked.

CHAPTER 16

GWEN

THE POKER ROOM WAS QUIETER THAN GWEN EXPECTED — NO jangling slot machines, no blaring music. Just the steady shuffle of cards, the low hum of conversation, the occasional groan when someone folded too early. It felt like a library for degenerates.

Pete and Izzy, naturally, stuck out like neon signs in matching floral print button-ups.

"Raise," Pete declared after barely looking at her cards, tossing in a chip like she was starring in a mob movie.

Izzy side-eyed her. "You don't even know what you have."

"I have *confidence*," Pete shot back. "Which, incidentally, always beats math."

Across the table, a middle-aged guy in a Hawaiian shirt smirked, calling her bluff without hesitation. Gwen sighed, sliding in her own chips, while Lillian sat poised beside her, sipping a martini as though this was exactly where she belonged.

The hand played out predictably: Pete bet way too high,

Izzy teased her, Lillian kept her face calm, and somehow Gwen walked away with the pot while Pete looked personally betrayed.

"This is rigged," Pete muttered, stacking her dwindling chips like they might multiply if she stared hard enough.

"It's just strategy," Gwen said mildly, though she hadn't done much more than wait out their antics.

They went a few more rounds before Pete leaned back, rubbing her temples theatrically. "Okay, I'm officially bad at poker, I think."

Izzy tilted her head, watching her. Then, softer than her usual snark: "What are you most excited about? You know… when you're married."

For once, Pete didn't have a quip ready. She fiddled with a chip, staring at it like it might bail her out. Then her mouth curved, smaller, almost shy.

"Honestly?" she said. "Waking up next to her every day, knowing I get to keep choosing her, and she keeps choosing me."

Izzy blinked, surprised by the sincerity.

Pete shrugged, still fidgeting with the chip. "She's the best thing that ever happened to me. Makes all the dumb stuff feel easier. Even when I'm messing everything up, she… I don't know. She makes me feel like I'm not."

For a moment, the table went quiet except for the shuffle of cards. Even Hawaiian Shirt Guy gave her a faint smile.

Lillian lifted her martini, her voice smooth. "To knowing when you've already won the only game that matters."

"When did you get so good at toasts, Lil?" Pete grinned at that, sheepish and proud all at once, and Izzy reached across to squeeze her hand.

Gwen looked away, focusing on her own chips, but her chest ached in a way she didn't care to name.

Pete ducked her head, still pink around the ears, and

gestured wildly at the dealer. "All right, let's play before Izzy starts journaling about my feelings."

Izzy leaned back in her chair, smirking. "Too late. I already drafted the chapter: *Petra Pancott Learns Vulnerability*."

Pete groaned. "You're insufferable." The cards slid out, and she grabbed hers like she'd been born at the table. "Okay, okay. This hand's mine."

It wasn't.

Pete went all in after the flop with nothing in her hand, bluffing with the enthusiasm of a game-show contestant. The guy in the Hawaiian shirt across the table blinked once, cool as ice, then flipped over a full house.

Pete's jaw dropped. "This is bullshit."

Izzy nearly fell out of her chair laughing. "You've got to stop betting like you're in *Casino Royale*, Pete. You're not Daniel Craig — you're like... the guy who accidentally gets shot in the cross fire."

Lillian hid her smile behind her martini glass. "Darling, not everyone gets to be James Bond."

Pete slumped dramatically, head in her hands. "Fine. I'll just die broke and in love. At least Danica still thinks I'm charming."

That earned her a round of chuckles, even from Hawaiian Shirt Guy, who pulled the pile of chips toward himself with the detachment of someone who'd seen this a hundred times.

Izzy tipped her drink toward Pete, grin softer now. "Hey, if she thinks you're charming, you've already won."

Pete peeked up at her, still flushed, and gave a crooked smile. "Yeah. Guess I have."

The table quieted for a moment, the sweetness of it lingering in the air.

Gwen stacked her modest pile of chips with careful precision, keeping her expression unreadable. But inside, something twisted. Because it was impossible not to see the truth in Pete's sheepish little grin — that sometimes love was worth looking like an idiot for.

And that truth pressed against Gwen's ribs in a way that had nothing to do with poker.

Pete was still sulking theatrically, Izzy egging her on, and Lillian calmly placed her next bet with the confidence of a card shark. Gwen should've been watching her cards, but her mind slid somewhere else entirely.

Back to the space between "yes" and forever.

She remembered the night before the wedding — how her hands had shaken lacing up her shoes, how Maggie had paced the hallway outside the hotel room like she might combust from nerves. Gwen hadn't been scared, not exactly. Just wired, restless, like her whole body was a live wire stretched too tight.

And then afterward. The dizzy relief of it being real. The cheap champagne in plastic flutes, the way Maggie had kissed her so hard she'd knocked her own veil askew.

Their honeymoon hadn't been Paris or Bali, not even close. They'd scraped together enough for a week in Santa Fe, splitting enchiladas at hole-in-the-wall restaurants, sharing one decent bottle of wine for the whole trip. Their hotel had creaky pipes and floral bedspreads older than they were, but Maggie had insisted it was perfect. She'd called it "romantic in a grad-student-budget kind of way," and Gwen had believed her.

She could still picture it — the two of them lying on a borrowed blanket under a too-bright desert sky, Maggie laughing at nothing, Gwen certain they'd built something that would last.

Even now, there was the heat of Maggie's breath outside the piano bar. The soft, stunned look in her eyes just before that kiss. Then, on the helicopter, the press of Maggie against her, their hands entwined, needing her.

Different moments, same pull. That unsteady gravity

between them, tugging her off-balance no matter how care-fully she'd tried to anchor herself.

Gwen told herself it was nothing more than nostalgia, but she knew better. Nostalgia didn't feel like this — sharp and bright, exhilarating and terrifying.

It had taken Gwen months to even realize the distance Maggie had put between them. Now she knew better: Distance was its own kind of ache. She knew she couldn't risk too much, not yet. Maggie was still skittish when the air got too thick between them. One wrong move, one word too tender, and Gwen could send her running.

The dealer's shuffle snapped her back to the present. Chips clacked, voices hummed around her, but her chest tightened anyway — aching with the hope she'd been trying to tamp down. She straightened her stack of chips, schooled her expression, and forced herself back into the game.

CHAPTER 17

MAGGIE

THE MOMENT MAGGIE STEPPED INTO THE SPA, SHE FELT HER whole body exhale. Cool air, quiet lighting, the faint smell of eucalyptus. It was like being dropped into another dimension. A blessedly *sane* dimension, with no helicopters, no champagne-soaked piano bars, no Gwen staring at her like she could see straight through her.

This was Maggie's element.

She loved spas. Loved the ritual of it. The plush robes, the way someone else fussed over her skin for an hour, the tiny porcelain cups of tea that tasted vaguely of flowers. After years of grad school, years of being broke, years of raising hell instead of resting, she had long ago decided that facials and massages were sacred, nonnegotiable self-care.

She stretched out on a cushioned lounge chair, cucumber-infused water sweating beside her, and let herself melt.

Danica wasn't quite melting. She sat stiff, still pale from the helicopter ordeal, hands folded primly in her lap. Even in a spa robe, she looked like she was calmly assessing a new patient.

Kiera, on the other hand, was already reclined, eyes closed, head tipped back with a towel draped around her hair. She let out a long, dramatic sigh. "I could live here."

Maggie smirked. "Same. Just bury me under hot stones and lavender oil."

Kiera cracked one eye open. "Noted for your funeral arrangements."

That made Danica laugh, a thin but genuine sound. She tucked her feet up under her robe, finally letting herself relax an inch. "I'm thinking let's always have spa days on vacation. Maybe a hundred percent less helicopters, though."

"It's a good thing these people could resurrect you from the dead with a facial peel," Maggie said.

Kiera chuckled. "Good, because Danica almost died on that helicopter."

"I did," Danica agreed solemnly, then ruined it by smiling.

Maggie tipped her head back against the chair, grinning. This — this was what she loved. The slow indulgence, the easy banter, the rare moment of stillness with her friends. No pretending, no chaos. Just the simple joy of being cared for.

Warm towels, soft music, the faint citrus scent of whatever serum the esthetician had brushed onto her skin — it all blurred into a haze that made Maggie's body feel heavier and her mind floatier. The kind of setting where secrets used to tumble out like beads from a broken string.

She thought of Telluride.

Another spa, another trip, another trio tucked away in white robes. Kiera had been the one to crack first, voice small but certain when she said her husband was cheating. Maggie could still picture Danica's hand shooting out to squeeze hers, how Kiera had crumpled then, the kind of pain you felt when you finally said the thing out loud.

Maggie remembered the silence after, the air thick and fragile. She'd filled it with her own truth, blurting it out before she could lose her nerve. That she'd been pregnant.

That she'd had to end it because there wasn't another choice. Because it hadn't been safe or viable, not for her.

She remembered how relieved she'd felt. That she wasn't carrying it alone anymore. That Danica and Kiera had listened and nodded and said all the right things, no judgment, no pity. Just the quiet kind of understanding that made her feel less like a failure and more like a person again.

Now, lying in the dim warmth of the Vegas spa, Maggie swallowed hard. She could still feel the relief of that moment, how necessary it had been.

But this wasn't Telluride. This was Pete and Danica's bachelorette trip. This was champagne toasts and chaos and pretending everything was easy. She couldn't drop something that heavy here, couldn't be the one to dim the lights with her grief again. Not now.

So she smiled into the towel at her throat, forcing her voice light when she said, "Spa days with you two are becoming our tradition. Just… minus the crying this time, okay?"

Kiera laughed, the sound muffled from under her face mask. "Not promising anything."

Danica giggled too, softer, but it was enough. The heaviness thinned, replaced by warmth.

Maggie closed her eyes, the relief sharper than she wanted to admit.

Steam hissed softly from some hidden vent, the kind of sound that made Maggie's body want to melt into the lounge chair forever. She was drifting, half dozing, when Kiera let out a long, audible sigh.

"Okay," Kiera said, her voice muffled through the towel across her eyes. "I wasn't going to bring this up, but… I'm anxious Izzy and I might never set a date for the wedding."

Maggie's eyes snapped open, staring at the ceiling.

Danica lifted her towel, blinking. "What? Why would you think that?"

Kiera shrugged, the fabric rustling. "I don't know. We've been together long enough. And yes, we're newly engaged, but it seems like she's really dragging her feet about wedding planning. She says she wants forever, but sometimes it feels like… forever in Izzy-language is just a concept, not a plan." Her voice wobbled, just slightly. "What if she just liked the idea of being engaged but didn't think about the reality of it?"

Maggie pressed her lips together, her chest tightening. She thought of Izzy whispering her worries to them.

Danica reached out across the space between their chairs and found Kiera's hand, squeezing gently. "She loves you. That's obvious. Maybe you should talk to her."

Kiera gave a soft, disbelieving laugh. "That sounds like something people say when they don't know the answer. I just can't help but worry that I'm too much. Divorced single mom carries a lot of baggage, you know?"

Maggie swallowed, forcing her voice steady. "Or maybe she's just worried she's not enough?" Her heart ached with guilt as she reached blindly for Kiera's other hand, squeezing just as Danica had. "If there's one thing I know about Izzy, it's that she doesn't do anything halfway. If she says forever, she means it. She's just… Izzy about it."

Kiera exhaled, tension bleeding out of her shoulders. "I really hope so. I love her so much."

Maggie leaned back against the cushion, closing her eyes again, her heart pounding. *Elowen will have a field day with this one.*

Danica was still glowing, hands clasped like she was already at the champagne toast. Kiera, though — Kiera had pulled the towel fully back over her face, as if hiding might protect her from how much she wanted.

Maggie's stomach turned.

She'd basically told Izzy love was a lie and not worth it. She'd meddled, like she always did, charging in with her own read of the situation, certain she was protecting everyone from disaster.

But she'd been wrong.

What did that mean for the lie she'd also been telling her friends?

Her throat burned. She forced herself to breathe slowly, to lean back in the chair and let the esthetician paint another layer of mask across her skin.

It was the same pattern, wasn't it? Charging in, thinking she knew best, only to make the wrong call. With her friends. With Gwen. With herself.

Maggie pressed her lips together under the cooling mask, fighting the sudden sting in her eyes. If Danica or Kiera looked too closely, they'd see it, and she couldn't bear that. Not today. Not here.

So she stayed still, the perfect picture of spa-day calm, while inside she wanted to crawl out of her own skin.

Maggie had almost managed to settle into the quiet again — mask cooling, hands folded loosely in her lap — when Danica shifted on the next chair over, turning her head toward her.

"So," Danica said, her voice soft, careful. "How are things with Gwen?"

Maggie's eyes flew open. "What do you mean?"

Kiera tilted her head on her towel pillow, not unkind, just curious. "We mean... when we were there for your mom's funeral, things felt... off. Between you two."

Danica nodded gently. "Yeah. Obviously that was a tough time for you, but we just want to make sure it's okay now."

The room suddenly felt hotter under the robe. Maggie's pulse picked up, trapped between the sting of memory and the fact that they were looking at her like they *knew*. They kept using the word *we*, like they'd spent time discussing it.

She forced a smile, the kind she used to wear at corporate Christmas parties with Gwen — polite, polished, deflective.

"Things are great," she said lightly, waving a hand. "We're fine."

Kiera studied her for a second longer, like she was weighing whether to press. Then she nodded, settling back under her towel. "Good. That's good."

Danica closed her eyes again, relaxing into the warmth. "You both deserve that."

Maggie's throat tightened. She let her head fall back against the cushion, staring at the soft glow of the ceiling lights, willing her face to stay smooth under the mask.

Because the truth was too messy, too jagged for this quiet spa. And lying — well, she'd been lying about Gwen for months now. What was one more?

Maggie was still staring at the ceiling, rehearsing the fine art of pretending, when Kiera shifted beside her. She reached across the narrow space between their lounge chairs and gently closed her hand over Maggie's.

"You know," Kiera said softly, her voice steady in the hush of the spa, "after my divorce, therapy really helped me work things out. Have you... have you tried therapy since your mom passed away?"

The question landed like a strike to the chest.

Maggie's mouth opened, but no sound came. Shock hit first — like, *what? here? now?* — and then something in her just... gave. The mask on her skin felt suddenly too tight, the room too warm, her chest too heavy.

Before she could stop herself, her eyes blurred. Tears spilled fast and hot down her temples, cutting clean tracks through the expensive serum.

"Oh—" Kiera squeezed her hand tighter, alarmed but gentle. "Maggie — hey, oh god, did I say something?"

Danica sat up halfway, wide-eyed.

Maggie shook her head, the laugh that tried to escape breaking halfway into a sob. "No — it's not you — it's just—" Her breath caught, hitching hard. She dragged her free hand over her face, smearing tears and spa mask alike. "God, I'm sorry. I don't even know why I'm crying."

But she did know. She knew exactly why.

Because she hadn't tried therapy. Because she hadn't done anything except run away. Because she was so tired of pretending, she was fine when everything under her skin still hurt.

Danica leaned closer, voice soft, steady. "You don't have to be sorry."

Kiera gave her hand another squeeze. "You don't have to hold it together all the time, Maggie."

Maggie closed her eyes, more tears slipping free, her breath shaking. For once, she didn't bother to wipe them away.

Maggie swiped at her face with the edge of the towel, but more tears just kept coming, hot and humiliating. "God," she choked out, half a laugh, half a sob. "This isn't... this isn't supposed to happen. We're on a spa day. A bachelorette trip. We literally just said this was a no-crying zone."

Danica's eyes softened, but she didn't push. "Maggie..."

"I mean it," Maggie barreled on, her voice cracking as she tried to wrestle it back under control. "This is supposed to be facials and cucumber water and stupid gossip about Pete. Not me..." She waved her hand at her wet face, the streaks running through her mask. "Not me being the *downer*."

Kiera shook her head, gentle but firm, still holding Maggie's hand tight. "You're not a downer. You're our friend. And if you need to cry, then that's part of this too."

Maggie's chest squeezed so hard she thought she might crack open. She wanted to believe her, but guilt sat like a stone in her throat — guilt for ruining the lightness, guilt for crying when she was supposed to be celebrating, guilt for feeling too much, always too much.

She laughed again, broken and wet. "I'm a cucumber mask disaster."

Danica reached for her other hand, her grip warm and steady. "You're not a disaster. You're human."

Maggie shut her eyes tight, trying to breathe, trying to stuff the tears back where they belonged. But they kept slipping free, traitorous and hot, as her friends held her hands like it was the most normal thing in the world.

And for one terrifying, relieving moment, Maggie let herself feel all of it — the grief, the guilt, the impossible relief of not being alone in it, even if her friends didn't know all of it just yet.

Maggie sniffed hard, dragging the towel under her eyes, smearing her mask. "Okay," she said, voice still wrecked but trying for light. "This is officially too much vulnerability for one spa day."

Kiera squeezed her hand again, steady. Danica gave her a look that was equal parts concern and tenderness.

Maggie exhaled a shaky laugh, forcing her mouth into a crooked grin. "Danica, don't you want to add some trauma to even the score? Really balance the energy in here?"

Danica blinked, startled, then let out an incredulous laugh. "What, like… 'Surprise, I once shoplifted lip gloss in high school'?"

"That doesn't count," Maggie said, managing a smile. "Trauma minimum is at least a dead relative or failed relationship."

Kiera groaned into her towel. "You're impossible."

Danica shook her head, but her smile softened. "Nice try. But no. Today's not about keeping score."

"Damn," Maggie muttered, sinking back against the chair. "Worth a shot."

The tension thinned, the heavy air giving way to quiet chuckles, and Maggie let herself close her eyes, grateful for the reprieve. Grateful that they let her crack and then let her laugh it off, too.

The laughter softened, fading into the hush of warm air

and faint music. Maggie let her eyes fall closed again, her hands still tangled with Kiera's and Danica's, the three of them a little cocoon of quiet.

Then Danica's voice wavered into the stillness. "I just need to say something, and you can't make fun of me."

Maggie cracked one eye open. "Okay, here it comes."

Danica sniffled already, cheeks flushed pink beneath her mask. "I'm just... I'm so thankful for you two. For both of you. For this." She gestured vaguely at their linked hands, her robe sleeve slipping down. "Like, do you know how rare it is? To have friends who've seen every version of you, even the ugly ones, and still stay anyway?"

Kiera blinked rapidly, her mouth twitching. "Danica—"

"No, I'm serious." Danica's voice shook, but she plowed on. "You've been there through everything. Through the worst. And you still show up. And I don't know what I did to deserve you, but I... I love you both so much."

Maggie felt the sting immediately, hot behind her eyes. She pressed the towel to her face, laughing helplessly as tears welled again. "Damn it, Danica."

Kiera was already crying, too. "You're not allowed to do this while I've got a seaweed mask on, you monster."

Maggie was gone again, tears sliding, shoulders shaking, laughing and crying all at once. The three of them sat there in spa robes with their faces tear-streaked, masks ruined, clutching each other's hands like lifelines.

They sat there a moment longer, sniffling and holding hands, the estheticians probably horrified behind their polite smiles.

Danica hiccuped through her tears, and Kiera dabbed uselessly at her face with the edge of her towel. Kiera laughed wetly, shaking her head. "We're a disaster. A very expensive disaster."

Danica let out a choked laugh of her own. "This has to be the ugliest spa brochure photo in history."

Maggie sniffled again. "We should ask for a group discount. Three-for-one breakdown special."

That broke them all — laughter bubbling up through the tears until they were doubled over in their robes, shoulders shaking.

Maggie gasped, clutching her stomach. "I swear, if one of you starts sobbing again, I'm demanding a refund."

"Too late," Kiera managed, still laughing, wiping at her cheeks.

CHAPTER 18

THE FACETIME WINDOW WENT BLACK, REPLACED BY MAGGIE'S reflection in the screen. For a moment, the suite was quieter, leaving Gwen still blinking at where the kids' faces had been, her heart both full and aching.

Maggie began, "Did you see how Arlo—"

Gwen's phone buzzed with a work email notification. She swiped it open before she could think better of it, her inbox spilling across the screen.

Maggie groaned, dramatic, tossing herself back against the cushions. "Can you go ten seconds without bringing work here?"

"It's an important project." Gwen didn't look up. She had dropped everything to be here this weekend for Maggie, and in the past, staying calm had worked. Until it hadn't. Still, they were on tenuous ground after last night's kiss and this morning's softness, the ease with which Maggie was holding her hand and being around her.

Maggie's head snapped toward her. "Yeah, you've been on an 'important project' for about ten years, Gwen."

The edge in her voice caught Gwen off guard, sharp in a room that was otherwise humming with soft chatter of people who were definitely straining to listen from all corners: Pete and Danica laughing in the hall, Izzy refilling drinks at the little bar cart, Kiera humming in approval at whatever playlist she'd queued.

Gwen typed out her reply to Melinda as fast as she could, then closed her phone, setting it face down on the coffee table, forcing calm into her voice. "There, all done."

"You're always only *half* here with me," Maggie shot back, quieter now but no less pointed.

The words hung there, heavy, too loud for how soft they'd been said.

Gwen's jaw tightened. She reached for her glass of wine, more to occupy her hand than because she wanted it. "This isn't the place, Maggie."

"I know," Maggie muttered, folding her arms across her chest.

For a moment, neither of them moved. The laughter from the other side of the suite swelled, masking the silence between them. But Gwen felt the tension buzzing like static, familiar and unwelcome, even here. Especially here.

Gwen pressed her lips together, staring at the rim of her glass. She could feel the heat creeping up her neck, the tightness that always came when Maggie jabbed a little too close.

What stung most was the timing. They'd had such a good morning sitting close on the helicopter, Maggie white-knuckling her hand the whole flight, both of them pressed shoulder to shoulder in a way that felt almost affectionate. And later, when Maggie came back from the spa, she'd seemed genuinely glad to see Gwen again, like the distance between them had thinned for a while.

They'd settled into a call with the kids, the boys tumbling over one another to talk about soccer practice, Rosie proudly announcing she'd made grilled cheese "all by myself,"

Gwen's mom popping in to insist with a laugh that she hadn't let their child use the stove alone. Jude had looked between them thoughtfully and said, "You're together." Maggie had gotten teary in that soft, unguarded way that always made Gwen want to reach for her, to tuck a strand of hair behind her ear, to remind her she wasn't carrying that missing alone.

For a few minutes, it had felt good. Like maybe they were finding their way back to something steadier.

Now, this.

Of course she'd been working. What did Maggie expect — that she could just leave in the middle of a deadline?

The project depended on her. Her team depended on her. This was the biggest project she'd ever taken on, and a promotion depended entirely on her doing well. Dropping the ball wasn't an option. Not when she'd spent years proving herself, climbing rung by rung until she was close — *so close* — to the position she'd worked for her entire career.

Maggie knew that. She'd always known that. Yet somehow, every time Gwen picked up her phone, it turned into an argument about her priorities.

Gwen clenched her jaw, her fingers curling tight against her knee. She wanted to shake it off, let it slide, but the sting of Maggie's accusation sat heavy in her chest.

She wasn't half here. She was here *and* working. Carrying both, like she always did.

And wasn't that enough?

The conversation with Maggie sat between them, sharp and unfinished, but the suite didn't give them room to stay there.

Because suddenly Pete came barreling out of the bedroom with Danica in tow, both of them dressed head to toe in white — white shirts and slacks for Pete, a white sundress for Danica, white sneakers, white sashes across their chests that glittered *Queerly Beloved* in rhinestones.

Pete spun in a circle, arms wide. "Behold," she crowed. "Bachelorette power couple."

Danica beamed, smoothing her sash. "We coordinated."

"Obviously," Maggie said, beaming with a smile.

Izzy let out a low whistle. "You look like you're about to either get married or lead a cult."

"Both," Pete said, entirely unbothered. "Anyway — bachelorettes don't sit around drinking wine in a hotel room all night. Tonight, we bar crawl."

Kiera groaned, tugging at the hem of her dress. "Define crawl."

"Crawl until our livers give out," Pete said. She produced a folded neon-pink flyer from her pocket like she was unveiling the Dead Sea Scrolls. "I mapped the route. Five bars. Five themed shots. Zero shame."

Lillian arched an elegant brow, sipping her gin. "Do any of these establishments have seating?"

Pete grinned wolfishly. "Nope."

The room buzzed with the kind of frenetic energy Gwen had come to expect from this weekend. Glitter, chaos, too much eyeliner. Everyone shouting over each other about who had to carry the emergency water bottles, who was most likely to vomit in an Uber, whether Pete's plan actually had any chance of survival.

Gwen sat back, watching Maggie get pulled into the excitement despite herself. Her heart thudded with something complicated... relief at the distraction, and that same ache that never really left, even in the noise.

Pete was still waving the flyer like a war banner when Gwen finally spoke up, voice dry. "I don't know if my liver can take this, Pete."

Pete flopped dramatically onto the arm of the couch. "Don't worry. If you pass out, we'll just Weekend-at-Bernie's you from bar to bar. You'll look incredible in sunglasses."

Maggie smothered a laugh behind her hand, shaking her head.

Before Gwen could retort, Lillian rose gracefully from her chair, setting down her gin and slipping her arm through Gwen's with a sigh. "Honestly, I don't know how you keep up with these wild women," she murmured, low enough for Gwen alone. "They've got the stamina of Olympians. I prefer to drink sitting down."

Gwen felt her lips twitch before she could stop it. "You and me both."

Pete, oblivious, pointed at them with delight. "See? Team Responsible already forming. We'll need you two to carry the rest of us home."

"Speak for yourself," Danica said, patting Pete's arm like she was indulging a child. "I have hand sanitizer at the ready."

The chatter swelled again, sashes glittering, laughter bouncing off the suite walls. And even as Gwen felt the familiar thrum of tension low in her chest, with the unfinished fight with Maggie and three new work emails still unopened on her phone, she let herself lean into the absurdity, just for now.

The crawl began like every bad idea — with enthusiasm and sequins.

At the first stop, Pete ordered a round of "Bachelorette Bombs," which turned out to be tequila dropped into Red Bull. Danica laughed so hard at Kiera's horrified face she nearly spilled hers. Maggie didn't even flinch — tossed hers back in one go looking incredible in a green two-piece dress that showed off her midriff, her blonde hair loose around her shoulders.

By the second bar, Maggie was on a table dancing with a pack of strangers while Pete egged her on like a hype man. Gwen nursed a vodka soda at the edge of the chaos, her stomach twisting.

"You look like you're calculating her blood alcohol content," Lillian murmured, appearing at her elbow with her gin and tonic.

"I might have to be," Gwen said.

At bar three, the group had acquired glow sticks, plastic tiaras, and at least one inflatable flamingo Pete refused to explain. Izzy was leading Kiera in a conga line. Maggie spun into Gwen's orbit for half a second, cheeks flushed, grinning in that reckless, magnetic way that had once undone her entirely. Then she was gone again, swallowed by the crowd.

Lillian steered Gwen toward the quieter end of the bar. "They're exhausting," she said, almost fondly. "Like watching a litter of puppies knock over furniture."

"Puppies don't usually order Jell-O shots," Gwen muttered, though her lips twitched.

Pete made Danica pose under a neon sign that read *TIL DEATH DO US PARTY*. Maggie photobombed, flashing double peace signs, a tiara sliding down her forehead. Gwen caught the moment in her periphery and felt a familiar pang — half fondness, half worry.

By the time they staggered into bar four, the energy was ragged but still loud, all sequins and slurred declarations of eternal friendship. Gwen stayed close to Lillian, the two of them orbiting at the edges, trading dry commentary while the rest of the crew spun themselves out.

Maggie was still in the center of it, reckless and shining, like the whole world was a dare.

And Gwen, steady as ever, could only watch.

By the fifth stop, Gwen's ears were ringing from bass-heavy playlists and too many shrieks of *"Shots! Shots! Shots!"* She stood near the edge of the bar with Lillian, who had somehow remained elegant despite the chaos — her lipstick intact, her martini glass perfectly balanced.

She was glad for Lillian's company in the trainwreck that was this bar crawl. Someone who hadn't lived through the college stories, who wasn't fluent in every inside joke. The group had always tried to fold Gwen in, but she'd never quite shaken the sense of being on the outside. With Lillian beside her, at least she wasn't the only one.

"They're unstoppable," Lillian murmured, leaning close so Gwen could hear her over the music. "I'm convinced Pete runs on battery acid."

Gwen huffed a laugh, tilting her head toward her. "You're not wrong."

Lillian's shoulder brushed hers. "You don't even look tired."

"I am tired," Gwen said, dry. "I'm just good at hiding it."

Lillian's smile curved, amused. "No wonder you've survived in this circus for so long then."

CHAPTER 19

MAGGIE SLAMMED THE REST OF HER DRINK HARDER THAN SHE meant to, the cheap plastic cup crunching in her hand. Across the room, Gwen and Lillian were tucked in a corner, all low voices and leaning shoulders. Lillian with her perfect skin and her *oh, I'm effortlessly cool in every situation* vibe, laughing at something Gwen said like she'd just been handed the world's best secret.

It was infuriating.

In front of her. In front of *everyone*.

"Hey." Kiera's voice cut in beside her, warm and concerned. She nudged Maggie with her elbow, eyes searching her face. "You okay? You look like you're about to light something on fire."

Maggie barked a laugh, sharp and flippant. "Just admiring Gwen's type. Guess I should've started wearing one-piece swimsuits and quoting poetry about now."

Kiera frowned, glancing around. "What? Maggie—"

Before she could finish, Pete swooped in, tiara lopsided, cheeks flushed from her last round of shots. "Are we talking about Lillian?" she crowed, catching only half of what Maggie had said.

Maggie stiffened. "Unfortunately."

Pete threw an arm around Maggie's shoulders, nearly knocking her off-balance. "Best person you'll ever meet. Dead serious. She's solid. Kind. Smart as hell. No drama. She's like…" Pete searched for the word, her drunken brain working hard. "Like if a golden retriever could do advanced calculus."

Kiera laughed, but Maggie just tightened her jaw.

"Great," she muttered. "Perfect. Exactly what Gwen needs. Thanks, Pete."

Pete didn't catch the bite in her tone, already weaving toward the DJ booth to request another terrible song.

Maggie forced a smile, but the jealousy was simmering hot in her chest, too loud to ignore.

Across the room, Gwen was still in that corner with Lillian, smiling like Maggie wasn't even there.

The music was pounding, bodies pressed together on the dance floor, lights strobing in dizzy colors. Maggie had finally let herself get pulled into the crush, hair flying, her skin damp with sweat and liquor.

And then she caught it.

Out of the corner of her eye — Gwen by the bar, Lillian leaning close, her manicured hand brushing Gwen's. A quick flick of white, small and rectangular. A hotel key card.

Maggie's stomach dropped, heat flooding her chest so fast it made her dizzy. No way. No way Lillian was that bold. No way Gwen would…

She didn't even think. She turned, found the nearest warm body — a man in a cowboy hat, grinning at her like he'd won the lottery — and grabbed his hand.

It wasn't about him. It wasn't about fun.

It was about Gwen. About making sure Gwen saw her —

saw that Maggie could still burn brighter, command attention, take up more space than anyone else in the room.

Her pulse thudded in her ears, wild and reckless, as she let the stranger spin her, her laughter sharp and glittering.

All the while, her eyes kept darting back toward the bar, waiting to see if Gwen was watching.

Cowboy Hat spun her again, his grin sloppy and delighted. Maggie laughed too loudly, head tossed back, tiara sliding down her hairline. Her pulse was still hammering from that flick of a key card, the image burned into her mind.

She was mid-twirl when two familiar bodies pressed in on either side of her — Danica, sash glittering across her chest, and Kiera, already laughing as she looped an arm through Maggie's.

"Excuse us, sir," Danica said politely, even as she shouldered Cowboy Hat out of the circle. "We are too gay for this."

Kiera tugged Maggie closer, her voice pitched high over the music. "Come on, dance with us instead."

Maggie blinked, then barked a laugh, too sharp around the edges. "I was only trying to get close enough to steal that hat."

"Clearly," Kiera deadpanned, shimmying beside her.

Danica spun her in a messy circle, her laugh bright and earnest. "The hat was hideous anyway, babe."

Maggie let them pull her in, their laughter tugging her out of her spiral, even if just for a beat. She moved with them, matching their silly spins, their flailing arms, letting the tension ease by inches.

Still, her eyes darted back to the bar. To Gwen. To Lillian.

Her friends were keeping her anchored, distracting her, but the jealousy sat hot in her chest, fizzing just under the surface.

Time blurred under the lights. Maggie let Danica and Kiera whirl her until her lungs burned, until sweat dampened the sash Danica had forced over her shoulders. The music shifted again, a pulsing remix of something early 2000s, and before she could catch her breath, Pete and Izzy barreled onto the floor like a wrecking crew.

Pete zeroed in on the still lingering Cowboy Hat instantly. "Well, howdy there, partner," she drawled in the worst fake accent Maggie had ever heard. She yanked the hat clean off his head and plopped it on her own, grinning like she'd just won a prize pig at a county fair.

The guy didn't even seem to mind. He laughed, clapping his hands, clearly charmed by Pete's chaos.

Pete threw one arm around Izzy, spinning her in a dizzy circle, then shoved her toward Maggie. "Spin her, cowboy style."

Izzy, already laughing too hard, twirled Maggie sloppily, nearly knocking into Kiera, who squeaked but managed to stay upright.

"Yeehaw!" Pete bellowed, switching partners again, grabbing Danica by both hands and swinging her wildly until her sash nearly flew off.

"Pete," Danica shrieked, laughing so hard she could barely stand.

Pete tipped the cowboy hat low over her eyes and did a terrible boot-scootin' shuffle in the middle of the crowd. "Ladies, you're all lookin' mighty fine tonight," she said in a bad Southern baritone. "Step right up, I'll twirl ya proper."

And she did — one by one, spinning Maggie, then Kiera, then Izzy, then Danica again, each turn wilder than the last.

By the time Pete yanked Cowboy Hat guy himself into the circle, twirling him so fast the whole dance floor cheered, Maggie was doubled over, gasping with laughter.

For a few minutes, the jealousy and the ache slipped out of focus, lost in the chaos of Pete's hat-stealing rodeo routine.

Maggie's legs were rubbery and her cheeks hurt from laughing. This last bar was a Coyote Ugly knockoff — sticky floors, twangy music blasting from blown-out speakers, and bartenders in cutoff denim dancing on the bar with bottles raised like weapons, women dancing beside them.

"Don't you dare," Gwen's voice said faintly behind her, steady, warning, drowned out by the music.

Maggie grinned, wild and reckless, and promptly hauled herself onto the bar anyway.

The crowd whooped, the bartenders cheering her on like she'd passed initiation. One slid a half-empty bottle her way, and before Gwen's voice could even cut through again, Maggie tipped her head back and let the liquor pour straight from the spout into her mouth.

The burn hit instantly — sharp, sweet, wrong. Mystery alcohol. Rum, maybe. Whiskey. She didn't care.

The room roared approval. Pete was pounding on the bar like she'd just witnessed the second coming. Kiera buried her face in Izzy's shoulder, half laughing, half mortified. Danica was shouting something Maggie couldn't hear but looked suspiciously like her full name.

Maggie wiped her mouth with the back of her hand, tiara slipping sideways, arms thrown wide. "Vegas, baby!" she shouted, her voice ragged, her grin blinding.

As the song ended, she crouched to climb down from the bar. Strong arms swept around her waist, steady and sure, pulling her down before she could wobble on her heels.

Gwen's arms.

The crowd whooped, but Gwen barely glanced at them, her focus only on Maggie as she set her back on solid ground, one hand still braced at her hip. "You doing okay?" she asked, low enough that only Maggie could hear.

Maggie's heart lurched at the gentleness, at the steadiness, at how much she wanted to collapse into it. Instead, the bitterness ripped out of her, sharp and ugly.

"Where's Lillian?" she snapped. "Aren't you more inter-ested in her tonight?"

Gwen blinked at her, slow and steady. "I'm asking about

you," Gwen said finally, voice even, almost swallowed by the roar of Shania Twain blaring from the speakers.

Maggie laughed, sharp and ugly. "Sure. Because you're suddenly so concerned." She tried to wrench her arm back, but Gwen's grip on her elbow tightened just slightly — not rough, but not soft either. Just like she knew Maggie was a flight risk and had no intention of letting her bolt into the neon.

Behind them, Pete was trying to convince Danica that riding the mechanical bull was a good idea. Izzy was egging her on with solemn nods, as if this were a sacred rite. Danica had her phone out, recording the chaos. Kiera was trying to wrangle them toward the exit. The whole scene buzzed with laughter, shouting, stomping boots.

And still, Maggie could only hear Gwen's voice. Low, careful. Always careful.

"You're drunk," Gwen said.

"No shit," Maggie snapped. "That was sort of the point of a party."

Gwen's mouth twitched — whether with irritation or something softer, Maggie couldn't tell. God, she hated that she still looked for softness.

"Come on." Gwen angled her body closer, guiding her toward the side of the bar where it was marginally less mayhem. Her hand slid down from Maggie's elbow to her wrist, warm against her pulse. Maggie tried not to notice the heat curling low in her stomach. She tried even harder not to notice that Gwen's thumb brushed once, just once, against her skin before pulling back like it hadn't happened.

"You don't get to do this," Maggie said, her voice breaking just enough that she had to laugh to cover it. "You don't get to swoop in like... like some gallant knight pulling me off the bar when five minutes ago you were practically undressing Lillian with your eyes."

That got a reaction. Gwen's jaw clenched. She looked

away, toward the crush of people, then back at Maggie. "What are you talking about? I wasn't—"

"Save it," Maggie cut in, throwing up her hands. "She's perfect, right? Tortoise biologist, saves the desert, doesn't dance on bars—"

"Maggie." Gwen's voice was sharp now. A warning. The kind that used to stop her mid-rant, back when they still knew how to fight fair.

Maggie's chest ached. Her throat felt tight. She held up her hands. "Relax. I get it. We're separated, technically, so I'm not asking for explanations. You don't owe me those anymore."

The words landed heavy between them. For a second, Gwen just looked at her with a searching expression, and Maggie hated the way that felt, like Gwen was memorizing her, like Gwen still cared.

Danica's voice cut through, high and gleeful: "Mags, Pete is gonna try the mechanical bull."

The group erupted in laughter again. The ridiculousness of it all should have been enough to drag Maggie back into the frenzy, but she was still pinned by Gwen's gaze.

"Are you okay?" Gwen asked again, quieter this time.

Maggie swallowed hard. She tried to say yes. She wanted to say no. This feeling was freaking her out... this pull between them. Surely it was just their history that made her jealous, made her want all of Gwen's attention. It was the muscle memory of love, nothing more. She rolled her eyes and pulled her wrist free. "I'm fine. Go rescue someone else."

She pushed past Gwen toward the rest of the group, heart hammering like she'd just sprinted.

Gwen's fingers wrapped around her elbow again before she could vanish into the crowd. Firm. Not up for debate.

"No," Gwen said, voice low, close to her ear. "We're going back to the hotel."

Maggie barked out a laugh that sounded like it belonged

to someone else. "We? Since when is there a *we*?" She yanked, but Gwen didn't let go. "I saw you take Lillian's card. I know what you have planned."

Gwen blinked, eyes narrowing just enough to register a hit. Then, maddeningly calm: "What the hell are you talking about?"

"Oh, please," Maggie shot back. "I'm not blind. You think you're subtle? You think I didn't notice her sliding that little hotel key into your hand like some… some key-card harlot?"

Around them, the group whooped. Pete had managed to half climb the bull and was already yelling, "This is for feminism!" Izzy and Danica were doubled over laughing. Kiera was filming, muttering about liability insurance. The whole bar was vibrating with noise, but Maggie could only feel Gwen's hand, solid and warm, holding her in place.

Gwen's mouth twitched — anger, not amusement this time. "What the fuck, Maggie."

"What?" Maggie lifted her chin, defiant. "If you want to go sleep with Saint Lillian of the Tortoises, go ahead. You don't need my permission. Just don't… don't stand here acting like you give a damn about me." There it was, the crack in her voice. She wanted to swallow it back down, but it was too late. Gwen heard it. Maggie saw the flicker in her eyes, the one that said she still cared, that she still felt *everything*.

Gwen leaned in, close enough that Maggie caught the clean, sharp smell of her perfume over the stale beer of the bar. "You're drunk. Let's get you out of here."

Maggie yanked her wrist, finally tearing free. "I know exactly what I saw."

But she didn't. Not really. And the uncertainty was almost worse than the jealousy.

"Yeah. She gave me her card," Gwen said, though her tone was more fact than confession.

Maggie froze. The bar noise blurred into static. Her

stomach dropped so fast she nearly laughed. Confirmation. Proof.

But Gwen kept going, sharper now. "Because she wasn't staying there. She has a house here, Maggie. The card was for me — for us. Lillian thought I might want…" Gwen exhaled, frustrated, like she hated how the words sounded out loud. "I asked her if we could have her room for the night for some time alone."

That landed like a slap. Maggie's head snapped back, eyes narrowing. "What?"

"It wasn't her idea to… fuck." Gwen raked a hand through her hair, still holding Maggie's wrist with the other. Her composure was slipping, the polished veneer cracking at the edges. "It was *her* idea to give me the card. Because she could see that I—" She cut herself off, jaw tight. "God, Maggie. You really thought I'd hook up with your best friend's sister? Here? Now? Who do you think I am?"

The floor seemed to tilt under Maggie's boots. She wanted to scoff, to double down, to toss out something sharp about Gwen's new Vegas bestie. But Gwen's voice — low and rough — lodged in her chest like an arrow.

Who do you think I am?

Behind them, Pete hollered something unintelligible from the bull. The crowd roared. Izzy yelled, "Stay on, cowboy," and Danica was crying with laughter.

"I don't know what you're trying to say," Maggie said, frustrated as she tried to piece apart all that Gwen had just confessed. She blinked hard, trying to focus. The neon lights didn't help — they smeared Gwen's face into something unreal, like a portrait half-wiped away. "You want to be alone with me? Why?"

Her voice cracked on the last word. Perfect. Exactly the kind of raw, pathetic note she didn't want to give Gwen. And maybe she was too drunk to follow the conversation, maybe she'd invented the whole thing — except Gwen was still holding her wrist, still looking at her like Maggie was both impossible and essential.

Gwen didn't flinch. She leaned closer, her breath warm against Maggie's temple. "Because I miss you," she said, low. Almost drowned out by the whooping from Pete's bull ride. "Because I don't know how to be around you when everyone else is there, and I want to spend time with you without an audience."

Gwen's hand slid down, past Maggie's wrist, and laced firmly with her fingers. Not tentative, not asking. Claiming.

"Come on," she said, and the steel in her tone left no room for argument. "We're going."

Maggie's stomach lurched. "What — no. No, I'm not—" She tried to pull back, but Gwen was already tugging her through the press of bodies, weaving toward the door like she'd mapped the exit in advance.

The air outside hit Maggie like a slap — dry desert night, cooler than the sweaty chaos inside, but her skin still buzzed, hot. "I didn't agree to this," she said, stumbling a little in her boots as Gwen kept hold.

"You will." Gwen didn't even glance back, just tightened her grip when Maggie resisted.

Maggie huffed in frustration and... something else lower in her belly that she would not be admitting to. She should've ripped her hand free, made a scene, stomped right back in and climbed on the damn bar again if only out of spite. But her feet kept moving, matching Gwen's stride. Her pulse thudded in her throat, in her palm where Gwen's fingers pressed against hers.

Half a block from the bar, the noise dimmed enough for Maggie to hear her own ragged breathing. "This is kidnapping," she muttered. "Highly illegal."

That earned her the tiniest curve of Gwen's mouth, quick as lightning.

Maggie swallowed down the sound clawing its way up

her chest, half laugh, half sob. "You think you can just, what, drag me out like this, and I'll, what? Just listen? Just—"

"Yes," Gwen said, cutting her off. Simple. Certain.

Maggie hated how much her body obeyed that certainty, even as her brain screamed at her to turn back.

The Uber ride and the elevator up to the room was silent, but not calm. Maggie could feel her pulse in her ears, in her fingers still tingling from Gwen's grip. She stared at the glowing floor numbers like maybe they'd tell her everything would be all right.

By the time they reached the room Gwen had apparently "borrowed" from Lillian for the night, Gwen had shifted into full crisis-management mode. Door shut. Lights on. Shoes off. And then, maddeningly practical, she steered Maggie straight into the bathroom.

"Shower," Gwen said, flipping on the water like it was the most obvious thing in the world.

Maggie snorted, half-hysterical. "Oh, sure. Just a casual shower at two a.m. Totally normal."

Gwen was already adjusting the temperature gauge, testing it with her wrist — her *wrist*, like Maggie was a toddler she didn't want to scald. The familiarity of it made Maggie's throat tighten.

"Come on," Gwen said softly. "You'll feel better."

Before Maggie could muster another protest, Gwen was undressing her from behind, unzipping her top and sliding it down Maggie's arms, then unzipping her skirt and holding onto Maggie's hip as she stepped out. Her hands were so warm on Maggie's skin, and her touch wasn't sexual, but caring. Comforting. The touch Maggie had felt one thousand times in crowds and parties and city sidewalks. A guiding hand of the person she trusted most in the world.

"I can undress myself," Maggie snapped, but she still leaned forward to hold onto the wall, her eyes closing as Gwen slipped her underwear down her legs. Then, without ceremony, Gwen led Maggie over the shower ledge and under the spray.

When the water hit, it was a shock. Too cold at first, then easing into warmth, running over her face, soaking her hair. Maggie pressed her palms to the tile, eyes shut tight.

Behind her, Gwen's voice: "I'll be right back."

The door clicked shut, and suddenly it was just her and the water.

Maggie let her head fall forward, forehead against cool ceramic. Her stomach twisted. Every nerve in her body was still sparking from the night, from Gwen dragging her here, from Gwen's hands slowly and carefully undressing her, from that ridiculous, impossible confession — *I miss you.*

She should feel lighter, rinsed of it. Instead she felt like she might drown standing up. She hated that her first instinct was to want Gwen back in the room. Hated how much of her was still tethered, knotted, raw. Her chest clenched, messy and overwhelming. Wanting too much. Always too much.

She whispered, just to hear it over the water: "What the hell are we doing?"

And of course, no answer came.

The bathroom door opened again, and Gwen's voice cut through the rush of water. "I brought your pajamas."

Maggie cracked an eye. Sure enough, Gwen was standing there like it was the most natural thing in the world, holding up the soft cotton set Maggie always packed for trips — navy shorts, striped tank. The domesticity of it made her want to laugh and scream all at once.

"You planning to dress me, too?" Maggie shot back, stepping out and grabbing a towel a little too aggressively. Water dripped down her legs, pooling at her feet. "What's next? Bedtime story? Glass of warm milk?"

Gwen didn't flinch. Just held out the pajamas. "You can barely stand up."

"I'm *fine*." Maggie snatched them, tugging the tank over

her damp skin, the fabric clinging. "You know what, Gwen? You don't get to—" She broke off, pulling the shorts on, fumbling with the drawstring. "You don't get to swoop in like this. Not after months of silence and complacency."

"I wasn't silent." Gwen's jaw tightened, her voice still maddeningly even. "I was giving you space."

Maggie laughed, sharp and ugly. "Oh, is that what we're calling it now? Space?" Her wet hair was seeping into the fabric of her shirt. "Funny, because from where I'm standing, it looked a hell of a lot like you were giving your attention to Lillian."

The silence that followed was worse than shouting. Gwen's eyes darkened, her mouth a thin line.

Maggie hated the way her chest heaved, hated how close Gwen was standing, hated that she could still smell her perfume under the steam. She wanted to shove her. Kiss her. Both.

"Say something," Maggie snapped, voice breaking.

Gwen did — finally. Quiet, but cutting. "I never chose anyone over you. Not once. You're the one who walked away."

The words hit harder than the water had. Maggie swallowed, throat raw. Her fingers fumbled at the towel like it might shield her from the truth in Gwen's voice.

"What was I supposed to do?" The words ripped out of Maggie before she could corral them. Her chest hurt, tight and messy, but she powered through. "You're married to your job. You never prioritized me."

The second it landed, Gwen's expression shifted into something sharp, jaw tightening, like Maggie had hit the precise nerve she'd been aiming for.

"That's not fair," Gwen said, voice clipped. "I worked so hard for *us*. For our life."

Maggie barked out a laugh, wet hair plastered to her cheeks. "*Our* life? What life was that? The blueprints you spent nights with while I—" She cut herself off, biting down hard before she admitted too much, before she confessed how many nights she'd lain awake staring at the empty side of the bed, wondering if Gwen would even notice if she left.

"I did it for us," Gwen said again, quieter this time, like repetition would make it true.

"No," Maggie whispered, shaking her head, the fight leaking into something softer, smaller. "You did it for you. And maybe I was supposed to understand, to wait around forever, but I—" Her throat closed. "I couldn't."

The silence that stretched between them was unbearable. Steam curled in the air, water still dripping from Maggie's hair to the tile. Gwen looked at her like she wanted to argue, like she had an entire courtroom of evidence stacked up in her favor — but underneath, Maggie swore she saw something else. Regret. Ache.

"You think I'm on this fucking trip for my own benefit?" Gwen's voice cut sharp through the steam. Her cheeks were flushed, eyes blazing in a way Maggie hadn't seen in months. "I'm here for you."

Maggie blinked, thrown. "Why? Why now?"

"I'm here because I—" Gwen broke off, hands flexing at her sides like she didn't trust herself with them. "Because you scare the hell out of me, Maggie. And I fucking love you."

The words lodged in Maggie's chest like shrapnel. She wanted to throw them back, twist them into something ugly. But her mouth was dry, her pulse wild.

And then — she wasn't sure who moved first.

One second, there was a gulf of air between them, and the next, it was gone. Gwen's mouth was on hers, desperate and sure, Maggie's hands fisted in the fabric of Gwen's shirt, pulling her closer like she could somehow climb inside the steadiness she both craved and resented.

It wasn't gentle. It wasn't careful. Months of silence, weeks of tension, years of history poured out in the press of lips, the scrape of teeth, the muffled sound Maggie made against Gwen's mouth.

The towel slipped from her shoulders, pooling at her feet, but Maggie didn't care. Didn't care about anything except that Gwen was kissing her like she'd been starving, like all that restraint had finally cracked open.

And Maggie kissed back, messy and hungry, because despite everything — despite the anger, the jealousy, the endless ache — god help her, she still wanted her.

The kiss turned feral in seconds. Gwen's hands were on her face, then her neck, then sliding down, urgent, like she'd been holding back so long she couldn't remember how to stop. Maggie gasped against her mouth, her back hitting the bathroom wall hard enough to make the mirror rattle.

"Jesus, Gwen," she muttered, but her hands betrayed her, yanking at Gwen's shirt, tugging her closer. Anything between them was suddenly too much. She wasn't sure if it was her or Gwen who removed her pajama top. Months of anger didn't matter, not when Gwen's body pressed flush against hers, not when her tongue slid against Maggie's and she moaned like she'd forgotten how to breathe.

Maggie couldn't stop touching — Gwen's shoulders, her jaw, the smooth line of her back. All the restraint, the distance, the cold civility of the past months — gone. Torched.

Gwen kissed her like she was reclaiming something. Maggie kissed back like she was setting fire to it.

Then Gwen lifted her, easy, strong. Maggie let out a startled laugh that dissolved into a groan as Gwen carried her into the room, dropping her onto the untouched of the two queen beds.

"You still mad?" Gwen asked, hovering above her, voice low and ragged.

Maggie stifled a grin, still defiant but breathless. "Furious."

And then Gwen was on her again, and the rest dissolved

into heat, hands, mouths, years of longing crashing into the present.

They were all teeth and hands and years of frustration, every kiss edged with anger, every touch like proof they still knew each other's bodies too well to pretend otherwise. Gwen's mouth dragged down her throat, sucking hard enough to bruise, and Maggie arched into it, half moan, half challenge.

"You're infuriating," Gwen muttered against her skin.

"Good thing you like that," Maggie shot back, gasping as Gwen's hands gripped her hips, holding her down.

It wasn't soft. It wasn't sweet. It was frantic, clawing, Maggie's sleep shorts and Gwen's pants stripped and tossed aside like none of it mattered except skin against skin. Gwen's weight pressed her into the mattress, solid and grounding, but her touch was everywhere at once — urgent, greedy, like she couldn't get enough.

Maggie clawed back, nails in Gwen's shoulders, teeth at her jaw. The taste of her, the heat of her. It was too much and not enough. They rolled, Maggie straddling her, riding the line between fury and hunger. Gwen's hands gripped her thighs, guiding, demanding, as if neither of them could decide who was in charge.

They kissed until Maggie's lips ached, until her chest heaved, until she was sure she'd break apart from the sheer force of it.

She shifted until she was riding Gwen's thigh, taking her own pleasure from Gwen's body, her hair dripping and Gwen's fingers tracing the droplets down her breasts, her stomach.

It was all sensation — skin slick with sweat, the rasp of Gwen's hair against her cheek as she bent, the salt of her collarbone under Maggie's tongue. The hotel sheets tangled around them, twisting as they fought for control, neither giving it up, both desperate to win and desperate to lose at the same time.

"You drive me insane," Gwen muttered, and Maggie could feel the words hot against her ear, could feel the tremor of it all the way through her.

"Good," Maggie gasped, rocking against her harder, reckless, drunk on the power of Gwen's hands clutching like she'd never let go.

It wasn't tender. It was raw and fast and too much, every movement building like a storm, their breaths colliding, bodies slamming together like they were trying to bruise the distance out of each other.

The intensity of Gwen's eyes as she watched Maggie was enough to make Maggie squeeze her eyes shut. Gwen finally held her hips, pushed her over the edge of orgasm. When everything broke open, it was with a desperate, angry tenderness that undid her.

Maggie clung to Gwen, trembling, hating and loving her in the same breath.

Gwen kissed her like she was angry about it, teeth scraping Maggie's lower lip hard enough to sting. Maggie bit back, a hiss against Gwen's mouth, and the sound only seemed to make her hungrier.

But they didn't stop. Couldn't stop. Because months of restraint had snapped, and now they were just two people devouring each other, desperate to feel, desperate not to lose the thread.

Every time Maggie thought they'd die from exhaustion, Gwen pulled her back under, mouth at her neck, hands roaming like she was memorizing every inch all over again. And Maggie gave it back — messy, greedy, biting hard enough to make Gwen curse against her skin.

The room smelled like sweat and perfume, the sheets kicked half off the bed, tangled around their legs. Maggie was vaguely aware of her own gasps and broken sounds she would've been embarrassed by if Gwen hadn't been answering them with her own.

They flipped again, Maggie pressed into the mattress, Gwen above her, steady and relentless as she spread Maggie's knees, watching as her fingers slid inside, her thumb circling exactly where Maggie needed it. Then Maggie clawed at her, dragged her down, rolled them over, the two of them locked in this constant struggle of want.

By the third orgasm — or fourth, she lost count — her body was trembling, slick with heat, throat raw from moaning Gwen's name like it was the only word she still remembered.

And Gwen — god, Gwen — looked wrecked. Hair plastered to her temples, lips swollen, eyes dark and unguarded in a way Maggie had never seen.

They kept going until sleep finally overtook them, until Maggie's limbs were heavy and her skin hummed, until she collapsed against Gwen's chest, too wrung out to move. Gwen's arms came around her automatically, pulling her in, holding her tight.

Maggie wanted to protest — wanted to remind her that she was still furious — but her eyes slid shut instead. The last thing she felt was Gwen's hand smoothing over her damp hair, steady even now, before sleep pulled her under.

CHAPTER 20

THE ROOM WAS QUIET, THE KIND OF QUIET ONLY VEGAS mornings allowed — air conditioner humming, faint traffic far below, the curtains letting slivers of dawn light bleed at the edges.

Gwen lay on her back, wide awake, staring at the ceiling. Maggie was curled against her side, bare skin pressed warm along her own, one arm flung across her stomach like it had always belonged there.

It should have felt right. It *did* feel right. And that was the problem.

Her chest ached, heavy with the certainty that she'd crossed a line. Maggie had been drunk — angry, jealous, reckless, all sharp edges and glassy eyes. Gwen should have gotten her into bed, pulled the blankets over her, let her sleep it off. She should have been the responsible one.

Instead, she'd kissed her. And then kept kissing her until neither of them had the sense to stop.

Maggie stirred, mumbling something unintelligible, burrowing closer, and Gwen's throat went tight. The way she fit against her was so familiar it was unbearable. Years of muscle memory, sliding back into place like it had never left.

And yet it had.

Gwen let out a breath through her nose, careful not to wake her. She stared at the ceiling and waited.

Her hand twitched, wanting to smooth over Maggie's hair again, but she forced it still against the sheets. She didn't get to touch her like that. Not anymore.

Maggie let out a soft sigh in her sleep, her lips brushing Gwen's shoulder. And Gwen — stoic, controlled, practical Gwen — closed her eyes against the guilty flood of want. Because no matter how much last night had felt like love, this morning it felt like betrayal.

Gwen stayed put. She told herself it was because moving might wake Maggie, that sliding out of bed would risk the inevitable confrontation too soon. But the truth was simpler, uglier: She didn't want to let go.

Maggie shifted against her, breath warming the hollow of Gwen's throat.

Any second now. She braced for it — the recoil, the angry what-the-hell-did-you-do, the look that would tell her Maggie had finally realized how wrong last night had been.

Instead, Maggie blinked up at her, eyes still heavy with sleep, hair wild after sleeping with it wet. For one suspended heartbeat, Maggie just looked at her. No anger, no judgment. Just raw, unguarded, too close.

Gwen's pulse roared in her ears. She almost spoke, almost blurted out *I'm sorry, you were drunk, I shouldn't have touched you.* But then Maggie's hand moved, slow and deliberate, sliding across Gwen's chest, splaying wide like she was testing if this was real.

"Morning," Maggie whispered, her voice rough, blinking blearily up at her. Her smile was small, crooked, so intimate it made Gwen's chest seize. "You're still awake."

"I never really slept." Gwen's voice was rough, too honest.

Maggie hummed, pressing her face back into Gwen's shoulder. "You always were terrible at turning your brain off."

Gwen let out a low breath, trying to steady herself. Because the guilt was there, just under her ribs, pressing hard. The memory of last night — how drunk Maggie had been, how reckless it all was — threatened to sour everything.

"You should hate me for last night," Gwen murmured before she could stop herself.

Maggie shifted again, lifting her chin just enough to look at her. Her eyes were clear now, if tired. "Why would you think that?"

She reached out, brushed her thumb over Maggie's cheekbone. "I don't ever want you to feel like I took advantage of you."

Maggie studied her, quiet for a long moment. Then she shook her head, hair tickling Gwen's skin. "You didn't."

Gwen wanted to believe her. Needed to. The sunlight was creeping in, illuminating the room, and for just a second, she let herself pretend. Pretend this was morning-after, not some fragile truce in a city built on illusions.

Maggie sighed, settling back against her chest. "Stop thinking so loud," she muttered.

Gwen's throat worked. She nodded once, because words would've cracked her open.

And then Maggie kissed her. Soft, almost tentative at first — so wildly different from the frantic collision of last night that it shattered something in Gwen's chest. Gwen kissed back before she could think better of it, the guilt still there but drowned under the pull, the impossible sweetness of Maggie choosing her even for one more moment.

It deepened gradually, like they'd both agreed not to rush this time. Maggie's fingers curled into Gwen's hair, tugging gently, and Gwen let her hand slip to Maggie's waist, holding her steady, grounding them both.

This wasn't fury, wasn't jealousy. It was slower, surer. Like rediscovering something they'd once built together and thought they'd lost. It was familiarity in morning breath and bedhead and pillow lines on cheeks.

And when Maggie climbed over her, lips trailing lower, Gwen couldn't stop the broken sound that escaped. She let herself believe, just for now, that this wasn't a mistake — that maybe, impossibly, they were finding their way back.

The difference was staggering. Last night had been a wildfire in a reckless, consuming, dangerous way. This morning was a slow burn, steady and devastating in its own way.

Maggie kissed her like she was relearning the shape of her mouth, patient and intent, every brush of lips more deliberate than the last. Gwen's chest ached with it, her hand sliding up Maggie's back, fingers tracing familiar ridges of bone and muscle as if they hadn't been apart.

Maggie straddled her, hair falling in a curtain around their faces. She was smiling, and Gwen nearly broke apart right there. How long had it been since she'd seen that smile directed at her, unguarded, without bitterness shading the edges?

"You're staring," Maggie whispered against her mouth.

"I know," Gwen admitted, voice hoarse. She didn't look away.

Their movements were slower, unhurried, but no less desperate. The urgency had simply shifted — less about punishment, more about proof. Gwen's hands mapped her body like she was committing it to memory, Maggie's touch lingering, dragging, savoring. Every sigh, every shiver, every whispered word sank deep.

Maggie shifted until their thighs were entwined, their centers slick and sliding against one another. As close as their bodies could possibly be, like they were two halves reconnecting into a whole. Maggie was gentle, careful as she circled her hips, and Gwen pushed up into her, greedy with want.

The room was still quiet — only their breaths, the rustle of sheets, the occasional half-choked laugh when a kiss missed its mark. Gwen let herself get lost in it, let the guilt recede for a moment. This wasn't taking advantage. This was Maggie choosing her, Maggie coming back, Maggie pressing close and murmuring her name like it still meant something.

Gwen's own climax peaked quickly, the visual of Maggie atop her unwinding every bit of self-restraint she'd ever had.

When Maggie finally trembled and gasped and collapsed against her, Gwen wrapped her arms tight around her and didn't let go.

The blackout curtains didn't hold forever. By the time it was over, a gray-pink line of dawn had found its way into the room, cutting across the sheets, softening everything it touched.

Maggie lay draped over her chest, skin warm, breaths shallow with exhaustion. Gwen stared at the ceiling, the ache in her body nothing compared to the ache everywhere else. She'd forgotten how Maggie loved to sleep after sex — messy, all limbs and weight, claiming every inch of space like it belonged to her. And god help her, Gwen had missed the heaviness of it. Missed the way it tethered her to the bed.

She brushed a wild strand from Maggie's temple without thinking. Old habits were treacherous like that.

Maggie's breathing evened against her chest again, the weight of her body warm and anchoring. Gwen kept perfectly still, afraid to disturb the fragile peace. But something in her chest was changing, almost painfully light, like the first break of sun after weeks of gray.

Maggie had kissed her. Chosen her. Not in anger this time, not in desperation, but in the slow, steady way Gwen remembered from the beginning. And if Maggie could do that — if she could climb back into Gwen's arms and smile like that in the faint pink of dawn — then maybe they weren't lost.

Maybe they had a chance.

The thought spread through her like champagne bubbles, effervescent and ridiculous. She almost laughed at herself, lying there half-naked in a wrecked hotel bed, smelling like sweat and liquor and Maggie's shampoo, feeling lighter than she had in months.

For the first time since Maggie left, Gwen didn't feel like she was bracing for impact. She felt... hope. Sharp, giddy, impossible hope.

She glanced down at Maggie's face, soft in sleep, lips parted just slightly. Gwen traced the line of her jaw with her eyes, committing it to memory all over again.

Yes. They could overcome this. They had to.

The champagne-bubble lightness lasted all of ten minutes.

Gwen was tracing the curve of Maggie's shoulder with her eyes when her phone buzzed across the nightstand. Once, twice, insistent. The sound cut straight through the quiet.

She considered ignoring it. Just let it die out, stay cocooned in the warmth of Maggie's body. But her gut twisted. Monday morning. Work didn't care that she'd spent the night tearing herself open and stitching herself back together again.

She leaned, careful not to jostle Maggie too much, and squinted at the screen.

MELINDA

Can you jump on a quick call about the
zoning revisions?

Of course. How she wanted to say no, to bask in this moment forever... But she couldn't. She owed it to the project and to herself to see this through. She'd been having visions all weekend about what she'd rather be doing to the area — revitalizing instead of scraping the entire block and the history of the area. Melinda would say she was being too romantic about the past, about code issues and the immense cost of repairing older buildings instead of building something new, safe, efficient.

Melinda was probably right. Gwen was just romanticizing.

Gwen patted Maggie's shoulder. "Hey, I'm sorry to wake you, but I just need to hop on a quick call with Melinda."

Maggie stirred, blinking awake as Gwen exhaled sharply. "Seriously?" she rasped, hair wild, eyes narrowing on the phone.

Gwen felt the bottom drop out. "I just need ten minutes," she said quickly, already hating how it sounded like a script she'd performed a hundred times before. Reassure. Compartmentalize. Slot Maggie into the waiting room of her priorities.

Maggie pushed up onto one elbow, her expression flattening. The dawn light caught the crease in her forehead, the set of her mouth. "Unbelievable. We just—" She broke off, shaking her head.

Gwen's chest tightened. She reached for the word that had always soothed, the one that came before apology, before explanation. "Baby—"

"No. You don't get to 'baby' me."

It landed like a slap. Gwen flinched, pulse rattling in her throat. She searched Maggie's face, desperate. "But last night... what was last night if not..." She swallowed hard, hearing how pathetic it sounded, but she pressed on anyway. "I kind of thought last night meant we were back together. Or at least this morning."

Maggie's laugh was sharp, brittle, a blade disguised as humor. "Last night was... fun. A bit of nostalgia. Let's just call it what it was."

The words carved into her. Gwen's phone slipped in her hand, the screen dimming as her grip went slack. "Mags—"

"It didn't mean anything," Maggie said.

Gwen's vision blurred. She wanted to argue, to call the bluff, to pour out every unsaid thing she'd been holding down for months. To tell Maggie that nothing about last night had been casual, that it had cracked her wide open. But her throat locked up. All she managed was a nod — thin, brittle, cowardly. And the second it left her, she hated herself for it.

Maggie swung her legs out of bed, pulling on her clothes with jerky, furious motions. "You should take that call, Gwen. Wouldn't want me to get in the way of your calendar."

Panic flared. Gwen sat up, reaching instinctively for her. "Mags, wait—"

But Maggie was already walking into the bathroom, her voice echoing sharp against the tile. "Don't."

Gwen's chest burned. "It's not—" she started, but the words came out too small, swallowed by the room.

Maggie stumbled back out, tugging her shorts into place, muttering, "Should've known better than to think I came first, even for a morning. You know what? Maybe last night, and this morning, maybe it was a mistake. Clearly nothing has changed for you, so nothing can change for us."

Each word was a gut punch, one after another. Gwen couldn't move fast enough to stop her, couldn't form a response before Maggie was at the door, yanking it open.

A whirl of wild hair. Leftover anger. The muted click of the door.

And then silence.

Gwen sat frozen on the edge of the bed, phone buzzing again in her hand, its glow cutting across the sheets where Maggie had just been.

The champagne bubbles were gone. Just like that.

CHAPTER 21

MAGGIE STOMPED BAREFOOT DOWN THE HALL, HER HAIR STILL damp, Gwen's scent clinging stubbornly to her skin like evidence. She hated that she wanted to scrub it off and bottle it at the same time.

She took a moment to compose herself. She felt all of her old defenses rising. Last night had been a lot of things, but this morning had been only one. This morning had been the slow realization that she still unequivocally loved Gwen, the chemistry of two people still desperately tied to one another. *A mistake. Nothing more than nostalgia.* The words tasted like ash. She'd seen the flicker in Gwen's eyes, the hurt she'd landed. It should have satisfied her, should have built the wall back up, but instead it hollowed her out.

By the time she keyed into the suite, she had her face set in a mask — nonchalant, casual, nothing-to-see-here. But the second the door swung open, she knew something was off.

Not morning-after hangover giggles. Not even the sluggish silence of too much tequila. The energy inside was taut, electric, like the air right before a summer storm.

At the dining table, Izzy and Kiera sat close — too close — hands tangled under the table, both looking like they'd swallowed a secret and were about to burst.

Pete and Danica were hunched together on the couch, a laptop balanced precariously between them. Danica's perfect bun had collapsed sideways, and Pete's jaw was tight enough to cut glass. Was Danica… crying?

Maggie blinked, hurrying to Danica. "What's wrong?"

Four sets of eyes swung her way at once.

Danica sniffled. "Our venue. It's gone. Double-booked. They gave the date to another couple."

Pete groaned, dragging her hands down her face. "Six weeks before our wedding."

Maggie's stomach pitched. She thought about the logistics immediately — flight refunds, hotel refunds, travel plans already paid for, vendor deposits that would be a nightmare to recover. The ripple effect of it all pressed in on her chest, the kind of adult chaos that couldn't be fixed with a laugh. It was money, time, expectation — an avalanche of headaches disguised as one flat sentence.

"Fuck," she said, wrapping an arm around Danica's shoulders. "Do you need listening or problem-solving?"

"Just comfort for now," Danica said, burrowing her face into Maggie's shoulder. Pete caught Maggie's eye and looked so miserable that Maggie reached out to set a hand on her shoulder, too.

The suite stilled for a moment, and Maggie was selfishly grateful to be holding two of her friends while her own heart was aching as well.

Her gaze drifted to Izzy and Kiera, who were glowing with a dangerous kind of glee. Definitely not the mood of the moment. "Why do you two look like you just committed a felony?"

Kiera went crimson, lips twitching. Izzy leaned back, smug as a cat. "Nothing."

Pete's head snapped up. "Wait, that does not answer the question."

Danica sniffled and let Maggie keep an arm around her shoulder as she glanced toward Izzy and Kiera.

"Now's not the time," Kiera whisper-scolded Izzy.

"You set a date," Danica announced, all of her bad mood thrown off like a blanket. "You picked a date for your wedding?"

They both nodded, positively beaming.

A flurry of excited yelling erupted from the couch and then all five of them were on their feet, hugging and yelling and gushing over the emerald-cut sparkle on Kiera's finger.

"When?" Pete asked, hugging Izzy so fiercely her feet were lifting off the ground.

"Last night." Kiera glanced toward Izzy.

"Immediately after Kiera went down on me," Izzy announced.

Kiera yelped, smacking her arm. "Oh my god, Izzy. You cannot tell people that part."

"I think it adds important context," Izzy said serenely.

"No, what's the date you chose?" Danica said, shaking her head.

The group erupted — shrieks, cackles, embarrassed and amused giggles until the tension broke like a dam. Izzy and Kiera pulled up their phone calendars and pointed to a July date nearly two years in the future. Everyone was teasing and laughing and celebrating, and Maggie felt it bubbling up inside her too, the absurdity of it all — the lost venue, her own mess with Gwen, and now this. She doubled over, wheezing.

And before she could stop herself, she blurted, "And I had sex with my ex-wife last night."

The laughter screeched to a halt.

Pete froze, mouth open. Danica's hand moved to her chest like she was reaching for pearls to clutch. Kiera blinked rapidly. Izzy's eyebrows looked as though they might raise right into her hairline.

"What?" Maggie demanded, defensive now. "Don't look at me like that."

But instead of shock, Pete just gave a low whistle. "I think that means you three owe me ten dollars each."

Danica pressed her thumb and forefinger to the bridge of her nose. "Pete…"

Izzy shook her head. "No way, last night was *my* bet. I won."

Maggie frowned. "Wait. What are we betting on?"

"When you and Gwen were going to get over your own egos and just admit that you're too in love to separate," Kiera explained, holding up her hands like Maggie was holding a weapon. "I didn't bet, but we were all pretty confident."

"How did you know we were separated?" Maggie asked, her voice rising in confusion.

Izzy leaned forward. "Of course we knew. Why do you think we pushed so hard for Gwen to come on this trip?"

Maggie held a hand to her chest. Heat surged inside her — anger, humiliation, betrayal, grief, longing, and something sharper she didn't want to name. It crashed in waves, hot and disorienting. Part of her wanted to scream, part of her wanted to laugh at the absurdity, and part of her wanted to crumple into tears. "You… meddled? For *me*?" Despite all of the turmoil, there was still a part of her filled with genuine delight to know that her friends had set up a Meddling Maggie-level scheme.

"Gwen thinks the sun shines out of your ass, babe," Pete said, all elegance.

Danica rolled her eyes. "And we knew you were still in love with her. So yes, we meddled." She lifted her chin, soft but firm. "We want you happy, Mags. And because Gwen is more than her job, whether she sees it yet or not. We weren't going to sit by and watch you two let it die without a fight."

Izzy crossed her arms, blunt as ever. "You think we didn't notice? The way you look at each other? The way you clearly still love each other? Come on. You've both been miserable for months, and you're too stubborn to admit it. Somebody had to push."

"So, does the sex mean you're back together?" Kiera asked, a gentle hand on Maggie's arm.

Maggie shook her head. "I mean, I thought maybe. But you don't get it. Gwen always chooses work. Always. I'm just the thing she squeezes in around deadlines. And I won't do it anymore."

Danica looked sympathetic, but Izzy was already crossing her arms, looking ready to play devil's advocate.

The suite door opened, and Gwen stepped inside.

Her hair was damp from a shower, her shirt crisp, her phone clutched loosely in one hand. She looked impossibly composed, as if the night before hadn't happened at all.

The air thickened. Everyone froze.

Maggie crossed her arms, pulse hammering. "They know about us," she said to Gwen. "They've all known."

Gwen's gaze softened but stayed steady. "Oh."

The silence that followed was unbearable — everyone holding their breath, Gwen's eyes locked on hers, Maggie vibrating with fury and shame.

And then, a knock at the door.

"Room service," a cheerful voice called. Gwen stepped to open the door.

Three attendants wheeled in carts laden with silver domes and enough carbs to quell a riot. The smell hit first — maple syrup, butter, coffee strong enough to file down teeth. The attendants did a practiced ballet around the island, setting down plates: pancakes the size of steering wheels, an architectural stack of waffles, a glistening mound of bacon, an omelet that looked like it had ambitions beyond breakfast.

"Bless you and your tiny cloches," Pete told the nearest server, deadly serious.

Danica was already organizing like a field marshal. "Plates first. Then proteins. Syrup last. Coffee… oh my god, that's *real* cream. Hand it over." She hugged the stainless carafe to her chest.

Izzy constructed a mimosa pyramid with the single-minded focus of a person who had not yet suffered consequences.

Kiera slid the pyramid a crucial inch back from the edge. "We would like to keep the deposit."

"Deposit is a social construct," Izzy said, topping her glass.

Maggie looked around the room, at everyone's desperation to tame the tension in the air. She grabbed a plate and started with pancakes. The ritual of it worked like a reset button: butter, syrup, a reckless scoop of berries. Her hands finally had something to do besides shake.

Pete tried to swipe Danica's bacon with the subtlety of a raccoon. Danica smacked her knuckles without looking. "Get your own."

"I was just testing the crispness for your safety," Pete lied, already chewing.

"Uh-huh," Danica said, guarding the bacon like crown jewels.

The group's noise rose and fell in waves. Someone found hot sauce, someone else found jam. Pete attempted to explain the idea behind "tooth butter" or "butter so thick that when you bite into it, you can see your teeth marks." Danica moved through them like a benevolent hurricane, refilling coffee, preventing small disasters, issuing tiny, efficient kisses to Pete's shoulder as she passed.

Gwen stayed at the periphery, at the counter by the sink, taking orders. "Black? Cream? Sugar?" She poured without spilling, without asking for thanks.

Maggie didn't look at her. Not directly. She let Gwen exist in the blur of the room — competent hands, quiet voice, the familiar rhythm of her moving through domestic chaos as if it were a puzzle she could solve with steadiness alone.

"Who ordered eggs?" Gwen asked, and three hands shot up at once.

"They're vegan," Izzy said, mouth full.

"Absolutely not," Danica said, pushing the vegan omelet toward Izzy. "Boundaries."

Pete popped a grape into her mouth and spoke around it. "Vegan eggs are like the weirdest breakfast suggestion."

"You're a breakfast suggestion," Izzy shot back.

For ten breaths, it almost felt like the morning could be ordinary. Plates slid, napkins unfolded, syrup stayed, mercifully, in its lane. Even the ache in Maggie's chest settled under the weight of butter and routine.

Then the first plate was empty and the second was possible, and the chatter drifted toward the unsolvable: wedding venues.

It started as a joke and then turned into a brainstorm the way all their best ideas did — loud, over-caffeinated, half-sincere.

"Will it be too difficult to find somewhere else in Bulgaria?" Maggie asked, sipping her coffee.

"I mean, I could fly out there and try to figure it out, but this venue was already like pulling teeth. I'm sure there's something in Sofia we could find," Pete began.

Danica's shoulders dropped. "I don't want you to have to plan the whole thing. Maybe we should just elope."

"You could get married by Elvis," Maggie suggested, glancing out the window.

Pete looked excited by the idea, but Danica shook her head. "My parents would kill me."

"What about planning something Stateside? Hotel refunds should still be available, and I'm sure most people could get flight credits, if not full refunds," Gwen said, infuriatingly realistic. "You could do something in Denver to keep the planning easier."

"Let's have a joint wedding," Izzy said with a grin, and Pete high-fived her as Danica and Kiera rolled their eyes.

"What about Telluride?" Kiera suggested. "Aspens, mountains, snow in the winter. Really take it back to the beginning."

"I mean, I'm sure Aunt Jade has other properties in her empire," Maggie said, reaching for another slice of bacon. "She's probably sitting on three wedding venues and a haunted monastery."

That got a ripple of laughter, but Kiera's eyes lit. "Wait. Aunt Jade has a lake house in Michigan. Wouldn't it be hilariously full circle if you two actually got married at another of Aunt Jade's properties?"

Danica hesitated, but Maggie saw it — the gleam in her eye. The wheels were already turning.

The chatter spun into happy chaos. Izzy argued for cornfields with the conviction of a person who had never met a bug. Kiera stole a hotel pen and began sketching a lakeside arbor on a napkin, labeling it with arrows like a crime scene diagram. Danica pretended to be noncommittal, which was how Maggie knew she was already planning the power grid for the tent. The table buzzed with warmth again, laughter spilling over like champagne.

Pete raised her fork, pointing it like a gavel. "We could hire a Prince impersonator for Michigan. Bring a little Vegas magic to the Midwest."

Izzy practically spit out her coffee. "Yes. Elvis for vows, Prince for reception. Iconic."

Danica groaned. "We're not having a theme wedding based on Vegas impersonators."

"Fine," Pete said. "But we're getting a fog machine."

Kiera rolled her eyes, but she was smiling. "Only if we

also rent bug zappers the size of small planets. Have you met Michigan mosquitoes?"

Maggie chimed in, smirking. "I'll bring citronella candles. Maybe Aunt Jade has those tiki torches."

Izzy tapped her chin. "Lakefront wedding plus cornfield reception after-party. Tell me I'm wrong."

"You're wrong," Danica said primly, but her lips twitched.

The banter spiraled — Pete insisting she'd rather wrestle a bear than battle mosquitoes, Izzy pitching a corn tuxedo for the officiant, Kiera countering with a lakeside lantern release. The food dwindled, coffee refilled endlessly, and laughter layered over the lingering tension like plaster on cracked walls.

Maggie laughed at the right moments, stole bites from Izzy's plate, and raised her glass to the ridiculous Michigan plan. She pitched in — "string lights across the dock, picture it" — and ignored the way her voice thinned when it carried across to Gwen. On the surface, it felt easy, just like them.

But under the syrup and chatter, her chest tightened. She caught Gwen's gaze across the table — steady, waiting, hopeful — and she looked away, a bitter taste in her mouth battling against the sweetness of pancakes.

Because she knew the truth. No matter what anyone else believed, Gwen would never choose her.

CHAPTER 22

THE AIRPORT WAS ALL WHITE NOISE — WHEELS CLATTERING ON tile, boarding announcements echoing off high ceilings, people hurrying all around them.

They stood in a loose circle near the security checkpoint they'd just shuffled through, between where their gates diverged, everyone rumpled and puffy-eyed from too little sleep, arms looped around carry-ons like lifelines. Pete and Izzy, the seasoned fliers of the bunch, looked calm and relaxed, while Danica held her boarding pass and her passport in her hand despite only being on a domestic flight. They were all traveling to Denver together, and Maggie and Gwen's gate was in another area, leaving slightly later.

The hugs started. When it was Maggie's turn, Gwen watched as she folded each of them tight into her arms, mascara smudging at the corners of her eyes. By the time she pulled back from Kiera, her voice cracked.

Pete patted Maggie on the shoulder, looking like a proud dad with a belt bag around her torso. "This is the first time we all made it to the airport at the end of a trip without someone weirdly bailing first."

"And I didn't want to jinx it, but this is also the first time I've made it through a trip without a terribly embarrassing injury," Maggie added.

They laughed, because it was true. Maggie had come home from their Telluride trip with a broken arm and showed up after the San Diego trip with a broken nose and two black eyes. Gwen also knew that usually someone disappeared before the last night, sneaking out early to avoid conflict or resolution. This time, against all odds, they were all here.

Gwen watched Maggie wipe at her cheeks, laughing through tears. It hit her in the chest — how much Maggie loved this group, how much she was already mourning the end of this trip, how much Gwen wasn't sure she could give her.

She wanted to reach out. Say something. But she only adjusted the strap of her bag, keeping her face carefully composed.

"Text when you land," Danica said, hugging them both again for good measure before tugging Pete toward their side of the gates. Izzy and Kiera trailed after, still hand in hand, still glowing with their renewed wedding excitement.

And then it was just Gwen and Maggie, the noise of the terminal rushing back in around them.

The others melted away, swallowed by the shuffle of shoes and the hollow calls of the boarding agents over the loud-speaker. It was just the two of them now, hovering by a row of molded plastic chairs, their bags at their feet.

Maggie sniffled, swiping at her cheeks with the heel of her hand. Gwen's chest squeezed.

Without thinking, she reached out, brushing her fingers over Maggie's shoulder. "Hey," she said softly. "It's okay."

Maggie flinched — not a big movement, just a shrug sharp enough to make the contact fall away. Her mouth twisted into something that was almost a smile but didn't reach her eyes. "I'm fine," she said, voice raw. "Don't you have some work to catch up on?"

Gwen's hand fell back to her side. She swallowed, steadying herself against the sudden hollow. "Maggie..."

But Maggie was already grabbing her bag, eyes narrowed on the departure board like it had personally wronged her.

Gwen stood there for a beat, rooted, the ache settling in her ribs. All her giddiness from that dawn light was gone now, replaced by the sharp reminder of why they were here, why Maggie had walked away in the first place. Gwen shouldered her own bag, forcing her face into its usual composure, and followed her toward their gate.

They walked in silence, past random clusters of slot machines with their volume up way too loud, families corralling kids, other couples dragging roller bags.

Maggie hitched her bag strap higher on her shoulder with a jerky movement. Her face was blotchy from crying, but her jaw was set.

"I think when we get back to Austin," she said suddenly, not looking at her, "you should get your own apartment."

The words sliced through the terminal din, clean and merciless.

Gwen stumbled for half a step before catching herself. She stared straight ahead, throat thick. She'd known this was coming — hell, she'd been bracing for it for months — but hearing it out loud was different. Final. "Maggie—"

But Maggie was already speeding up, weaving through a knot of travelers, not giving her room to answer.

Gwen forced her legs to move, her breath steady, her face composed the way she'd trained it to be. Inside, though, it was unraveling. The fragile hope she'd let herself taste in that hotel bed, the giddiness that had bubbled up at dawn — it all collapsed under the weight of Maggie's disappointment.

Her own apartment.

Separate keys. Separate lives.

By the time they reached their gate, Gwen's chest ached so fiercely she thought she might actually break open. She sat down across an aisle from Maggie, folding her hands in her lap, pretending she wasn't dying inside.

Gwen didn't argue. The words sat on her tongue, heavy and hot, but she swallowed them back. Maggie's shoulders were tense, her jaw locked — nothing Gwen said in an airport terminal was going to soften that.

So she stayed quiet.

Through boarding, through stowing their bags, through two and a half hours of recycled air and the low hum of the engines. Maggie leaned against the window, earbuds in, eyes closed. Gwen sat rigid in the aisle seat, staring blankly at the book in her lap she never turned a page of. Every so often Maggie shifted, brushing against her, and Gwen's heart would leap stupidly before it settled into the ache again.

They didn't speak once. Not in the air, not during landing, not while shuffling off the plane with the rest of the herd.

The silence didn't budge until they walked down the escalator into arrivals, the buzz of Austin wrapping around them — Spanish mingling with English, guitar licks from someone inexplicably playing electric guitar in an airport bar, the smell of coffee and BBQ from the food court.

"Mama! Mommy!"

Three voices at once, shrill with excitement.

Their kids came barreling across the terminal, backpacks bouncing, sneakers squeaking. Gwen barely had time to drop her carry-on before they collided into her legs, arms thrown tight around her waist.

Maggie crouched low, pulling all three kids against her, laughing through fresh tears. "I missed you, I missed you, I missed you," she said, kissing their hair, their cheeks, their sticky faces.

Gwen dropped to her knees beside them, smoothing a

hand over Rosie's hair, pressing her cheek to Arlo's as he hugged her, reaching to tug Jude into the fray. The ache in her chest shifted — still heavy, but different now.

Maggie glanced up, just once, eyes red and wet.

And then one of the kids pulled free, waving frantically toward the baggage claim. "Come on, Grandma brought cookies."

The spell broke. They all stood, moving as a family toward the carousel, the sound of the terminal folding around them. Side by side, but with miles still stretched between.

THE APARTMENT SMELLED like paint and carpet glue. Brand-new construction, all beige walls and echoing corners, the kind of place staged for the "empty, picture your things here" photos in a realtor's slideshow.

Gwen set her suitcases just inside the door and stood there, staring at the empty expanse of it. She'd signed the lease yesterday, filled out all the online forms, transferred the deposit with a few clicks. Efficient. Orderly. Necessary.

It didn't feel like hers.

She sat on the edge of the bed she'd panic-ordered to be delivered on time, palms pressed to her knees, and let her mind circle the weekend like a wound she couldn't stop touching.

Vegas. Two nights they couldn't keep their hands off each other, months of anger dissolving into heat and hunger. Then that angry sex, the slower love the morning after, sunlight soft across Maggie's bare skin, when Gwen had felt stupidly and recklessly certain. Certain they could find their way back, certain this wasn't the end. She'd let herself imagine rebuilding, one kiss at a time.

Now here she was, surrounded by beige walls and freshly

laid carpet, nothing but her folded clothes and the hum of the empty fridge to keep her company.

She reached for a laundry bin to begin to put a few things away, startled to find Maggie's Rice University shirt tucked near the bottom. A faint bleach stain near the hem, a stretched-out collar... She held the fabric to her nose, knowing it would smell like all of her other laundry, but she could have sworn the sweatshirt held just a hint of Maggie's perfume. Blinking back a tear, she tucked the sweatshirt onto a high shelf of the closet.

She'd thought separation would be big and loud, all slammed doors and shouted arguments. But it wasn't. It was silence.

Just her.

SHE LASTED LESS than an hour in the silence before picking up her phone. Her thumb hovered over Maggie's name, then her mom's, then finally landed on Logan.

Her brother answered on the second ring. "You sound like someone who's either drunk or about to be."

"Neither, unfortunately," Gwen said. Her voice came out steadier than she felt. "I just moved in to the new place."

There was a pause, a low whistle. "So it's official, then."

"Yep." She looked around the sterile one-bedroom — blank walls, bare counters, not a single thing that betrayed anyone with a personality had ever set foot inside. "It's official."

Logan let out a sigh that crackled through the line. "How's it feel?"

She swallowed. "Quiet."

"Quiet good or quiet bad?"

"Quiet... loud, somehow," she admitted. The words slipped out before she could stop them.

Logan didn't fill the silence right away. He never rushed

her, which was both comforting and unbearable. "You want me to come down this weekend? Help you hang shelves or… something?"

"No." Gwen rubbed her temple. "Thank you. But no. I need to… figure out how to live in this."

He made a low hum of agreement. "Just don't figure it out alone, okay?"

Her throat tightened. She glanced at the blank wall across from her, tried to picture Maggie's laugh bouncing off it, the kids' drawings taped up. She somehow couldn't.

"I'll try," she said.

They hung up a few minutes later after Logan gave her the update on the new couple he was dating. How her brother could handle dating two people when she couldn't even manage to make one woman happy was beyond her. Gwen set the phone face down on the counter and leaned back in the chair, the apartment yawning wide and empty around her.

THE NEXT DAY, Dr. Elowen's office couch was still too hard to sit comfortably. Maybe it was a psychological exercise, physically torturing her clients in this way before torturing them with the emotional warfare of being asked repeatedly, "And how did that make you feel?"

Gwen sat on the edge of the couch anyway, spine straight, palms pressed together in her lap like she was bracing for cross-examination. Maggie sprawled at the far end, one ankle hooked over the other, her body angled toward the therapist. A united front against Gwen, except Gwen didn't have the energy to mount a defense.

They'd already agreed to logistics. Alternating weekends with Gwen in the house with the kids, and Maggie staying with Colette during that time. It kept the kids in one place, settled and comfortable, which was one thing they could agree on. On paper it was clean, orderly, the kind of compromise Gwen usually thrived on. In practice, it felt like she was borrowing her own life in two-day increments.

"I think it's time to talk about the separation as a reality you're both experiencing," the therapist said gently, scanning between them.

"Yes," Maggie answered before Gwen could open her mouth.

Gwen nodded, slow. No resistance. She'd learned that pushing only made Maggie's jaw lock tighter.

"And how does that feel for you?" the therapist asked, eyes on Gwen now.

It would have been easy to recite something polished: *I want what's best for everyone. This is a healthy step.* Instead, Gwen surprised herself by saying, "Terrible."

Maggie shifted, arms crossing over her chest. She didn't look at Gwen.

The therapist gave her a small nod. "And for you, Maggie?"

Maggie blew out a breath. "Like I can finally breathe. I need… space. To not feel like I'm waiting on her job, or her schedule, or—" She cut herself off, shook her head. "Space."

Gwen stared down at her folded hands. She wanted to argue. Say she'd give her space without moving out, say she could change, say all the things she hadn't said at the airport. Instead, she just nodded again.

Because maybe Maggie was right. Maybe silence was safer than her promises.

The therapist let the quiet settle for a moment before saying, "Sometimes separation gives clarity. Sometimes it reinforces distance. The work is noticing which it's doing for you."

Maggie made a sound — something between a scoff and a laugh. Gwen kept her face still, but inside she felt something tighten, like a string pulled too far.

"You know, you never told me what you needed from me until it was too late. You never gave me a chance to fix it," Gwen said.

"Are you kidding me? I asked one thousand times." Maggie's voice sharpened, the words spilling faster. "I asked you to come home earlier. I asked you to take just one week off after we lost the baby. I asked you to stop putting me second. Do you even remember that?"

Gwen's throat went dry. She did remember. She remembered Maggie's voice in the kitchen doorway, low and frayed, asking if Gwen could reschedule a meeting, if she could just be there, and Gwen had said, *I'll try*. And then she hadn't. She remembered Maggie's texts during late-night flights, her careful phrasing — never demands, always requests. And still Gwen had brushed them aside, telling herself she'd make it up later. The stress of being the sole monetary provider for the family had been her constant, not Maggie's need for time together.

"I remember," Gwen admitted, her voice quieter than she meant. "I just thought… if I kept everything running at work, then I was protecting us. I thought I was taking care of you by taking care of us financially, and with health insurance, and all of those important things."

Maggie's laugh was sharp, incredulous. "You thought twelve-hour days and missed birthdays was taking care of me?"

The therapist leaned forward, hands folded in her lap. "This is good. This is important. It sounds like both of you were asking, but neither was hearing."

Inside, her mind reeled back through years of choices that had felt so rational at the time. She had told herself she was doing the right thing, always. If she worked harder, brought in more money, made sure the mortgage was covered, the kids' college funds padded, the medical insurance bulletproof — then she was protecting them. Protecting Maggie.

She'd convinced herself that being the steady one, the reliable one, was the same thing as being present. That a perfect balance sheet could stand in for sitting beside Maggie on the couch when she cried. That making partner would erase the sting of an empty chair at the school play. That her long hours were noble sacrifices, not betrayals.

But looking at Maggie now, arms crossed like armor, Gwen could see it plain: she had built a fortress around their life, and in the process, locked Maggie out.

Maggie's mouth twisted, hurt and tired all at once. "I wanted a partner. You kept offering stability when I needed intimacy."

The room went quiet again, the words sitting heavy between them. Gwen felt something tighten in her chest, like a rope drawn too taut. Because she had believed, truly believed, that steady meant safe. That safe meant loved. Now she was seeing all the ways she'd been wrong.

Maggie stared at her knees, blinking hard. Gwen wanted to reach across the space, wanted to uncross those arms and hold on until Maggie believed her. But she stayed still, nails biting into her own palms.

Because wanting wasn't enough.

Maggie's arms stayed folded, but her gaze flicked briefly toward Gwen before dropping again. Her voice softened, almost as if against her will. "I thought... I thought you taking unexpected time off to be with me for this Vegas trip was a good start." She exhaled sharply, shaking her head. "But then I felt triggered by you working at all hours of the day. And maybe that's on me, too."

Gwen blinked, the words catching her off guard. She hadn't expected that kind of honesty or self-awareness from Maggie when the real separation was so raw.

Maggie's throat worked. "It's like, every time your phone buzzes, I brace for impact. I don't give you a chance to prove it's different, because I've already decided what it means.

And maybe that's not fair. Maybe I'm clinging to the story I wrote about us, that I was always second place, because it's easier than believing you could change."

The admission landed in Gwen's chest with a confusing mixture of relief and devastation. Relief that Maggie still saw the attempt, still noticed her showing up in ways she hadn't before. Devastation that the moment her phone lit up, all of it crumbled.

The therapist nodded, her tone steady. "So you're both holding old hurts like evidence. Gwen believed working harder was protecting the marriage. Maggie believed being present was the proof of love. Neither of you said it clearly enough, and now both of you are guarding yourselves with stories that keep the other out."

Maggie looked up then, meeting Gwen's eyes for just a beat. There was weariness there, but also honesty. "I don't want to be stuck in that loop forever. That's why I need the separation."

Gwen's hands clenched in her lap. She wanted to promise she'd never answer another work call again, never touch her phone if Maggie was in the room. But the truth was messier than vows. The truth was they both had to rewrite the stories they'd been telling themselves for years.

And that, Gwen realized, was perhaps impossible.

The session wound down. Maggie grabbed her bag quickly, already halfway out the door before Gwen rose to follow.

On the sidewalk, the sun glaring off car hoods, Gwen finally spoke. "I'll see you Friday, then, to trade for the weekend."

Maggie nodded, curt, and slipped into her car.

Gwen stood there a moment longer, hands in her pockets, trying not to feel like she'd just been erased.

CHAPTER 23

MAGGIE

THE BEAR HEAD WAS GLARING AT HER.

Not a real one — though honestly, with Colette, who could say — but a fake taxidermy mount she'd dragged back from some West Texas flea market, swearing it was "the best kind of vintage Americana with a wink." The fur was stiff and uneven, the glass eyes too shiny. Maggie had been brushing it with a pet grooming glove for fifteen minutes, like she could coax it into looking less like it would consume its owner in the night.

It wasn't working.

"Stop fussing with it, it's supposed to look like a fever dream," Colette called from the back, where she was restacking enamel pitchers. "It's camp."

"It's cursed," Maggie muttered.

She gave the bear another pass with the brush, and her mind slid where it always did when she wasn't vigilant — back to therapy. Her own, not couples. She'd only been twice now, but she was already kicking herself for waiting so long. The first session with Lauren had been awkward, all intake and "I've experienced three major losses in the past three years" and a look she imagined Lauren was going to give her a lot, which was kind of a professional version of "yeesh." But by the second session, Maggie was crying freely and voluntarily connecting the grief of the termination of her pregnancy and the loss of her mother in ways she hadn't considered before. She had a feeling that therapy was going to be good for her.

Lauren had asked about Gwen, of course. Everyone did, in their own way. But Maggie had dodged, pivoted. And then Lauren had asked something worse: "You said you never stopped running. Running from what?"

Maggie had laughed, loud and sharp. "From the obvious. From the part where my mom dropped dead on a Tuesday afternoon and no one prepared me for how much it would hollow me out."

The therapist didn't flinch. "What did that loss mean for you and Gwen?"

And Maggie had said it. The thing she'd been carrying like proof. "She wasn't there. Not the way I needed. She was… somewhere else with the love of her life — her career. Leaving me to sit on the kitchen floor with casseroles I didn't eat and the strange bureaucracy of dealing with my mother's death."

Her throat had tightened, but she'd kept going. "And once you've lived through that? Once you've sat in that kind of silence without your person showing up? You don't forgive it. You can't."

The therapist had only said, "I want you to imagine that moment planted a seed, thinking that if she wasn't there then, then she'll never be there."

Maggie had blinked in confusion.

Her therapist continued. "And maybe that's a seed you've been watering every day since?"

Maggie hadn't answered. Couldn't. Because it felt true. It had calcified into her bones.

Now, brushing a bear that didn't need brushing, she muttered under her breath, "I'm not just watering some seed, that's ridiculous."

The bell over the shop door jingled. A couple wandered in — matching hats, matching tattoos — cooing over Colette's barware display. Maggie flashed them a smile, tossed out her usual line about *everything's twenty percent off today, except the cat,* then went back to the bear.

The truth was, she liked it here. Found & Chosen was weird and crowded and forgiving. She could sprawl, let her mess leak out without apology. The opposite of Gwen's world, where everything had to fit in neat rows and nothing was ever left unscheduled.

But grief had no schedule. It was the one mess she couldn't joke away.

She stared into the bear's glassy gaze, her own eyes stinging. "You get it, don't you?"

The couple glanced over, startled, then politely redirected to the shelves and away from the weird lady speaking to a taxidermied bear head that she was only seventy-three percent sure was actually fake.

Colette appeared from the back, hands on hips. "If you've bonded with him, I'll cut you a deal."

Maggie straightened, brushing hair out of her face. "Don't flatter yourself. I was just unloading my trauma onto his dead little eyes."

Colette didn't miss a beat. "That's what he's here for."

Maggie laughed, too loud, then pressed a hand to her throat. She wanted to believe it — that grief could be absorbed by a wonky, haunted bear and two sessions of therapy. That she could scratch the surface without ever digging deeper.

But the truth sat under her skin, relentless: She'd lost her mother, and she hadn't stopped running since.

And maybe, just maybe, she didn't know how to stop.

ROSIE HAD STOLEN her phone again. Maggie found her under the dining table, little legs splayed, cheeks smeared with peanut butter, holding the screen so close her nose was practically touching it.

"Hi Auntie Izzzzzy," Rosie shrieked into the camera. "Hi Auntie Keeeeera."

Izzy's face filled the screen, grinning. "Well, hello, my sweet angel darling girl. Can I buy you a pony?"

Behind her, Kiera leaned in, softer smile. "Hey, Rosie-posie. Where's your mom?"

"Rosie, that's Mama's phone." Maggie ducked down, tugging the phone out of sticky fingers before her kid could FaceTime-order a family pack of Taco Bell, not that that would be unwelcome.

Maggie was breathless as Arlo and Jude thundered through the living room, Nerf darts whizzing dangerously close to her head. She dropped onto the couch, kids orbiting like manic satellites, and gave the camera a look that said it all. "As you can see, it's been a quiet evening."

Izzy snorted. "Looks like a zoo."

"Correction," Maggie said, flipping the phone to show the trail of Goldfish crackers, LEGO bricks, and couch cushions strewn across the rug. "This is a *zoo after the apocalypse*."

Rosie crawled onto Maggie's lap, wedging herself into the frame again. "Show them Puck! Show them Puck!"

Maggie tilted the phone toward the wall, where Rosie's prized possession — Puck, an aggressively pink stuffed duck the size of a small ottoman — slumped in the corner. Izzy nodded, shrugging. "Puck the duck. Can't imagine how that could be mispronounced badly."

The kids whooped, then disappeared again in a flurry of Nerf fire. Maggie sighed, returning the camera to her face. Izzy and Kiera were tucked into what looked like their condo's kitchen, mugs in hand, rings of steam curling upward. They looked... good. Glowy. Happy in a way that twisted something tight in Maggie's chest.

"How's engaged life treating you?" Maggie asked.

Kiera smiled. "It's good. We haven't really started planning besides picking the date, but based off of how Pete and Danica are handling it, I think we're going to put that off as long as possible."

Maggie laughed. "That's wise."

"And," Izzy added, tone faux-casual. "How are *you*?"

Maggie forced a smile. "Oh, you know. Fine. Great. Totally thriving."

Kiera gave her a look — the one that screamed high school teacher. "Maggie."

Maggie tipped her head back against the couch cushion, staring at the popcorn ceiling. "It's like... the house feels different now. Quieter. Like something's missing, but you're not supposed to say it out loud because then the kids will hear you and realize it too."

Izzy's grin slipped. "It's wild that Gwen really moved out."

"Yeah," Maggie said, her voice dipping quieter as she eyed Rosie concentrating on a sheet of puffy stickers across the room. "She's... around. For the kids. We worked it out. Every other weekend with her, all weekdays with me. They don't know the details, not yet. To them it's just... Mama gets her sleepovers with Auntie Colette, and Mommy gets to make pancakes when she's here."

Kiera's brow furrowed. "And how are you doing with that?"

Maggie blew out a laugh that scraped at her throat. "Depends on the hour. Sometimes it feels like freedom, like I can finally breathe without waiting for her work calendar to clear. And sometimes it feels like... I don't know... like I left half my heart at the curb with her suitcase. But hey, at least the Wi-Fi still works."

They were both quiet for a beat, Izzy's mouth twitching like she wanted to crack a joke but couldn't quite get there. Maggie could feel the conversation tipping into territory she wasn't ready for. So she did what she always did. She swerved.

"Anyway," she said brightly, "enough about me and my thrilling divorcée sitcom."

Izzy's smile was laced with pity. "At least we'll be seeing you soon at the wedding."

"Hopefully," Maggie muttered, watching Arlo and Jude run into the room again. "If the Nerf crossfire doesn't get me first."

The kids shrieked again in the background, and Maggie held the phone steady, letting them wave and shout their goodbyes.

By the time she hung up, the living room was a disaster, Rosie was begging for cookies, and Maggie's chest felt scooped out and full all at once.

She closed her eyes for a moment, leaning back against the couch, hearing her therapist's voice again: *Is it true, or is it just the seed you're watering?*

But she shoved the thought away. Focused on the joy on her friends' faces. That was easier.

Much easier than the silence pressing at her from every corner of the house.

Danica named the conversation "Wedding Mayhem 🦆"

DANICA

Okay, Michigan venue is officially booked.
Walloon Lake, baby.

PETE

Hell yes. Midwest gay wedding supremacy.

IZZY

Can't wait to see cornfields and couture in
the same weekend.

Pete named the conversation "Corn to be Wild".

KIERA

She will not listen to me when I say there
aren't cornfields. It's a lake.

IZZY

Cornfields are never far away in the Midwest.
Don't ruin my vision.

MAGGIE

I'm sure we could get Izzy to a cornfield post
haste.

Pete named the conversation "Shucked Up".

KIERA

Flights into Traverse City? Or do we drive
from Detroit?

DANICA

Traverse City, unless you want a road trip. It's
4+ hours from Detroit. I will not be doing that.

IZZY

You don't want to christen another of Aunt Jade's properties with car sickness?

PETE

Oh we'll be christening it alright.

MAGGIE

Hell yeah, get it.

DANICA

KIERA

I'm scrubbing that from my brain so I can continue to look my aunt in the eyes.

MAGGIE

Okay but real question: what's the weather like in Michigan in October?

DANICA

Looks pretty brisk.

IZZY

Bring on the lesbian flannel fest.

CHAPTER 24

THE CONFERENCE ROOM SMELLED FAINTLY OF BURNT COFFEE AND carpet cleaner. Gwen sat at the head of the table, the blueprints spread before her like a map of someone else's life.

She folded her hands, blazer sleeves brushing against the cool surface. The stainless steel watch at her wrist caught the light. She rotated it slightly, a nervous habit she'd never broken, the way her thumb brushed the ridged bezel. Maggie had given it to her for their seventh anniversary — slipped the box across the table at a quiet restaurant, murmured, *You're always on time, might as well look good doing it.*

Across from her, Michael — one of the senior principals — beamed. "It's a legacy project, Gwen. You'll get promoted off this alone. The Board is ready to push you forward as Principal Architect."

The others chimed in, all praise and handshakes. Words like *visionary, leadership, career-defining.*

Gwen nodded at the right beats, even forced a smile. But the drawings blurred. The sleek glass towers they were proposing would level an entire historic neighborhood. Shops she'd walked past for years. Houses people had raised families in.

Back on her desk, she had dozens of sketches of what the neighborhood could be if they'd invested in upgrading structures, increasing affordable living spaces, prioritizing the residents who already lived there.

She should've been thrilled. This was what she'd spent two decades climbing toward. Proof of worth. The kind of title she could hang around her neck like a medal.

Now, it all felt wrong.

Instead, her chest was tight, her throat narrowing like a vise.

"I'll review the revisions tonight," she heard herself say, her voice steady even as the edges of her vision sharpened, tunnel-like.

The meeting broke with back slaps and congratulations. Gwen gathered her notes with mechanical precision, slipped into the hallway, walked past reception, and didn't stop until she'd locked herself in the bathroom.

The silence hit like a wave.

She braced her hands on the counter, knuckles white against the cold marble. Her reflection stared back — polished, professional, controlled. She hated this project. Oh god, she hated it so much. She hated that it stood for everything she'd fought against — rezoning historic neighborhoods, leveling legacy just to be shiny and new and expensive.

Her chest heaved. She couldn't get air down deep enough. The sound of blood rushed in her ears. She pressed a fist to her sternum like she could hold herself together physically, but her hands were trembling.

This isn't who I am.

The thought came unbidden, raw.

She tried to remember Maggie's laugh — loud, brash, alive. The kids' shrieks when they ran into her arms on the weekends. The way silence had swallowed her sterile apartment whole in the three weeks she'd been there.

The air caught, jagged, but it broke something loose. She slid down the wall to the tile floor, knees drawn up, breath coming in short, uneven gasps.

Someone knocked on the door. She forced her voice to be steady. "Occupied."

Here she was, panicked by the crushing realization that she didn't want the job she'd been killing herself for. That she'd spent years proving she was indispensable, only to discover she'd made herself disposable in her own life.

She buried her face in her hands and whispered it into the sterile air: "I don't want this."

Her phone buzzed in her blazer pocket. She fumbled it out, still sitting on the tile.

A notification: *Shared Calendar Update from Maggie Pierce.*

She opened it with trembling fingers.

Trip to Michigan — 4 days
Notes: *Kids with Gwen.*

That was all. Just logistics.

No explanation, no context. Just confirmation that while Maggie was off somewhere lakeside with their friends, Gwen would be here — parenting alone, filling the silence, pretending it was enough.

She closed her eyes against the screen's glow, letting the realization settle like lead in her chest. The promotion, the apartment, the calendar — it was all the same story: A life she'd built so carefully, and somewhere along the way, she'd managed to write herself out of it.

THE BAR WAS one of those sleek hotel lounges where the lighting was too dim and the martinis too sharp. Gwen didn't belong here, not tonight, but Melinda had texted — *Drinks? You could use one.* — and Gwen had said yes before she could think of an excuse.

Now she sat across from her boss, her mentor, the woman whose approval she'd chased for the last decade. Melinda in her tailored blazer, hair smooth as ever, the faintest smudge of eyeliner. Buttoned-up, inscrutable, always.

"You look tired," Melinda said simply, lifting her glass.

Gwen forced a small smile. "It's been… a week."

Melinda arched a brow. "Everything all right?"

The question was casual, but her eyes held her steady, and Gwen felt her defenses buckle in a way they rarely did. She could have lied. She usually did. But instead, she exhaled and said, "No. Not really."

Melinda didn't blink. Just waited.

"I'm separated," Gwen admitted. The word still felt foreign on her tongue, like she was trying out someone else's vocabulary. "We've worked out custody. I'm in a new place. It's… new."

"New?" Melinda echoed. "Is that good or bad?"

Gwen huffed a laugh. "It's really bright and soulless, but it's still nice at the same time. I don't know how to explain it right."

"Don't," Melinda said, taking a slow sip. "You don't have to."

Gwen wrapped her hands around her glass, fingers tight on the condensation. "I just… I thought I was doing it all for us. Working late, taking every project, building something big enough to carry both of us. And all she saw was me… gone."

It was more than she'd meant to say. She clamped her mouth shut, cheeks heating.

Melinda set her glass down with a precise click. "You don't owe me an explanation, Gwen."

"I know." Gwen hesitated. "I just — I can't say it to anyone else."

Melinda regarded her coolly, eyes sharp in the low bar light. For a long moment Gwen thought she wasn't going to answer at all. Then Melinda leaned back, her posture elegant, detached. "I do understand, you know. I've been divorced twice."

Gwen blinked. "Really?"

A faint, knowing smile. "Yes. Both times, the job came first. It always did. It always will."

The words landed like a verdict, unflinching. Gwen felt them settle heavy in her chest. "And you don't regret it?"

Melinda lifted her glass, swirling the liquid slowly before answering. "Regret?" She shook her head. "No. I'm proud of what I've built. My career gave me more than either marriage ever could. Stability. Recognition. Power. It's not romantic, but it's the truth."

She looked directly at Gwen, her gaze cutting clean through. "You can try to pretend you can give both the work and the marriage your all, but one will always suffer. I chose not to be mediocre at either. I chose to give my all to the work."

The truth of it pressed in on Gwen, sharp and suffocating. Maggie's face rose unbidden — her grief, her laughter, her warmth — and Gwen's chest seized. She'd always told herself she was the steady one, the provider, the ballast. But what had she really provided? She hadn't been carrying Maggie at all. She'd been carrying the job.

Melinda tipped her chin, eyes glittering. "It isn't compartments, Gwen. It's priorities. I think you and I are a lot alike in that way. We just find work to be the most rewarding part of our lives, and society says that's wrong because we're women, but only we get to say what's right for us."

Gwen nodded, mostly because Melinda was still her superior, and tried not to give in to her impulse to yell *No. I'm not like that. I'm more than that.* Instead, she sipped her drink in silence.

On the walk back to her car, Gwen's phone buzzed again. The calendar notification glowed: *Trip to Michigan — 4 days. Kids with Gwen.*

She clenched the phone in her hand, the bitterness cutting sharp. Maggie off with their friends, Gwen left behind with the silence again.

And for the first time, she wondered if Melinda's story wasn't a warning at all, but a prophecy.

Two divorces, a glittering career, the kind of résumé people pointed to with admiration — and Melinda had sat there in the dim light, unapologetic. No regret in her voice, no wistfulness. Just steel. The job had come first. Always. And she was proud of it.

The words echoed long after. Gwen had followed the same map: build walls out of deadlines, stack accolades like bricks, convince yourself it was noble to be the steady one, the provider. But pride didn't keep the apartment warm at night.

Her marriage hadn't ended in a single break. It was death by a thousand cuts. Missed birthdays. Canceled weekends. Her phone always within reach, Maggie's laugh sharpening until it lost its sweetness. And then the final cut: Gwen carrying her boxes into a sterile two-bedroom, while Maggie explained to the kids in careful phrases about "Mommy's new place" and "different houses, same love."

Now, the silence was everywhere. Custody schedules taped to the fridge. The coffee pot set for one. The kids' toothbrushes in a cup by the sink, a reminder of weekends that passed too quickly. She saw the outline of absence everywhere — the space on the couch where Maggie used to sit, the side of the bed that never dipped anymore.

She sat in the driver's seat outside her building, hands locked on the wheel, throat tight. She used to imagine growing old with Maggie, their kids loud around the dinner table, holidays crammed into a house that always felt too small. Now the image dissolved every time she reached for it. What remained was silence, and the weight of her own choices.

Maybe she was already too far down the road Melinda had walked. Maybe the truth was simpler: She had lost Maggie. She had lost the life they built. And prestige — the projects, the titles, the praise — wasn't going to fill the empty rooms.

CHAPTER 25

MAGGIE

COLETTE'S GUEST BED WASN'T BAD, BUT IT WASN'T HERS. TOO many pillows, too much lavender spray on the sheets, the mattress firm enough to remind Maggie she was supposed to be a guest, not a resident. She blinked awake to sunlight slicing between the curtains and the muted sound of Colette clinking around the kitchen downstairs.

An open sketchbook she'd been idly drawing in the night before lay open on her nightstand — the first time she'd sketched in a long time. The figure wasn't meant to be Gwen, and Maggie had abandoned the sketch the second she realized what she was doing.

Her head throbbed faintly — too much wine, too little water — and her chest carried that familiar morning-after heaviness, like grief and hangover had joined forces.

Couples therapy day. Thankfully, Maggie had requested this one be virtual, saving herself the stress of sitting in the same room as Gwen.

She dragged herself upright, pulled on a hoodie, and walked downstairs.

The coffee was already brewing, the kitchen smelling rich and warm. Colette stood at the counter arranging stems of eucalyptus in a stone vase, looking like a moody French lifestyle blog, and Maggie muttered, "Thanks," by way of good morning.

Colette only smirked, poured her a mug, and said, "Good luck."

MAGGIE BALANCED her laptop on her lap in the guest bedroom, still barefoot, still bleary, trying to center herself before Dr. Elowen's face blinked onto the screen. The little video squares populated — herself on the left, the therapist in the center, and Gwen on the right.

Gwen sat at the kitchen table. Their kitchen table. Sunlight streamed through the windows behind her, bouncing off the familiar cabinets, the fridge covered in crayon drawings and magnets from road trips. Maggie's stomach pinched, like she was trespassing in her own life.

And Gwen, immaculate as ever, hair neat, expression closed, as if she'd stepped into a deposition instead of therapy.

"Good morning," Dr. Elowen said warmly, her square lighting up in the center of the video screen. "How are we all doing today?"

Maggie shifted, the mattress creaking under her weight, someone else's life folded into crisp sheets. She took a sip of coffee to stall. "Peachy."

Across the screen, Gwen gave the faintest nod.

The therapist's eyes moved between them. "Last session, we touched on space — what it gives, what it costs. Today, I'd like to talk about communication. How you connect, especially as you navigate parenting together."

Maggie rubbed a hand over her face. "Well, we don't. Communicate, I mean. Not really."

"That's not true," Gwen said, calm. Too calm. "We coordinate schedules, drop-offs, school events."

"That's not communication," Maggie snapped, then sighed. "That's logistics."

Gwen's jaw flexed, but she didn't argue.

"Can you each describe what communication looks like, ideally?" Dr. Elowen asked.

Maggie gave a humorless laugh. "Ideally? I can tell her I'm falling apart without feeling like I'm burdening her. It's her looking up from her laptop long enough to actually notice." She glanced at her own square in the corner, the faint hollows under her eyes. "It's not me screaming just to get a reaction. Which I did. I weaponized how bad I felt, because at least then she couldn't ignore me. But it wasn't fair. To her. Or to me."

Gwen's gaze dipped down.

"And for you, Gwen?" Dr. Elowen urged.

"Clear. Concise. Without volatility. I need space to think before I respond. I don't want to be ambushed."

Maggie's laugh cracked sharp. "Yeah, well, news flash: Life doesn't schedule meltdowns for your convenience." Her voice softened as she tried to calm her own nerves. "I know I ambushed you. I wanted you to just… know what I needed without me saying it, and when you didn't, I came at you sideways. That's on me."

"Which is exactly why—" Gwen stopped, jaw tightening again.

Dr. Elowen lifted a hand. "Let's pause. What I'm hearing is that Maggie values immediacy and vulnerability, while Gwen values order and reflection. Neither is wrong, but they clash."

Maggie rubbed her temples. "They clash us right into the ground."

The silence stretched. Then Dr. Elowen said gently, "You

mentioned something happened on your Las Vegas trip. Would you be willing to talk about that today?"

Maggie paused, glancing to Gwen's stoic face, and she almost made a joke, but instead, she said, "We slept together. And I told myself it didn't mean anything." Her thumb worried the chipped rim of her mug. "But it did. For one night, it felt like I had her back. And then she woke me up to take a call, and I panicked, because I knew nothing had changed."

Across the screen, Gwen's throat worked. Finally, she said, "I thought it was a beginning. I thought maybe the pieces we broke could fit again. And when you said it didn't mean anything, it felt like losing you all over again." Her voice cracked before she steadied it. "I've spent years trying not to need more from you than you could give me. But that night? That morning? I wanted more. I still do."

Maggie pressed her palm to her chest, trying to keep steady. "And I can't trust that you'll ever put me first. You haven't shown me that. You didn't show me that when you had the chance."

The therapist nodded, voice calm. "What I hear is that night revealed there's still love between you. But love alone isn't enough. What you do with it matters."

"Yeah, well, what we do is fight," Maggie muttered.

Gwen's square flickered as she leaned closer. "We fight because you go for the jugular every time. You don't leave room for anything but your crisis in that moment."

"And you don't fight at all," Maggie shot back, her voice sharper than she meant, bouncing back tinny through her laptop speakers. "You shut down. You disappear into work, into silence, until I'm screaming just to hear something back. Do you have any idea how lonely that is? To be married and still alone?"

Gwen's voice rose, steadier than Maggie wanted. "Do you have any idea how exhausting it is to walk into a room and never know if I'm going to be greeted with love or a land mine?"

The guest room felt too small, her chest too tight. Maggie stared at the square of her own kitchen, the woman sitting in it, the life she used to live.

Her throat burned. "This is exactly it. You want order, I want connection, and neither of us is getting it. I think—" She forced the word out, jagged and final. "I think the only answer is divorce."

The word didn't echo. It just hung between their rectangles, heavy as stone.

Maggie's pulse thudded in her ears, louder than the faint hum of Colette's guest room radiator. Her cursor blinked at the bottom of the Zoom window, taunting her with *Leave Meeting* like an escape hatch she didn't dare use.

In Gwen's box, nothing moved. Gwen sat still, hands folded, as steady and unreachable as a statue.

Maggie tried to swallow, but her mouth was sandpaper. The word she'd said — *divorce* — still scraped at her insides, like it had hooked on something deep.

She hated how badly she wanted Gwen to interrupt, to argue, to refuse. To say *no, we can fix this, I still choose you.* But Gwen didn't even blink.

A wave of nausea rose sharp in her gut. She shifted against the headboard, grounding herself in the borrowed space: the lavender-scented sheets, the faint creak of pipes in the walls, nothing of hers. Not her room. Not her house. Not her life.

Dr. Elowen was sitting calmly in her own square, giving them time.

The silence grew unbearable.

She cleared her throat, voice shaky. "Say something."

Gwen's square stayed still, only the faint rise and fall of her chest proving the connection hadn't frozen. Maggie gripped her mug tighter, wishing she could reach through the screen, shake her, force her into motion.

Because silence had always been Gwen's sharpest blade.

Maggie blinked hard, vision stinging. Divorce. She'd meant it. She'd said it. But saying it out loud didn't feel like relief, didn't feel like strength. It felt like watching herself step off a ledge in slow motion, body waiting for the crash that hadn't come yet.

"Do you believe that too, Gwen?" Dr. Elowen asked softly. "That divorce is the only option?"

For a long moment, Gwen said nothing.

And Maggie — staring at the woman she'd once believed would always choose her — felt the answer settle in her bones, whether Gwen spoke it or not.

Gwen didn't look at her. She looked past the camera, at some fixed point only she could see, and said, evenly, "If that's what you want, I'll give it to you."

The words were clean. Bloodless. Like a doctor delivering terrible test result news.

Maggie's mouth went dry. For half a second she wanted to snatch them back — *no, not like that, not so easy* — but the reflex died as quickly as it came. Of course Gwen would make even this tidy.

Dr. Elowen's voice was soft. "What comes up for you hearing that, Maggie?"

She stared at the little square of her own face. Puffy-eyed. A hoodie with a ketchup stain. Colette's camp movie posters over the bed. "I don't know."

A beat. The therapist waited. Gwen's shoulders were so straight they looked painful.

"We don't have to decide anything final today," Dr. Elowen said. "A statement of intent isn't the same as filing paperwork."

Gwen nodded, still not meeting the camera. "I'll contact a mediator. It's cleaner."

There it was again: cleaner. Maggie pictured bleach wipes and color-coded folders and the way Gwen's hands had felt on her in Vegas, desperate and sure. The two images didn't reconcile. Maybe that was the point.

"Okay," Maggie said. The syllables felt like swallowing a coin. "A mediator."

When the session ended, Dr. Elowen thanked them for their honesty. The squares blinked: therapist gone, Gwen still there. For a second neither of them moved.

"Thanks for adding Michigan to the calendar," Gwen said finally. Polite. A stranger at a PTA meeting.

"Yeah." Maggie picked at a loose thread in the blanket. "I figured you'd want a heads-up."

Gwen's gaze flicked, just once, toward the camera. "I hope you have… a good trip."

A good trip. Like she was going to Cabo with a girls' group text and SPF 50, not to a wedding where her best friends would promise forever and she'd sit in the second row pretending she didn't believe in it anymore.

"Sure," Maggie said and killed the call before Gwen could be decent about anything else.

She stared at her black laptop screen until her own reflection came into focus. She didn't recognize the woman in it. She looked like someone who'd misplaced a life and was pretending she'd meant to.

"Divorce," she said out loud to no one, testing the weight. It just sat there, heavy as wet wool.

If that's what you want, I'll give it to you.

She closed her eyes, and for a rotten, traitorous second, wished Gwen had said anything else.

SHE LET herself into the house just after sunrise, the keys slipping soft in the lock. The quiet inside had a particular weekday-morning quality — not sleepy exactly, but waiting, as though the walls themselves knew the routine was about to start. The kids were still asleep upstairs.

It should have felt like coming home. Instead, it felt like trespassing.

Her own backpack slumped by the door, her jacket draped over the hook — small signs of her life scattered here like evidence. Yet as she walked through the kitchen, Maggie had the strangest sensation of sneaking, of stealing a moment she no longer had any right to.

Maybe this is how Gwen feels, she thought, *when it's her weekend. A guest in a house she built, tiptoeing through her own kitchen.*

The smell of coffee reached her first. Then she saw Gwen on the couch, legs tucked under her, hair still damp from the shower, a book open in one hand and a mug in the other. She looked… soft. Casual. Not the polished, armored version Maggie had last seen on the virtual therapy call — all even voice and mediation talk.

Gwen glanced up, startled at first, then composed in an instant. "You're here early."

Maggie hovered in the archway, suddenly unsure of what to do with her hands. "Yeah. Wanted to be here when the kids woke up."

Silence stretched between them, heavy but not sharp. Just strange. Maggie had said the D-word only two days ago, and now here they were, sharing air, sharing coffee steam and morning light. Her throat tightened.

"You can sit," Gwen said finally, voice low, cautious. Not quite an invitation — more like an allowance.

Maggie almost did. Almost crossed the room, curled into the other end of the couch, asked what she was reading. Muscle memory tugged at her. Instead, her feet stayed rooted.

"I should start breakfast," she said instead, already backing toward the kitchen.

Gwen's gaze lingered for a second longer, unreadable, before dropping back to her book.

By the time Maggie turned around, the front door had clicked shut. Gwen was gone.

She stood in the kitchen, palms braced against the counter, staring at the empty space where Gwen's mug had sat so many mornings. The quiet pressed in, thick as syrup.

Then came the thunder of little feet.

Arlo and Jude tumbled in first, already arguing about who had won their pillow fight, hair sticking up in every direction. Rosie followed, dragging her pink duck by the foot.

"Breakfast," she demanded, climbing onto her stool.

"Yeah, yeah," Maggie said, fumbling for bowls. "Cereal first, or we'll all regret it."

The twins groaned theatrically but sat. She poured cereal, added milk, slid bowls across the counter, marveling at how her kids could inhale food like they were auditioning for an eating contest.

Once spoons were scraping and tempers cooling, she leaned against the counter, sipping her own coffee. The morning still felt heavy, strange with Gwen's absence pressed up against her presence just minutes ago.

Rosie licked milk from her spoon and announced, "We should bake something today."

"Like what?" Maggie asked.

"Muffins," Arlo said instantly. "With chocolate."

"Yeah, muffins," Jude echoed, mouth full.

Maggie laughed, surprising herself with the sound. "Muffins it is. But you're all sous-chefs, and you have to follow the boss's orders."

Rosie puffed up, clearly pleased. "I'm the boss of sugar."

"Obviously," Maggie said, pulling the flour from the pantry. "Use your powers wisely."

Chaos bloomed instantly. Flour dusted the counters like first snow, Jude dropped half an eggshell into the bowl, Arlo tried to fish it out with his fingers, and Rosie dumped a mountain of sugar that could have fueled a small village. Maggie laughed, loud and unguarded, her heart tugging at the sight of all three kids orbiting her in their sticky, noisy way.

She was wiping chocolate from Jude's cheek when the front door opened.

Her chest hitched.

And then Gwen's voice floated in, tentative: "I just forgot a file for work."

The kids froze for a split second, then erupted like fireworks. "MOM!"

They barreled down the hall, feet pounding, Rosie nearly toppling off her stool in her rush to reach her. The twins collided with Gwen's legs, arms wrapping tight. Rosie climbed up her like a koala.

"You're here!" Rosie squealed, muffled against Gwen's blazer. "We never get both moms anymore."

The twins echoed her, chanting, "Both moms, both moms," until Maggie had to press her palm flat to the counter just to stay upright.

Gwen crouched, folder forgotten, arms full of their kids, her laugh breaking in that startled, fragile way Maggie remembered from a thousand small moments — birthday candles, spilled cereal, chaos that made her soften. A strand of hair had slipped from her clip, catching on her cheek.

And Maggie, standing with the spoon still in her hand, felt the ache hit bone deep.

Because Rosie was right. They didn't get this anymore. Not the noise, not the togetherness. Not both. Not for a long time.

"Hey," Gwen said finally, looking up at her. Just one word. Careful.

"Hey," Maggie answered, her voice rougher than she wanted.

The kids tugged at Gwen's hands, babbling about eggs and chocolate chips and Rosie's sugar coup. For a moment, it almost felt like before — like an ordinary Monday morning when the house was alive and whole.

Then Gwen straightened, folder in hand again, smoothing her jacket back into place. "I've got to get to the office."

A collective groan. Rosie's lip wobbled. "But… muffins."

Gwen kissed the top of her head. "Save me one."

The twins chorused promises. Rosie beamed through her pout.

The door shut, and the house felt too quiet, even with the kids still shouting about who got to lick the spoon.

Maggie stirred the batter hard, forcing a smile. "All right, sous-chefs. Let's make these the best muffins ever."

The house looked the same, smelled the same, sounded the same — and yet it wasn't.

CHAPTER 26

THE DINER HAD GONE THROUGH A GLOW-UP SINCE GWEN'S HIGH school years. No more cracked red vinyl booths or sticky Formica. Now there were reclaimed wood tables painted in chalky pastels, mason jar light fixtures, and chalkboard menus in looping script that made "Turkey Reuben" look like an artisanal delicacy. Each table had a thrift-shop mug filled with daisies or carnations. The bones were the same, but someone had slapped "shabby chic" on top of the grease.

Her mother sat by the big window, sunlight slanting across the table and catching in the steam from her coffee. She was already halfway through her first mug. Her mother never waited for Gwen to arrive before ordering coffee.

"Sit," she said, with that tone that was part command, part concern. "You look drawn."

Gwen slid into the chair across from her, tugging her blazer sleeves straight. "Good morning to you too."

Her mother stirred her coffee with a spoon she didn't need. "You're working too much again."

The waitress appeared, pad in hand, all easy warmth.

Gwen ordered coffee and dry wheat toast — her fallback when her stomach was knotted tight. Her mother ordered the short stack with a side of bacon, unapologetic.

When the waitress moved off, her mother gave her a pointed look. "So. How's work?"

The script hovered on Gwen's tongue — *fine, busy, a promotion is coming* — but the words came out different. "They're going to offer me Principal Architect."

Her mother blinked, then sat back. "Well. That's the top of the ladder, isn't it? Exactly what you've been killing yourself for."

"Yes." Gwen forced a small nod.

Her mother's brows knit. "But?"

Gwen swallowed. "But I can't breathe when I think about it." She looked down at the daisies between them, their cheeriness almost obscene. "It's this redevelopment. A whole historic neighborhood leveled. Families uprooted. They call it revitalization, and I sit there smiling, but all I can think about is Maggie. How she'd look at me if she knew all the details."

Her mother was quiet for a long moment, then set her spoon down. "So it isn't just about work. It's about who you want to be. At work, and at home."

The waitress returned with steaming plates. Gwen stirred cream into her coffee, her hands careful, deliberate, to keep them from shaking.

Her mother cut neatly into her pancakes. "And Maggie?"

The air thickened. Gwen heard herself say it flatly. "She said 'divorce' in therapy last week." Gwen's throat went raw. "And I didn't fight her."

Her mother set her fork down. "Do you want a divorce?"

The question slipped past Gwen's defenses. She swallowed hard. "No, not at all. But she's tired. She thinks I'll never choose her. And maybe she's right."

Her mother's gaze softened. "You've spent so much of your life proving yourself at work. Promotions, projects, presentations. But you don't have to prove yourself to Maggie. You just have to be present."

They ate in silence for a while. Gwen pushed dry toast around her plate. Her mother steadily worked through her pancakes, efficient as always. The diner hummed with low chatter, the hiss of the espresso machine, a toddler babbling two tables over.

Then her mother said, almost casually, "I almost left your father once."

Gwen's head snapped up. "You what?"

Her mother's gaze didn't waver. "He started making decisions for our life without me. Tried to move our family out of Austin without even asking for my opinion. I packed a bag one night." She sipped her coffee. "But he came home, and we talked until sunrise. About everything we were afraid of. It didn't fix it all at once, but it gave us a place to start again."

Gwen blinked. "You never told me that."

"You were a child. Children don't need to carry their parents' failings."

Gwen stared. "And now?"

Her mother folded her napkin, precise. "Now you're not a child. You can see me and your father as humans, and humans make mistakes. We worked hard to get our marriage back on track."

"How long did that take?"

"Take? It's not past-tense work. It's present tense, constant work," her mother quipped with a small smile.

The daisies in their chipped vase bobbed slightly as the air conditioner kicked on. Gwen stared at them until her vision blurred.

Her mother reached across the table, laying a hand briefly over Gwen's. "You don't have to be the best at both right now — career *and* marriage. But you do have to decide which one matters more in this moment. Because it seems like your marriage cannot exist with your current priorities."

Gwen's throat tightened. "I thought I was building a life for us. Every late night, every project. I thought if I built something big enough, it would carry us both."

"And maybe it could have," her mother said, not unkindly. "But if Maggie never felt carried, then it wasn't working the way you hoped. That doesn't mean it can't. It just means you have to build it differently."

Gwen looked at her, surprised by the note of compassion under the critique.

Her mother smiled faintly. "You're my daughter. I want you happy. Whether that's in the corner office or at home making muffins with your kids. But don't let this drift away without making the choice yourself. You deserve better than that. So does she."

Gwen gripped her mug tighter, the ceramic biting into her palms. She didn't answer. Couldn't. The question of *career or marriage* sat heavy in her chest, the kind of decision that promised to break her open either way.

Her mother, seeing the look on her face, reached for her coffee again. "You don't have to decide today."

The silence stretched until Gwen forced herself to breathe. "Thank you, by the way. For still helping both of us with the kids."

Her mother waved it off, as if the words embarrassed her. "You know I love spending time with those little angels." A faint smile tugged at her mouth. "I'm here whenever you — or Maggie — need me."

Gwen nodded, swallowing against the tightness in her throat. "I know."

For the first time, she admitted silently: she couldn't have both. The title. The life. One would kill the other.

And she didn't know which she was ready to let go.

CHAPTER 27

MAGGIE

THE TRAVERSE CITY AIRPORT BARELY COUNTED AS AN AIRPORT — two gates, one security line, carpet designed by someone's grandma in 1987. Maggie shuffled out with her carry-on dragging behind her and spotted Izzy immediately: standing on a bench, arms windmilling, yelling, "Maggie!"

Kiera tugged her down, mortified but grinning.

Maggie laughed, dragging her bag across the tile. "What, no sign?"

Izzy jumped down and enveloped her in a hug. "You're late."

"I'm on time."

"Which is basically late."

Kiera hugged her next, warm and grounding. "We're glad you're here."

"Better than Colette threatening to stage an intervention if I didn't get out of town," Maggie said and let herself be swept toward the parking lot.

The air outside was crisp and pine-tinged, carrying the

faint sweetness of lake water. Maggie inhaled like she could bottle it.

Izzy tossed her suitcase into the SUV. "All right. Buckle up. Lake house awaits."

"Wait," Maggie said, climbing into the back seat. "Snacks?"

"Better," Izzy said. "Pie."

They stopped at a clapboard bakery with a crooked sign reading *Grandma's Secret Pies*. The place smelled like butter and cinnamon heaven. Kiera carefully debated flavors like it was a test; Izzy just declared, "Cherry and apple, done."

"Blueberry," Kiera countered.

"Fine. Three. But we are not getting rhubarb. Rhubarb is a scam."

Maggie raised her hand like she was swearing in at court. "I'll eat anything you put in front of me."

They left with three warm boxes, the car filling with the smell of sugar. Maggie leaned back and sighed. "Already the best trip I've ever taken."

"You haven't seen the house yet," Izzy said. "It's stunning. No surprise, given it's Aunt Jade's."

"It's beautiful," Kiera confirmed, reaching across the console to take Izzy's hand.

Maggie was happy for them. She really was.

THE LAKE HOUSE looked like something out of a faded postcard — cedar siding, white trim, sagging porch, Walloon Lake glittering behind it like a sheet of glass.

Inside was chaos: Danica's mom darting around with a tea towel, barking instructions while chopping herbs, her stepdad silently perfecting a charcuterie board like it was a NASA experiment. Cousins hauling in wine, people stringing lights, laughter and voices overlapping everywhere.

Danica herself appeared, flushed from errands with

Gladys, her rescued pit bull, at her side. "You made it." She hugged Maggie tight as Gladys leaned against Maggie's legs, then lowered her voice. "I put you in the bunk room with Izzy and Kiera. Instant summer camp."

"The what?"

"The bunk room," Izzy said gleefully.

Kiera added, "I'm the counselor, Izzy's the delinquent, and you're the homesick kid writing letters."

"Rude," Maggie teased. "I definitely feel like I bring the best camp counselor energy." She reached down to scratch Gladys' ears.

"I'd hire you for my summer camp," Pete said from somewhere behind her, picking her up in a hug. "I'm so glad you're here."

Maggie looked around at all of her friends, people she'd known and loved for nearly half her life. "I'm so glad to be here, too."

"No crying," Danica shouted, seeing Maggie's eyes start to tear up.

Dinner was a blur: charcuterie, grilled fish, pies in the center of the table like trophies. Too many conversations at once, glasses clinking, laughter rolling out across the deck.

Later, with bellies full and cheeks warm from wine, the five of them gathered at the fire pit in Adirondack chairs. They dragged blankets out from the house, settled in with another bottle of wine. The air had that sharp fall edge to it, smoke curling up into the stars.

Izzy sat sideways in Kiera's lap, her head tucked against Kiera's shoulder, their laughter low and easy. Pete and Danica leaned close, hands linked between their chairs, the flames catching in their faces. According to Pete, Gladys had put herself to bed hours ago.

Maggie curled deeper into her blanket, letting herself pretend. Pretend it was just another trip, Gwen back home with the kids, everything intact. Not this hollow ache, not the lonely bed, not the word *divorce* echoing in her chest.

Danica's gaze flicked to her across the fire. "How are you, really?" she asked softly. "I mean — with everything."

Maggie bristled, taking a drink directly from the wine bottle. "Oh no. Nope. We are not talking about that."

"Mags—"

"Dan." Maggie leveled her with a look, then softened. "This is your wedding weekend. We're two days out. We are not making it about me." She reached for her glass, swallowed hard. "You're getting married. Let's all be happy. What happened to your no-crying rule?"

Danica hesitated, then let it go, leaning back into Pete's shoulder.

The fire cracked, sparks popping into the night. Somewhere down by the lake, a long, mournful honk carried over the water.

Everyone froze.

"What was that?" Maggie asked.

Pete shuddered visibly. "It's the fucking swan from hell."

Izzy snorted. "Maybe she just wants pie."

"Don't joke," Pete muttered, pulling her blanket tighter. She pitched her voice lower. "It's watching."

Maggie laughed, then realized she was the only one laughing. She cleared her throat. "Okay, so I did have an idea about the tablescape..." she began.

THE BACKYARD WASN'T MANICURED, exactly, but it didn't need to be. The grass rolled right down to the lake's edge, dappled with taller patches of native grasses and sections of clover. The house itself loomed behind them, big windows catching the morning sun, cedar siding weathered to gray. A tent company had rolled in just after breakfast, men in matching polos hauling poles and tarps across the lawn.

Maggie and Izzy were supposed to be "helping," which in practice meant stringing lights along the dock pillars.

"Higher," Izzy grunted, stretching on her toes.

Maggie leaned back from where she crouched, laughing. "Izzy, that's not higher. That's *closer to average human reach.* Want me to grab you a stool? Or maybe some stilts?"

Izzy shot her a glare, still trying to loop the cord around the weathered post. "Not all of us are giraffes, Maggie."

"You say that like it's an insult," Maggie said, knotting her end of the light string with ease. "You're just jealous I can reach the cereal on the top shelf without a ladder. Superior genes."

"Superior *ego,*" Izzy teased.

The lake glittered behind them, the autumn air sharp but clear, a breeze rippling through the trees. Somewhere behind the house, Danica's mom was scolding someone about folding napkins properly, her voice carrying across the yard.

Danica's mom had always been a sweetheart, like an older version of Danica, and she'd always reminded Maggie of her own mom. When Maggie had brought up that fact to her therapist, Lauren had nodded and said, "Sometimes when someone reminds us of who we lost, it's really just our way of noticing what we still need."

A noise interrupted her thoughts.

A long, trumpeting honk that sounded halfway between a bugle and a horror movie soundtrack.

The tent workers froze mid-pole. One of them muttered, "Oh god, not again."

From the far side of the yard, the swan appeared — white feathers gleaming, wings flapping like sails, black eyes locked in with unnerving intensity. It barreled straight through the workers, scattering the group of grown men like bowling pins.

"Run!" one of them yelped, dropping a mallet as the swan hissed, actually hissed, like some kind of viper.

Izzy ducked behind the dock post. "Oh no."

Maggie squinted. "That's it? That's the terror everyone's been talking about? It's just a goose with a nice suit and superiority complex."

Izzy's eyes widened. "Mags. Don't—"

"No, seriously," Maggie cut in, rolling up her sleeves. "Geese are terrifying, yes, but this thing? It just needs to know who's boss. Look at it — acting like it owns the lawn."

The swan honked again, louder, wings beating the air.

"See?" Maggie said, already stepping off the dock toward it. "I think it just responds to fear. I'll just herd it back into the water, easy."

Izzy warned, "Do not engage with the swan."

But Maggie was already halfway across the grass, arms spread like she was wrangling a toddler. "Shoo! Back in the lake, your highness. This isn't your runway."

For a second, it worked. The swan hesitated, wings half folding. Maggie smirked. "See? Just a bird with a god complex."

Then, the damn thing lowered its head, spread its wings, and charged.

Maggie's smirk evaporated as six feet of furious feather and rage thundered at her. She tried to stand her ground — *show no fear, it's just poultry, it cannot hurt you* — but the swan hissed like Satan's kettle and snapped its beak an inch from her knee.

She yelped and stumbled backward.

The tent workers were already retreating to the far side of the lawn, shouting warnings: "Don't turn your back on it" and "It goes for the ankles."

Izzy was doubled over on the dock, half laughing, half hollering, "I told you not to mess with the swan."

Maggie tried to recover, sidestepping, hands out like she

was negotiating with an unhinged and armed toddler. "Okay, okay, I get it, you're the boss, but—"

Out of nowhere, Gladys came to her rescue, barking and running after the swan.

The swan lunged toward Gladys, which made the dog pause. Maggie backpedaled, desperate not to get between Gladys and the swan, until her foot caught on the light string still snaking across the dock.

There was a half second where time slowed: Izzy shrieking her name, the swan's wings flaring wide like a demonic creature, Maggie's arms windmilling.

Then she pitched backward off the dock and hit the lake with a spectacular splash.

The water was shockingly cold, searing against her skin.

Maggie surfaced, sputtering, hair plastered to her face, lake water stinging her eyes. Above her, the swan strutted along the dock, honking like it had just won a jousting tournament.

When she pushed the wet strands of her hair from her face and blinked up, the first thing she saw was Pete doubled over, practically crying with laughter, and Izzy right next to her, gasping for air. Both of them were useless — clutching their stomachs, pointing at her like she was the best entertainment.

Gladys looked extremely proud, barking at the edge of the dock. Pete had to grab her collar to keep her from jumping in beside Maggie.

"Oh my god," Izzy wheezed. "You — you said — snobby goose — and now look at you—" She collapsed against Pete, the two of them shaking.

"Glad I could amuse," Maggie muttered, coughing up pond water.

From the dock, Danica knelt, reaching her hand out, face caught between worry and trying not to laugh. "Here, come on."

Kiera appeared beside her, more efficient, already bracing herself to haul Maggie up. Together, the two of them managed to drag her back onto the dock, dripping and indignant.

Maggie tried to stand, but the second she put weight on her left foot, pain shot up her ankle. She gasped in pain and nearly toppled again. She stayed sitting, instead.

"You okay?" Danica asked quickly, hand still steadying her.

"Totally fine," Maggie said through clenched teeth.

"You can't even stand," Kiera pointed out, brows knitting.

"Standing is overrated," Maggie shot back, forcing a grin. "Really, I'm great. Lake water's good for the skin. People pay a lot of money for lake water. Very refreshing. Five stars."

Behind them, Pete was still howling. "That swan has it *out* for us."

Izzy nodded, tears streaking her cheeks. "It didn't even hesitate. Straight for the ankles. It knew."

Gladys got in a few healing licks to Maggie's cheek. Maggie groaned, clutching Kiera's arm as Danica bent to examine her. "I'm fine. It's a mild—" She gasped as Danica touched her ankle. "Inconvenience. Barely a sprain."

"Barely?" Pete snorted. "You face-planted into the lake."

Maggie glared at her. "I tripped on the lights. Very different."

The swan honked again in the distance, as if to say *don't forget who's boss.*

Maggie shoved wet hair out of her eyes, muttering, "I am not losing a standoff to poultry."

Pete wiped tears of laughter from her face. "Oh, honey. You already did."

CHAPTER 28

GWEN

THE RENDERINGS SAT IN FRONT OF HER, GLOSSY AND triumphant. Whole city blocks reduced to neat rectangles and gleaming glass towers, parks like green stamps, traffic flow modeled in clean arcs. It was supposed to look inevitable. Progress made tangible.

Gwen tugged at the edge of her blazer sleeve, her thumb brushing over the watch Maggie had given her, the one she always wore to big meetings as a kind of lucky talisman. She needed the strength of it now more than ever.

She swallowed hard and said, calmly, "I'm declining."

The word dropped into the conference room like a stone into a pond.

Across from her, Melinda's head snapped up. "Excuse me?"

"I can't accept the Principal Architect promotion." Gwen kept her voice even, steady. "Not at this time."

The senior partner to Melinda's right blinked. The junior associate at the far end of the table actually dropped his pen.

Melinda recovered first, her tone sharp. "Gwen, this isn't a minor project. This is your moment. Years of work have brought you here."

"I know." Gwen forced herself to meet her eyes, rotating the watch against her wrist until the band pinched. "That's why I need to step back. I'd like to request a leave of absence instead."

Inside, her chest was a vise, each breath scraping. Her palms itched. Her pulse pounded hard enough she half expected someone to hear it, but her voice remained the measured, collected cadence she'd spent two decades cultivating.

Melinda stared. "A leave."

"Yes." Gwen smoothed a hand down the line of her charcoal trousers. "Effective immediately. I'll work with the team to transition my active projects."

"Gwen—" Melinda leaned forward, incredulous. "Do you understand what you're saying? This isn't a sabbatical. This is the culmination of your career. You've built a reputation for being unshakable, indispensable. And now you want to... vanish?"

The panic in Gwen's chest threatened to spill, but she anchored herself with the feel of the watchband biting against her wrist. "I'm not vanishing. I'm preserving my ability to return."

Melinda's eyes narrowed. "This isn't like you."

No, it wasn't. Not the Gwen who stayed late, who slept on office sofas during deadlines, who made herself a weapon of reliability. Except that Gwen had watched her marriage disintegrate in the quiet margins between projects. That Gwen had sat in sterile rooms with blueprints while Maggie sat on the kitchen floor with funeral potatoes and grief.

"This is what I need," Gwen said finally, voice low.

For the first time, she saw it. The flicker in Melinda's expression wasn't concern. It was disappointment. Irritation.

A calculation about how hard it would be to replace her. Gwen felt something inside her shift, like a lens snapping into focus.

Melinda wasn't her friend. She had never been her friend.

She was her boss. Her mentor, maybe, but only as long as Gwen performed. The loyalty Gwen thought they'd built — the long hours, the late-night takeout, the half confessions over martinis — it was all transactional. A currency of usefulness.

Her best friend had always been Maggie. Maggie, who teased her, fought her, knew her flaws and loved her anyway. Maggie, who'd seen her exhausted and brittle and still leaned in, still reached for her. Even now, even separated, even drowning in resentment — Maggie was the only one Gwen wanted in this moment. Sitting in that sterile conference room with the cold, flawless design plans between them, Gwen wanted nothing more than to hear Maggie's laugh, to feel her hand on her knee under the table, to have her say *It's just a job, Gwen. You're allowed to choose something else that's a better fit for you.*

The realization gutted her. Because Maggie wasn't here. Because Gwen had chosen wrong too many times.

The silence stretched. The others at the table looked everywhere but at her. Melinda's expression hardened into something Gwen didn't want to name.

"Very well," Melinda said at last, clipped. "We'll discuss the details with HR. But Gwen—" Her gaze cut sharp. "Think carefully. Some opportunities don't wait."

"I know," Gwen said again.

Her chest screamed, panic clawing at the edges. But outwardly, she sat still, composed. She gathered the glossy renderings, stacked them neatly, and slid them toward the center of the table.

Melinda's hand hovered, then withdrew.

The meeting ended in a flurry of awkward chair scrapes and murmured excuses.

Gwen walked out first, her dress shoes clicking across the polished floor, each step steady, betraying nothing. Inside, she was collapsing.

By the time she reached the elevator, her throat was tight, her breath shallow. Her reflection stared back from the stainless steel doors: blazer, trousers, the watch gleaming on her wrist. Immaculate. Unreadable.

She pressed the button, pulse racing, and whispered the words to herself, trying to make them true: "I did the right thing. I did a stupid thing, but the right thing. Oh my god. What did I just do? Was it the right thing?"

The parking garage was a half-empty echo chamber, the kind of place where footsteps ricocheted too loud. Gwen walked to her car with a measured pace. Inside, she was fraying apart.

She slid into the driver's seat, shut the door, and the silence collapsed around her like a vacuum. For the first time all morning, there was no hum of conversation, no scrape of chairs, no steady drone of HVAC. Just Gwen and the ringing in her own ears.

Her chest seized.

She dropped her forehead against the steering wheel and finally, finally let herself exhale. It came out ragged, almost a sob, though she forced it down before it could become one. She gripped the wheel until her knuckles whitened, then reached instinctively for the watch. She twisted it on her wrist, thumb pressing into the bezel, grounding herself in the weight of it. Maggie's gift. Maggie's taste. Maggie's reminder.

Her best friend, her anchor, the person she'd lost thread by thread.

She should call her. God, she wanted to call her.

The thought came like a flood: Maggie's voice in her ear,

Maggie teasing her for being dramatic, Maggie softening once she realized Gwen was serious.

Her thumb hovered over Maggie's name in her contacts, screen glowing in the dim light of the car. Just one more push and she'd hear her voice. Just one more push and maybe everything wouldn't feel like it was unraveling.

But then her stomach knotted, panic rising. What if Maggie didn't pick up? Worse — what if she did, and sounded tired, or polite, or worse still… indifferent? What if the only thing Maggie heard in Gwen's voice was desperation?

She swiped the screen off, tossing the phone onto the passenger seat like it had burned her.

Her breaths came shallow, tight. She pressed the heel of her hand to her eyes. She couldn't afford to want so much. Not when she was the one who had made herself a stranger in her own marriage.

Her phone buzzed against the seat. She startled, fumbling to grab it, answering without even checking the ID. "Maggie?"

But it was Izzy's voice, low and urgent. "Uh, no. Sorry. It's, uh, it's Izzy."

Gwen didn't like the tone in Izzy's voice. Her heart stuttered. "What's wrong?"

"I'm at the hospital," Izzy said quickly. "With Maggie."

Gwen's grip on the phone tightened until the edges cut into her palm. "Hospital? What happened?"

"Well, it's kind of a long story. She fell down off the dock. Danica was freaked it was broken. They're doing X-rays." Izzy's voice wavered, like she was trying to keep it breezy but couldn't. "She's fine, mostly. But I thought you should know."

Gwen's mind filled in too many details at once: Maggie laughing on the dock, Maggie's ankle folding, Maggie in pain, Maggie scared. Maggie without her.

"Is she—" Gwen swallowed hard. "Is she asking for me?"

"Not exactly," Izzy admitted softly. "She doesn't know I called. I'm out in the hallway. She'd kill me if she knew. But, Gwen—" Izzy hesitated. "She's stubborn. She's downplaying it. But she's in a lot of pain and…"

The silence stretched. Gwen's breath came shallow, panic clawing again.

She could stay. She could sit in this car and tell herself Maggie didn't want her there. That Izzy's call was meddling, that Maggie would be furious, that showing up would only make things worse. She could play it safe, respect the boundary Maggie had tried to draw.

Or—

She could go.

She could choose, for once, the opposite of what had wrecked them: showing up. Not with a blueprint or a plan or a neat solution. Just her, messy and present.

The thought terrified her. Because if she went and Maggie turned her away? That would be the final break. No ambiguity left. No thread to hold on to.

But if she didn't? If she stayed here, caged in her car, watching her life shrink down to an empty apartment and a title she no longer wanted? That was its own kind of death.

Her thumb rubbed the edge of the watch, the gift Maggie had given her when time had still been on their side.

She exhaled, steadying her voice. "I'll be on the next flight out."

Izzy was quiet for a moment, then whispered, "Good. That's what I was hoping you'd say."

They hung up with Gwen promising to send through details as soon as she had them.

Gwen sat in her car, phone still pressed to her ear, heart hammering. Then she lowered it, started the engine, and pulled out of the garage.

For once, she wasn't thinking about the cost. She was

thinking about Maggie. And she wasn't going to be too late this time.

At the first red light, she called her mom. "Gwen?" her mom's voice said, wary but warm.

Gwen gripped the wheel, throat tight. "Mom, you know how you said you'd watch the kids anytime?" She swallowed, her voice catching. "Well..."

CHAPTER 29

IT FELT LIKE THEY'D BEEN IN THE EMERGENCY ROOM FOREVER. Time stretched and folded strangely in hospitals — plastic chairs, buzzing fluorescent lights, the faint smell of antiseptic and burnt coffee. Maggie shifted on the stiff bed, trying not to wince as the paper crinkled beneath her. Her ankle was propped up on a pillow, swollen and bruised so badly it looked like someone had swapped it for a prop from a zombie movie.

Maggie tried for a grin at Izzy, who was slumped in the corner chair, head tipped back against the wall. "You know," she said lightly, "I jinxed it. Back in Vegas I thought the Maggie injury curse was broken. But no. Apparently the streak lives on. Fucking swan. Elitist jerk."

Izzy cracked one eye open.

Maggie added, "I mean, at this point the universe just thinks I'm greedy for attention."

That earned her a smile, but it was the tired kind — the one Izzy used when she was running on fumes.

"I'm the injured one but you look wrecked," Maggie said, softer now.

Izzy rubbed her eyes. "I'm fine."

"You're not. You're slouching like a teenager. You never slouch."

Izzy studied her for a beat, then sighed. "I'm worried about you, Mags."

Maggie blinked. "Me?"

"You're in the ER with an ankle the size of a softball," Izzy said. "You're making jokes, but I see you wincing. You've been hurting for a while."

Maggie looked away, throat tight. "It's just an ankle."

Izzy leaned forward, elbows on her knees. "It's not just an ankle. It's everything. And now you're talking divorce like it's already stamped. What's the rush?"

Maggie's head snapped back toward her. "Rush? Izzy, I've been living in limbo for months. Years, if I'm honest. Calling it divorce is the first honest thing I've done in a long time."

Izzy held her gaze. "So that's it? No room for anything else? You just burn it down?"

Maggie let out a brittle laugh. "You think I didn't try? That I didn't twist myself in every direction to make it work? You weren't there in our kitchen every night. You didn't hear the silence. You didn't feel how heavy it was just to breathe in the same room with her."

Izzy's voice was quieter now, but insistent. "I'm not saying it wasn't hard. I'm asking why you have to slam the door before you're sure."

"Because waiting is worse," Maggie said quickly. Her voice cracked anyway. "Because every time I see her, I still want her, and it kills me. And I can't keep living in the in-between. It's torture."

Izzy studied her for a long beat. "So you do still love her."

Maggie's chest constricted. "Of course I do."

Izzy leaned back, tipping her head against the wall again,

exhaling like the fight had gone out of her. "Then I guess I just don't understand how you let that go. I don't care what happened — I know you two still love each other."

Maggie blinked hard, eyes stinging, and pulled the blanket tighter around her shoulders. Her voice came out quiet but steady. "Sometimes that's not enough."

The words settled between them, heavy but final. Izzy didn't argue. She just reached across the space and squeezed Maggie's hand once, firm and warm, before letting her head tip back again.

Maggie let the touch linger, swallowing past the lump in her throat.

The curtain swished back before she could say anything more. A young doctor breezed in, clipboard in hand, her ponytail swinging. "All right, good news first — no fractures on the X-rays. Bad news"—she tilted her head at Maggie's swollen ankle—"that's one impressive sprain."

Maggie let out a half laugh. "I don't get a cast? Kinda feels like a rip-off."

"No cast." The doctor smiled. "But you will need a boot, crutches, and to stay off it. You'll follow up with your PCP back home in Austin — if they want to do an MRI, they'll let you know. For now, ice, elevation, and pain meds."

Izzy exhaled audibly, relief flooding her face.

Maggie felt it too, even if she tried to cover it with another joke. "Great. Nothing completes your wedding outfit like a Velcro boot."

The doctor chuckled, scribbled a few notes, and disappeared again.

They left with Maggie outfitted in her new orthopedic fashion statement, Izzy steadying her as she wobbled on crutches. The pharmacy in the hospital handed over a little white bottle of painkillers. Maggie made Izzy carry it, muttering something about her dignity already being in shreds.

On the drive back to the lake house, the fall air swept crisp through the cracked windows. Maggie rested her head against the seat, watching the trees blur by. "You know," she said, "I was reading that Hemingway used to summer at this lake when he was a kid."

Izzy snorted. "Hemingway was a real dick."

"Yeah," Maggie said, smiling faintly. "But it's still pretty cool, I guess."

Izzy tilted her head. "Yeah. It's still pretty cool."

BACK AT THE HOUSE, chaos was still in full swing — laughter, voices, clatter from the kitchen. When Maggie hobbled in on her crutches, everyone surged toward her with questions and exclamations. She waved them off, embarrassed, cheeks hot.

"Really, I'm fine," she insisted as Danica steered her toward the couch like a queen in exile. "A little sprain, nothing dramatic."

They piled blankets around her and shoved a pillow under her leg as Gladys set up as part guard, part nurse on the end of the couch.

Danica handed her a cardboard box full of plastic champagne flutes. "You can sit there and assemble these," Danica decreed. "It'll keep you busy while we set up outside."

Maggie sighed, snapping stems into bases while the TV murmured in the background. She felt ridiculous. Embarrassed. Sorry for herself. Everyone else was bustling with wedding prep and she was stuck on the couch, Queen of the Plastic Cups.

She was halfway through the box, lip caught between her teeth as she watched her third *Golden Girls* episode, when the front door burst open.

And there she was.

Gwen stood in the doorway, blazer rumpled, hair loose around her face, dress shoes scuffed like she hadn't stopped moving since she left wherever she'd been. Chest heaving, eyes locked straight on Maggie.

Gladys barely lifted her head, annoyed to be woken up.

For a second, Maggie didn't breathe. She held herself rigid, like maybe she could still bluff her way through this, keep the armor on. But then Gwen's gaze didn't shift, didn't soften, didn't blink — and the dam broke.

The tears came hot and sudden, blurring Gwen into shapes, spilling faster than she could swipe them away. Maggie pressed her palms hard against her face, but it was useless; the sob ripped through her chest before she could choke it back. The sound startled even her — ugly, unguarded, nothing like the brave, breezy front she'd been holding together for weeks.

She curled forward, shaking, words stammering out between hiccuped breaths. "Sorry — sorry, I'm fine, I'm okay —" But the words collapsed under the weight of her crying. For the first time, she wasn't fine. She wasn't pretending.

Gwen crossed the room in three strides, no hesitation now. She dropped her bag by the door, crouched, and pulled Maggie against her chest. Her arms were steady, anchoring, her blazer scratchy against Maggie's cheek, her heartbeat pounding hard and fast.

"Hey," Gwen whispered, low and rough, her hand threading into Maggie's hair. "You don't have to be fine."

That undid her all over again. Maggie clutched fistfuls of Gwen's shirt, sobs tearing loose in a way she hadn't allowed herself in months. Gwen just held her tighter, rocking them both in the stillness of the room, as if she could absorb the shaking right out of Maggie's body.

Because this — this was what she'd accused Gwen of never doing. Not showing up. Not putting her first. And now she was standing in a lake house two flights away from home, when she should've been in a glass tower conference room nodding at renderings.

The swell of relief was so sharp it almost hurt.

Then panic hit Maggie like a second wave. Her heart jerked. "Wait. Where are the kids?"

"The kids are fine," Gwen said quickly, her voice steady in a way that made Maggie's stomach twist. "My mom's with them."

Maggie exhaled, some of the panic ebbing — but it left her lightheaded, like standing too fast.

"Tell me everything. Start from the top," Gwen asked, softer now, eyes searching Maggie's face like she could read every hidden answer there.

Maggie blinked down at her, dazed. The champagne flute stem was still in her hand, forgotten, the cheap plastic biting into her palm. She wanted to say something sharp — *you don't get to swoop in now, you missed so much already* — but what came out instead was a shaky laugh.

"There's this demonic swan," she muttered. "That's the top."

Gwen's brow furrowed, like she thought Maggie was joking. Then she glanced at Izzy, who raised both hands solemnly. "True story. Swan's got a vendetta."

Pete walked in from the back deck and paused to proclaim, "Gwyneth!"

Gwen laughed, giving Pete a wave. Her gaze went back to Maggie's ankle, then up to her face, all careful intensity. The kind of look Maggie used to fall into. The kind of look that made her feel seen, even when she didn't want to be.

And damn it all, Gwen was here. Gwen had come.

CHAPTER 30

SHE'D LEFT THE OFFICE GARAGE WITH NO LUGGAGE, JUST HER blazer and her phone. At the airport, she bought a ticket for the first flight to Traverse City without even checking the price. When the agent asked if she had any bags to check, Gwen just shook her head.

She'd cut it close — sprinting down the terminal with her shoes slapping against the carpet as the final boarding call echoed overhead. She collapsed into her seat, heart pounding, and texted Pete and Danica with the bluntness of someone who couldn't sugarcoat it: *On my way to Michigan. I know I'm crashing the wedding.*

Danica had immediately sent a string of exclamation points, followed by *YES* in all caps. Pete replied with a promise of free rein in her closet, which had almost made Gwen laugh out loud at the absurdity.

Her layover in Dallas had been exactly forty-two minutes — just enough time to find a sandwich she barely tasted before boarding the second leg. Then Traverse City, an absurd minivan rental car, the drive north with Google Maps droning at her. She'd broken at least half a dozen speed limits on those winding roads, gripping the wheel hard enough to leave dents in the leather.

Then she'd been standing in the doorway of the lake house, chest heaving, blazer wrinkled from travel, Maggie staring at her with wide eyes.

It had been… heartbreaking, in a way she hadn't expected. Maggie had crumpled at the sight of her, like Gwen's presence had torn down all her defenses.

Their friends had joked for a moment, but then the air shifted and suddenly everyone seemed to remember something urgent to do in the kitchen. Within seconds, the room had emptied.

It was just the two of them.

Gwen let out a breath she'd been holding since Austin.

Maggie shifted against the pillows, her eyes flicking to Gwen's and then away, like it was too much to look straight at her. "You didn't have to come."

"Yes, I did." The words left Gwen before she could edit them, sharper than she intended.

Maggie scoffed lightly, though her voice wavered. "No, really. It's such a hassle for you to get here."

"It really wasn't."

Her head snapped toward her. "But—"

"Maggie." Gwen reached for her hand before she could overthink it, covering her fidgeting fingers with her palm. "Shut up." She said it with a smile, soft enough to break the tension.

Maggie's shoulders eased, the faintest laugh escaping her. For the first time since Gwen walked in, she looked a little less braced for impact.

"What do you need? Ice? Tylenol?" Gwen asked.

"Well," she said, gesturing weakly at the open box of champagne flutes, "if you're going to be here, then help me with these stupid cups."

Gwen took the plastic stem from her hand, snapped it into place, and set it neatly in the box. "Done."

Maggie smirked, shaking her head, but she didn't pull her hand away.

For a moment, Gwen let herself believe this was what showing up felt like — quiet, ordinary, and right.

THE REST of the afternoon blurred — tasks traded hand to hand, laughter ricocheting across the yard, Maggie perched on the couch like a reluctant monarch while Gwen fetched, carried, and quietly logged her pain med doses in her phone under a note called *Mags Meds*. She typed the timestamps like they were sacred, as if recording them could keep her from slipping through Gwen's fingers again.

Pete had insisted Gwen borrow something from her suitcase. Ten minutes later Gwen was wearing a faded neon T-shirt that read *I Survived Girls Gone Wild, Key West 2004*. Pete had tossed it with a grin. "Iconic," she'd said. Maggie's laugh when she saw it made the whole thing worth it.

By late afternoon, the tent was glowing with strings of lights, tables laid with mismatched vases of dahlias and roses cut from Danica's mom's garden. The air had the sharp bite of October, and more sweaters and thicker jackets appeared one by one as the sun slid lower.

That was when Lillian showed up.

She came up the drive with a tote bag slung over one shoulder, her easy grin widening the second she spotted Gwen. "Well, if it isn't my favorite architect," she said brightly, setting down the bag to pull Gwen into a hug.

And Gwen hugged her back — because she was genuinely happy to see her, because Lillian had been kind and uncomplicated in Vegas when everything else had felt thorned. But the minute she pulled away, her eyes flicked to the couch, where Maggie was smiling up at Lillian and accusing her of pulling an Irish Goodbye on their last night.

"I heard it was tradition for the group to have someone disappear," Lillian joked.

Pete gasped. "*All* of the travel curses live on."

DINNER WAS LESS "REHEARSAL" and more "family cookout" — platters of grilled fish and corn on paper plates, bottles of wine sweating on the tables, kids darting in and out from the dock. Danica's mom flitted like a benevolent general, her stepdad beaming over an elaborate salad no one had the heart to say wasn't needed.

By the time everyone had a plate, Pete stood with her glass raised, Danica rising beside her, cheeks flushed pink from wine and happiness.

"We just want to say how thankful we are," Danica began, her voice catching. "For every single one of you — for showing up, for laughing with us, for putting up with swans and family chaos and Michigan weather. It isn't Bulgaria," she added with a wry smile, "but we are truly honored to celebrate with you anywhere."

Pete slipped an arm around her, nodding. "Yeah. Family isn't just blood, and this..." She gestured at the long table, the mismatched plates and noisy cousins and friends pressed shoulder to shoulder. "This is our family. Every one of you. Even when it's messy. Especially then."

Her gaze landed on Gwen for a heartbeat — pointed, not sharp, but steady. Then to Maggie, then down to Izzy and Kiera tucked together at the end of the table, sharing a blanket.

"To family," Pete finished softly.

Glasses lifted. *To family* rose around them, uneven but whole.

Gwen lifted hers too, the stem trembling slightly between

her fingers. And when Maggie's boot nudged her ankle under the table, whether by accident or not, Gwen let the warmth of it sit with her.

She didn't know what tomorrow would bring, but tonight, at least, she wasn't on the outside looking in.

By the time the plates were cleared and the last bottle of wine was uncorked, Maggie shifted in her seat. "I'm done," she announced, voice pitched casual but eyes half-lidded with fatigue. "The day has defeated me. I need sleep before the swan comes back for round two."

There was a ripple of laughter, but Gwen was already moving to her side, offering an arm without comment. Maggie didn't protest. She leaned into Gwen's shoulder as they made their slow way inside and to the bunk room, crutches awkward under one arm, blanket trailing. Gwen got her settled into the bottom bunk with a handful of pillows to prop up her ankle and tugged the quilt over her. When Maggie sighed — long, content, too tired to fight — Gwen felt something loosen in her chest.

"Night, Mags," she said softly.

"Night," Maggie mumbled, already half under.

For a moment, Gwen let herself linger, watching the slow rise and fall of her chest. Then she slipped back out, shutting the door with a quiet click.

The fire pit was glowing by the time Gwen returned, Adirondack chairs pulled close, smoke curling up into the night sky. Danica sat on Pete's lap, Kiera and Izzy leaned into each other, laughing at some story Lillian was relaying.

When Gwen settled into an empty chair, blanket wrapped around her shoulders, Kiera leaned forward suddenly, eyes bright. "I'm so glad you came," she said, earnest in the way only tipsy people could manage. "Really. It's..." She gestured helplessly at the circle of chairs, at the laughter and the crackle of the fire. "It wasn't the same without you."

Izzy nodded. "She's right."

Danica smiled across the flames. "We mean it, Gwen. We're glad you're here."

Even Pete, who usually preferred her sentiment wrapped in sarcasm, lifted her glass in a small salute. "To the *whole* crew back together."

The warmth of the fire pressed against Gwen's face, but it wasn't just that. For the first time in what felt like forever, she let herself sink into it — the laughter, the easy chatter, the simple fact of being wanted. Not as a title. Not as a function. Just as Gwen.

DANICA NAMED THE CONVERSATION "BRIDEZILLA SUPPORT GROUP"

DANICA

GOOD MORNING IT IS MY WEDDING DAY

PETE

my future wife is in full caps lock mode both in the chat and in real life

IZZY

Can confirm. Heard the squeal through the wall.

MAGGIE

Through the floor, actually. Thought a raccoon got in.

KIERA

Please don't put raccoon energy into the wedding chat.

IZZY

Too late. Pete is raccoon energy.

PETE

rude. but also accurate.

LILLIAN

Some of us were trying to sleep, you know.

PETE

Gladys is up and at em, so you can be, too.

GWEN

It's 8:15.

LILLIAN

But it's only 5:15 in my body.

DANICA

no sleeping!!! it's wedding day protocol!!
waffles and mimosas by 9, hair and makeup
by 10.

PETE NAMED THE CONVERSATION "WARM FEET, COLD MIMOSAS"

MAGGIE

You sound like a cruise director.

IZZY

Except instead of shuffleboard, it's eternal
love.

PETE

eternal love sounds like a game I would win.

LILLIAN

Unlike poker, which you never won.

PETE

wow RUDE

DANICA

🙂 you're marrying me. you already won.

KIERA

Okay but... did you both remember to bring
your vows?

PETE

relax. mine are hidden in a very safe place.

MAGGIE

Oh god, where.

PETE

maggie's boot

MAGGIE

y. She means booty.

IZZY

Ooh sexy!

PETE

sorry you had to find out this way, gwyneth.

GWEN

It's a great booty, I can't blame you.

KIERA

I'm nervous that neither bride confirmed nor denied they have the vows.

DANICA

okay I love you all but everybody GET UP. waffles are hot. champagne is cold. let's get married!!!

PETE

to carbs and matrimony

CHAPTER 31

Maggie

By morning, the lake house had transformed.

Danica had taped a color-coded schedule to the fridge, complete with little boxes to check off like the most polite Bridezilla of all time. Maggie hobbled in on crutches, still bleary-eyed, and read it twice before muttering, "Scheduled to the minute mark? Unfair."

"Organization," Danica corrected sharply, sweeping by with a garment bag over one arm. "Hair and makeup in the dining room. Florals delivered at eleven. Pete's tux steamed by noon. Pictures at three sharp."

The dining room, formerly a place for pot roast and mismatched placemats, now looked like the backstage of a Broadway show. Curling irons, hairspray cans, lip glosses, and enough eyeshadow palettes to paint a mural were spread across the table. Danica's mom, already in a silky robe, sat with hot rollers in her hair, gossiping with Danica's aunt. Annie — the neonatologist colleague Maggie had heard about but hadn't officially met until yesterday — was perched on a chair with a mimosa in hand, laughing at something Danica's mom had said.

The whole house smelled like hairspray and perfume, layered over coffee and blueberry muffins.

Meanwhile, Pete, Lillian, Izzy, and Gwen had been "banished" to town for massages. Maggie knew the real purpose was to keep them out from underfoot, though she had to admit the thought of Gwen lying face down on a massage table while some stranger dug elbows into her back was more amusing than it should've been.

She was halfway through sipping her coffee when Danica's mom appeared in the doorway, eyes warm. "Maggie," she said, clasping her hands to her chest. "I just think it's the most romantic thing I've ever heard. Your wife flying across the country to be here with you? To take care of you?"

Maggie nearly choked on her muffin. "Oh, I — well—"

Her aunt joined in, fanning herself with a curling iron instruction sheet. "Truly. Like a movie. You should've seen the way she was looking at you last night. Oh, my heart."

Maggie forced a smile, cheeks heating. "She, uh… yeah, it was sweet." She waved her crutch vaguely toward the chaos of curling irons. "But let's not get distracted. Today is about Danica, not about me."

The diversion worked — for about thirty seconds.

From across the room, Kiera piped up dryly, eyes glinting. "Didn't look very divorced to me."

Danica, sitting with a stylist brushing through her curls, smirked into the mirror. "Agreed."

Maggie gaped at them. "Oh, you two are *menaces*."

"We prefer the term 'meddlers,'" Danica corrected with a prim little shrug. "Lovingly."

"Lovingly, my ass," Maggie muttered.

• • •

By MIDDAY, robes were discarded for dresses, and the energy in the dining room shifted from frantic to giddy. Maggie leaned on her crutches by the mirror, smoothing the fabric of her dress down over her hip.

"I'm just saying," she argued, pointing at her ankle. "I don't *have* to wear the boot. It doesn't go with the outfit."

Danica spun in her chair, half a curl pinned to her head. "You absolutely have to wear the boot."

"It ruins the aesthetic," Maggie protested.

"It prevents further injury." Danica raised one eyebrow. "Nonnegotiable."

Maggie groaned. "You think your big fancy med school degree makes you a medical expert?"

"Yes, in fact, it does," Danica answered firmly but with a sweet smile.

"Fine. But you're letting me take at least one picture without it."

Danica considered, then sighed. "One. Just one. And if you so much as twitch wrong, it's going back on."

"Deal." Maggie grinned in triumph.

As the florals arrived, Danica was pacing in her robe, wringing her hands. "What if it rains? What if the tent collapses? What if Pete changes her mind at the last second?"

Kiera set down her mimosa, calm as a mountain. "You're fine. It's fine."

Maggie leaned against the table, tapping her crutch like a gavel. "You're nervous because you're in love. That's normal. If you weren't jittery, we'd be worried."

Danica shot her a wide-eyed look. "Really?"

"Really," Maggie said firmly. "Also, you're marrying Pete. The only thing she's going to change her mind about is whether or not to wear socks with her dress shoes."

That got a laugh, enough to break through Danica's nerves.

Kiera reached over, squeezed her friend's shoulder.

"Besides, nervous brides make the best photos. Very cinematic."

Danica groaned, but she was smiling again, cheeks flushing.

Danica's schedule ticked forward, boxes checked, hair curled, makeup powdered. The hum of women in various stages of preparation filled the air — laughter, teasing, the occasional yelp as a curling iron got too close. Maggie sat back in her chair, ankle propped, watching it all with a warmth flowing through her.

This was what she'd missed — the buzz, the belonging, the messy, loud little family that wasn't hers by blood but hers anyway.

And then, like it always did in moments like this, the ache came sharp: Her mom would have been here, sitting next to Danica's mom and laughing along. She would have been here, fussing over Maggie's hair, telling the wrong stories at the wrong time, sneaking her a tissue before the vows even started. Maggie could almost hear her laugh blending into the noise, could almost feel her hand on her shoulder — and then it was gone again, just absence taking up space in her chest.

Even with the boot strapped to her ankle, even with Gwen just a room away somewhere in this house, Maggie let herself think that maybe things weren't as broken as she'd convinced herself. But god, she wished her mom could've seen her like this — surrounded, not alone.

THE CEREMONY itself felt like a blur, the kind you almost want to hit rewind on just to catch every detail.

By late afternoon, the lake had turned to liquid silver, the sky streaked with pink. The tent glowed from the inside, lights strung like stars overhead. Guests gathered on the lawn, bundled in shawls and cardigans against the October chill, their breath puffing faintly in the air.

Pete and Danica had insisted on keeping things simple — no cathedral-length trains, no complicated readings — but somehow the simplicity made it perfect. The aisle was just a wooden walkway lined with jam jars of dahlias and roses from Aunt Jade's garden. Maggie had a front-row seat, ankle propped on a pillow, tasked with "sitting still and looking pretty," which she found both insulting and oddly nice.

The music started, something acoustic and bright, and everyone craned their necks as Pete walked in with Gladys on a floral-embellished leash from one side, Danica from the other. They met halfway down the aisle, both grinning like idiots, and proceeded together. Of course they did.

Danica's curls caught the last of the sunlight, her dress simple and perfect, the kind of thing that didn't overwhelm but suited her exactly. Pete looked sharp in her tux, though Maggie caught the glint of mismatched socks peeking from under her hem of her trousers.

Their vows were equal parts sweet and ridiculous. Danica's made everyone tear up with soft words about finding someone who saw her for exactly who she was, even when she was obsessing over medical information at midnight. Pete's started with "Wendell, you are objectively the hottest doctor alive" and ended with "I can't wait for every little thing with you." Gladys lay down and snored loudly through the event.

The guests laughed, sniffled, laughed again. Izzy actually wiped her eyes, though she tried to disguise it by tugging Kiera closer. Maggie pretended not to notice.

When the officiant — Danica's aunt, ordained online for the occasion — pronounced them married, Pete dipped Danica so dramatically it made the crowd roar. Danica squealed into the kiss, clutching Pete's lapels, and even the swan — lurking ominously somewhere unseen — let out a honk that sounded suspiciously like approval.

The applause rolled across the lawn, glasses clinked, and

Maggie found herself laughing through the ache in her ankle, clapping harder than she should've. Because really, it was impossible not to.

It wasn't Bulgaria. It wasn't the grand European wedding Pete had once wanted. But here, on the edge of a Michigan lake with fairy lights swaying and family buzzing all around them, it was exactly right.

Maggie leaned back against her chair, warmth swelling in her chest, and thought if this is what love looked like — messy, funny, loud, and entirely imperfect — then maybe there was hope for her too.

Applause echoed across the lawn, and Maggie felt the familiar tug in her chest — joy tangled with ache. Like every wedding, it made her remember her own.

It hadn't been this. Not fairy lights over a lake, not mismatched jam jars and socked tuxedo ankles. Hers had been in Austin, on a sticky June evening where the air clung to every dress shirt and her curls wilted within ten minutes of walking down the aisle. They'd chosen an art gallery that doubled as an event space — exposed brick, polished concrete, the kind of venue that looked chic in pictures and echoed in real life.

She remembered the way Gwen's hand shook when she slid the ring on her finger.

She remembered the way she'd felt: so, so certain.

Certain that she'd chosen right, that whatever life threw at them, Gwen would always be there. That this was their foundation, unshakable, permanent.

But sitting on the edge of Walloon Lake, applause fading, her ankle throbbing inside the boot, Maggie couldn't help but think about how fragile permanence had turned out to be. How a foundation could crack slowly, invisibly, until one day you looked down and realized you were balancing on rubble.

She pressed her lips together, blinking hard, forcing her

attention back to the newlyweds who were glowing under the fairy lights.

It wasn't about her. It was about them.

Still, as Danica laughed into Pete's chest and the crowd cheered, Maggie couldn't help slipping a glance to her left — where Gwen sat quietly, hands folded around her glass, eyes fixed on the couple.

For a flicker of a second, Maggie thought Gwen looked just as lost in memory as she was.

CHAPTER 32

MAGGIE HAD NO BUSINESS LOOKING THAT HAPPY WITH A BOOT strapped to her ankle and a pair of crutches tucked under her arms, but somehow she did.

The music blasted out of the rented speakers — something loud and joyfully ridiculous — and Maggie was in the middle of the dance floor, swinging her crutches like extended legs. She used them as props for dramatic can-can kicks, then twirling one like a baton, earning a circle of laughter and cheers around her.

Gwen couldn't stop laughing. Not just because Maggie looked like some kind of injured yet genius choreographer, but because it was so her. Messy, dramatic, refusing to let anything — not even a swollen ankle — keep her out of the spotlight.

She told herself she was imagining it, the tiny shift between them. The way Maggie's gaze had softened when Gwen had tucked her into bed the night before, the way she'd let her hand linger on Gwen's arm when Gwen fussed over her boot earlier. She kept replaying the ceremony in her head too, waiting for a moment that hadn't come. Maggie always cried at weddings. Always. Gwen had almost hoped that this time, Maggie would slide her hand into hers like she had at every other wedding they'd been to together. This time, Maggie hadn't. And Gwen had sat there, waiting, fingers brushing her knee, feeling like she'd been left holding an empty space.

The song ended, and Gwen's throat felt too tight. She pushed herself up from the table and headed toward the pop-up bar tucked in the corner of the tent.

Izzy and Lillian were already propped against the portable bar, half leaning, half holding it up, while the volunteer bartender — a bored-looking cousin with a bow tie askew — poured vodka sodas like he regretted volunteering in the first place.

Izzy was explaining something, her hand carving arcs through the air as she talked, Lillian tilting her head with that easy, slow smile she always had, like she was in on the joke before it landed.

They both turned when Gwen approached.

"Well, if it isn't Miss Surprise Guest of Honor," Izzy said, her voice singsong, eyes glittering in a way that was about two glasses of wine past mischief.

Lillian's grin widened. "How's Reconnection 2.0 going?"

Gwen felt her shoulders tense. "Uh, what do you mean?"

Izzy raised her glass like she was toasting, her tone shifting from playful to pointed. "We're all just waiting for you to go get your girl."

Her words cut through the music and chatter, straight to the bone. "Haven't I already been doing that?"

Lillian nodded, sipping her drink. "You can't wait for her to make the next move. Sometimes you just have to say what you mean."

Gwen laughed under her breath, low and dry, but the

sound didn't carry conviction. "You two rehearsed this, didn't you?"

Izzy arched a brow. "We're very good at interventions."

And just like that, Gwen felt the weight of it pressing against her chest — the choice she'd been circling for months, the words she'd swallowed every time Maggie looked at her with hurt or fire or both.

For once, she didn't roll her eyes, didn't argue, didn't dodge. She just nodded, slowly, as if to herself.

Gwen found her near the edge of the crowd, Maggie's head tipped back, laughing at something Danica had just said. It would've been easier if she hadn't looked so alive in that moment, if Gwen could've told herself she was doing this for efficiency's sake. No, she had to push through the knot in her throat anyway.

She leaned in, voice pitched low so only Maggie could hear. "Something's wrong with the lights on the dock. Can I get your help?"

Maggie blinked at her, caught between suspicion and curiosity. "The lights?"

"Yes." Gwen didn't give her time to question it, just started making her way to the edge of the tent. Maggie was slow as she followed, still frowning.

Outside the tent, the air was cooler, threaded with the sharp tang of the lake. The strings of bulbs Maggie had insisted on draped neatly from post to post, glowing without a single flicker. Perfect, of course. Gwen had known they would be.

Maggie stopped short. "They look fine to me."

"Hmm, weird. I could have sworn..." Gwen let her voice trail off as she continued down the dock like she was inspecting each bulb.

There was nothing wrong with the lights, of course. Gwen just needed an excuse — any excuse — to get Maggie away from the noise and the crowd.

By the time they reached the end of the dock, Maggie's crutches and boot clicking in tandem on the warped wooden planks, the chill had settled in for the night. The string lights twined along the poles glowed soft, golden, reflected in the black ripple of the water. Someone had scattered jars of flowers out there earlier, dahlias that bobbed gently when the boards shifted beneath their feet.

Gwen steadied Maggie with a hand on her elbow, guiding her to the small covered portion at the very end. A wooden bench waited, draped in a plaid blanket. The music from the reception floated faintly over the water — something low and romantic now, muffled by distance.

Gwen turned, pulse stuttering, and asked, "Would you like to dance?"

Maggie blinked at her, then gestured down to the crutches leaning against the bench. "I can sway at best."

"Right." Gwen's mouth curved in a smile that was more tender than amused. "Then we'll sway."

Maggie eased herself onto the bench instead, patting the space beside her. "Or we could sit and pretend. Same effect, less chance of me face-planting into the lake."

Gwen grinned and sat. The wood creaked under their combined weight. Out beyond the glow of the lights, the lake stretched into darkness, endless and still.

"Wasn't today perfect?" Maggie asked after a moment, her voice quiet, almost reverent.

Gwen swallowed, staring at the shimmer of light on water. "Almost."

Maggie tilted her head, studying her. "Almost?"

Gwen's throat went dry. She twisted her watch on her wrist, the familiar ritual grounding her, and then forced the words out. "Listen. I have something to tell you."

Maggie's expression sharpened, but she didn't interrupt.

"I quit my job," Gwen said. Then amended, "Kind of. I think."

The words tumbled into the night air, heavy and light all at once.

Maggie's eyebrows shot up. "You what?"

"I… turned down the Principal Architect promotion." Gwen inhaled slowly, fighting to keep her voice steady. "I asked for a leave of absence instead. Indefinite. I don't know if they'll take me back."

The silence stretched between them, broken only by the water lapping against the dock. Gwen forced herself to keep going, the way she'd rehearsed in her head on the flight, in the car, pacing in the airport terminal. Maggie just watched her, face half in shadow.

"I've spent years building everything around work. And I told myself it was for us — for stability, for the house, for the kids, for you. But the truth is, it was for me. For my pride. For the part of me that thought being indispensable meant being loved." She finally turned, meeting Maggie's wide, startled eyes. "And it cost me everything. It cost me you."

Maggie blinked at her, eyes wide, lips parted like she was about to speak but the words didn't come. For once, Maggie, who always had a quip, a deflection, a half joke at the ready, was speechless.

Gwen pressed her palms against her thighs, willing herself not to look away. The string lights above them hummed faintly, casting Maggie's face in warm shadow, and something in Gwen broke open.

"I can't keep doing it the way I was," she said, the words tumbling now, raw and unedited. "I kept telling myself I was sacrificing for us, but it wasn't a sacrifice. It was avoidance. I made my work the excuse for every time I wasn't there for you. Every time you needed me and I thought another late night at the office mattered more."

Maggie's throat worked, but still, no words.

Gwen twisted her watch again, the one Maggie had given her, the metal digging into her skin. "When Melinda looked at me in that meeting, I realized she wasn't my friend. She never had been. You were. You're the only one who's ever been. And I let you carry everything alone while I buried myself in blueprints and told myself that was love. That terrifies me. I don't want to live for my work. I want to live life with you."

Her voice caught, but she forced it steady. "I don't want a corner office or a title. I want mornings with the kids. I want you to call me in the middle of the day just because. I want to sit on a dock with you and not feel like I'm stealing time from something else."

She exhaled, long and shaky, and finally looked directly at her. "I love you, Maggie. I always have. And if there's still a chance for us, even the smallest one, I want to come home. Not to the house. To you."

The lake was so still it felt like it was holding its breath with them. Gwen's heart pounded, waiting for Maggie to say something, anything. Waiting to find out if she'd just given everything up for nothing.

CHAPTER 33

IT WAS EVERYTHING SHE'D EVER WANTED GWEN TO SAY.

Every single thing Maggie had dreamed of hearing in every fight, every lonely night, every quiet hour she'd spent convinced she'd never get it. Now Gwen was sitting beside her under the soft buzz of string lights, voice steady and raw, saying the words like she meant them. Maggie believed her, believed that she really did mean everything she was saying.

Maggie blinked hard, but it was useless. The tears came fast, spilling hot down her cheeks. She tried to laugh, to wave it off, but instead she hiccuped, choked on a sob, and suddenly she was crying so hard she couldn't breathe.

"Whoa, hey—" Gwen's hand was on her shoulder instantly, her face tight with alarm. "Talk to me. What's wrong?"

Maggie swiped at her face with the heel of her palm, shaking her head. "No — I—" Her voice broke. "It's just—"

More tears, more hiccups. Words came out mangled, soggy, impossible. "You — *snff* — said all the things — *hkkh* — always wanted—"

Gwen leaned closer, brow furrowed, like she was trying to decipher a foreign language.

That only made Maggie cry harder. She buried her face in her hands, shoulders shaking, half laughing through the sobs. "I'm sorry," she hiccuped, cutting out the middle of her sentence. "A mess."

Gwen's hand rubbed slow circles between her shoulder blades, warm and steady. "Then be a mess," she murmured. "I've got you."

Maggie peeked at her through her fingers, tears streaking her cheeks, mascara probably halfway down her face by now. Gwen was still watching her — earnest, soft, eyes shining like she meant every word she'd just confessed.

And it gutted Maggie all over again, because she wanted to believe it. She wanted to believe every syllable.

Her chest felt too full, her heart breaking and mending at the same time.

The words clawed their way out of her throat between sobs, wet and inelegant but true. "I love you, too."

Gwen froze, like she hadn't dared to hope she'd hear it again. "Even if I don't have a job and we lose everything?" she asked softly, voice trembling at the edges.

Maggie lowered her hands, blotchy and red-faced, tears streaking freely now. "You'll land on your feet. You always do. And maybe... maybe this time you'll land somewhere better. Somewhere meant for you. Something more fulfilling."

Gwen's lips parted, as if the words were too much to take in. "And us?" she whispered.

Maggie inhaled, ragged, the night air cold in her lungs. Her gaze dropped to the surface of the lake, because saying it while looking at Gwen felt impossible. "I wasn't dealing with my stuff," she admitted, voice thick. "With losing my mom, and the pregnancy before. With how much it gutted me. I just... shoved it all down, and when it spilled out, I aimed it at you."

Her throat worked, the confession scraping raw. "I weaponized my sadness. Made it your fault. Punished you for not being able to fix me. But, I'm making some really good progress in therapy."

Gwen's hand was still warm on her back, steady. She didn't flinch. She didn't argue. She just listened, like maybe this was what Maggie had been waiting for all along, space to finally say it out loud.

Maggie swiped at her eyes again, hiccuping another half laugh. "So, yeah. We're both disasters."

Gwen leaned in, her forehead resting gently against Maggie's temple. "Maybe, but we're disasters who still love each other."

For a long moment they just sat there, shoulders touching, the string lights humming above them and the water stretching into endless dark. Maggie's breathing evened out, though her cheeks were still damp, and Gwen didn't move except to keep her hand steady against Maggie's back.

Maggie turned, finally, meeting her eyes. Gwen looked wrecked in the best way — rumpled from travel, tired around the edges, but wide open in a way Maggie hadn't seen in years. No walls. No office face. Just Gwen.

And Maggie leaned in.

Slow. Careful. The opposite of Vegas, where they'd collided like fire and gasoline. This was soft, tentative, the kind of kiss that felt like a question and an answer at the same time.

Gwen's lips were warm against hers, the faint taste of wine lingering. Maggie sighed into it, her chest loosening, her hands trembling as she cupped Gwen's jaw. The world narrowed to that one small point — the press of her mouth, the solid heat of her shoulder, the steadiness Maggie had missed so much it hurt.

When they pulled back, Gwen kept her forehead resting

against Maggie's, eyes closed, breath mingling in the cold night air.

"Promise me," Maggie whispered, voice breaking.

"Anything."

"Don't disappear again."

Gwen's thumb brushed the damp trail of tears from her cheek. "I won't."

And then they kissed again, softer still, like sealing it. Not a grand gesture. Not fireworks. Just the quiet truth of finding each other again at the edge of a lake.

The kiss lingered, slow and soft, until Maggie pulled back just enough to see her. Gwen's tie was crooked, her dress shirt rolled up to her elbows, and somehow it made her look devastatingly good — like the version of Gwen Maggie always wanted to keep for herself, stripped of polish but still steady, still hers.

"I wish those bunk beds weren't singles." Maggie whispered, the words spilling out before she could think.

Gwen blinked. "What?"

"Because you look so hot right now," Maggie said, her voice shaking but sure. "And I've missed you so much, and I have to have you right now."

For half a heartbeat, Gwen just stared at her, stunned. Then her mouth curved, slow and dangerous. "I mean, the rental car is a minivan."

Maggie's laugh came out breathless. "What?"

"The seats fold down," Gwen said, and there was something dark and wicked in her tone that Maggie hadn't heard in so long it nearly undid her.

Heat pooled low in her stomach, her heart pounding. "Lead the way."

Gwen stood first, offering her a hand. Maggie grabbed her crutches with her other, hobbling to her feet, her ankle screaming in protest but her body buzzing with urgency.

The lake stretched behind them, silent witness, as Gwen helped her off the dock and toward the driveway.

The walk up the gravel drive was ridiculous. Gwen steadying her elbow, Maggie swinging on her crutches like a deranged circus act, both of them half laughing and half tripping their way toward the parked rental minivan. By the time Gwen popped the back open with the fob, Maggie was breathless, clutching at her side.

"This is the least sexy setup in history," she wheezed.

"Give me thirty seconds," Gwen muttered, yanking at the seats, trying to fold them flat. The headrest caught, she swore under her breath, and Maggie started giggling uncontrollably.

"Wow," Maggie said, leaning on her crutch, eyes dancing. "The big romantic gesture ruined by child-lock engineering."

"Shut up," Gwen growled, but she was laughing too, breath puffing in the chill night air. She gave the seat one final shove, and it collapsed with a clang. She turned back, cheeks flushed, hair mussed, grinning in triumph. "Ta-da."

"Hot," Maggie said. "Truly, nothing gets me going like a minivan."

"Get in here," Gwen said, low and urgent.

Maggie's crutches clattered to the ground outside as she climbed into the back of the van, Gwen's hands on her waist, guiding her down onto the folded seats. The back of the van beeped in warning as it closed, and they both paused for a moment to laugh, until their mouths were back together. The kiss hit like a match — hungry, messy, years of want compressed into one impossible moment. Maggie gasped against her mouth, laughing and moaning all at once as Gwen pressed her back into the upholstery.

"Careful — ankle—" Maggie squeaked, grabbing for Gwen's shirt.

"Got you," Gwen promised, adjusting, bracing her hands so Maggie could settle without jostling. Her jacket hit the floor first, then Maggie's cardigan, their laughter breaking through the desperate rhythm of kisses.

Maggie tugged at Gwen's tie, fingers fumbling.

"Oh my god, just rip it," Gwen panted, and Maggie grinned, tugging roughly until the knot finally gave way and the tie fluttered to the carpeted floor.

The van rocked faintly as they shifted, Maggie pulling Gwen down on top of her, gasping when Gwen's mouth found the line of her throat.

"Do you realize," Maggie managed between kisses, "how absolutely absurd this is? We're — oh god — making out in a Dodge Caravan."

Gwen laughed against her skin, the sound dark and warm. "Would you rather be back in the bunk beds?"

"Fair point," Maggie groaned, tugging her closer.

The cold outside contrasted with the heat building between them, windows already fogging as their clothes hit the floor. Maggie couldn't stop giggling — half from nerves, half from the sheer relief of Gwen's weight pressing her into the seat, Gwen's hands sliding under her dress, Gwen's voice rough in her ear.

Their laughter tangled with moans, raw and breathless. Gwen's mouth slid against hers, wet and hungry, their teeth clashing once before Maggie laughed through it, tugging her closer anyway. The kisses were sloppy, unpracticed, but there was no hesitation — just urgency, the kind that said *we've waited too long for this.*

Maggie clutched at Gwen's shoulders, reveling in the hard press of Gwen's chest against hers, the steady weight she'd missed so much it made her dizzy. Her ankle throbbed in protest, but the ache was drowned out by everything else — the way Gwen's hands were greedy and reverent all at once, sliding up her thighs like she couldn't decide whether to claim or worship.

And there was something else, too. The intimacy of

knowledge. Gwen's hands finding her like they always had, without fumbling, without hesitation. The tilt of her jaw, the exact pressure of her mouth, the way her thumb stroked the inside of her thigh like she knew Maggie would shiver because she always had. That familiarity made it sharper, sweeter. Not just want but knowing. Not just heat but history.

Her fingers dug into Gwen's hair, messy and soft between her hands, holding her close, grounding herself in the solidity of her. And then the words tumbled out without her permission, whispering against Gwen's mouth between frantic kisses:

"Missed you, missed you, missed you."

It came out like a prayer, desperate and holy, half-choked with tears, her lips trembling against Gwen's as she said it again and again. Each repetition loosened something tight in her chest, untying knots she hadn't even realized she'd been carrying.

Gwen groaned low, almost breaking, and Maggie felt it vibrate through her whole body. She pulled her back into another kiss — softer this time, but no less intense — because it wasn't about proving anything anymore. It was about the relief of being known, of being touched by someone who had always seen her, always understood exactly what she wanted, what she needed. The way Gwen's hands moved like they still had a map of her drawn somewhere under her skin, every brush and press precise, not careful but confident, and Maggie felt herself unraveling faster because of it.

She gasped into Gwen's mouth as Gwen shifted down, pressing hot kisses across her collarbone, tugging the neckline of her dress lower. "You — always know—" Maggie panted.

"Of course I know," Gwen murmured against her skin, her voice rough. "You're mine." She slid her mouth over Maggie's nipple.

Maggie groaned at that, arching up, fingers clutching the back of Gwen's neck. It was the kind of line that should've sounded possessive, but in Gwen's mouth it felt like truth — like a promise, like a claim Maggie had been waiting to hear again.

Her giggles slipped through even as her breath caught. The van seat squeaked when Gwen moved lower, and Maggie burst out laughing. "Oh my god — this car is going to be so loud—"

"Then be quiet," Gwen said, smiling against her stomach, and then pushed her dress higher.

Maggie bit down hard on her lip, stifling the sounds that rose up anyway. She reached down, threading her fingers through Gwen's hair, tugging, guiding, desperate for more.

Gwen groaned in response, low and vibrating as her tongue slid against Maggie, and that sound almost undid her. Maggie gasped and laughed at the same time, pressing a hand over her mouth, her whole body trembling as Gwen worked her the way only she could. Not tentative. Not experimental. Just knowing. Exact. Perfect.

Maggie moaned, lost in the sensation. She'd forgotten what it was like — to be touched by someone who could read her without asking, who didn't have to guess, who knew her body like it was muscle memory. Every shift, every flicker, Gwen anticipated it, answered it, pushed her higher until Maggie was dissolving, crying out, her laughter catching on sobs as the release ripped through her.

She slumped back against the seats, hair stuck to her damp face, chest heaving. Gwen slid up, kissing her messily, tasting her smile.

Maggie tugged her closer, fumbling with Gwen's belt until Gwen swore softly and helped. Clothes shifted, another flurry of kisses, and then her fingers were slipping into Gwen's wet heat. Gwen reached for Maggie, fingers gentle as they slid over Maggie's clit, then inside.

"More," Maggie gasped, her own fingers matching Gwen's rhythm.

Gwen groaned, hips rocking. "I'm here. I'm not going anywhere."

That line broke her. Maggie clutched her tighter, hips stuttering, and then she was falling again, crying out into Gwen's mouth with ragged sounds of pleasure.

When Gwen followed, groaning her name, Maggie held her through it, heart pounding so hard it felt like her whole chest was lit up.

After, they collapsed into each other, a heap of limbs and sweat and laughter in the back of the fogged-up minivan.

Maggie pressed her face into Gwen's neck. "Enterprise is going to blacklist us for life."

Gwen chuckled, lips brushing her hairline. "Worth it."

Maggie tugged her back for another kiss, softer now, smiling into it. "So worth it."

THE NEXT MORNING, the lake was bright as glass, the sun already warming the autumn chill. Maggie hobbled out under the tent on her crutches, still flushed with the memory of the night before, and paused.

A long table had been pulled together, mismatched chairs tucked around it, covered in a patchwork of tablecloths. Platters of fruit and scrambled eggs and still-steaming biscuits filled the center alongside pitchers of orange juice and carafes of coffee. Someone had even set out jars of dahlias, a little wilted but cheerful anyway.

Everyone was there.

Pete, hair sticking up, still glowing from the night before, was feeding Gladys cantaloupe as Danica took pictures. Danica's mom and aunt were bickering gently over whether the bacon was too crisp. Kiera and Izzy sat pressed shoulder to shoulder, Izzy stealing bites off Kiera's plate while Kiera pretended not to notice. Lillian was across from Annie, animatedly telling some story with her hands, while Annie laughed so hard she snorted into her coffee.

And Gwen — Gwen was already seated, a mug cradled in her hands, watching Maggie come toward the table. When their eyes met, Gwen's smile was small but sure, a private thing Maggie felt in her chest.

For a second, Maggie just stood there, taking it all in.

Her friends. Her family. Her people.

The last few days had been chaos — swan attacks, ER visits, tears, confessions, laughter so loud it rattled the windows. But this... this quiet hum of voices, the way the morning light slanted through the tent, everyone calm and happy, felt like a calm exhale.

She eased herself into the seat Gwen had saved beside her. Gwen's hand brushed her knee under the table, steady and grounding.

Pete cleared her throat, raising her glass of juice. "We feel so lucky to be here with you, to share our love with you, and to feel your love in return. To yesterday. To today. To all of us making it through this weekend without losing any more limbs."

Everyone laughed, glasses lifted, the sound carrying out over the lake.

Maggie raised hers too, her chest so full it almost hurt.

Because for the first time in a long time, she believed it: They were going to be okay.

All of them.

Pete and Danica, already falling into the rhythm of teasing and tenderness that would carry them through. Izzy and Kiera, buzzing with contagious, reckless joy. Danica's mom and aunt, fussing like they'd adopted the whole table, which — honestly — they probably had. Even Lillian, who had shown up late but with her whole heart, sliding in like she'd been part of this crew forever.

And Gwen.

Gwen, who'd come when Maggie needed her most, who'd sat with her on the dock and finally said the words Maggie had been dying to hear. Who was sitting beside her now, their knees brushing under the table, her smile quiet and steady like it had nowhere else to be.

Maggie let the sounds wash over her — the laughter, the clink of forks, the gentle lap of the lake against the dock. For once, no sharp edge waited to cut through it. No lies hidden. Just warmth. Just presence.

She didn't know exactly what came next — therapy, hard talks, maybe another move or two before they found their footing again. But that was the point. She could finally imagine a future without flinching.

She took another sip of her juice, smiled into her glass, and thought: *This is what love feels like.*

This table. These people. This love — messy, bruised, stitched together with laughter and grace and forgiveness.

All of them.

EPILOGUE

MAGGIE

ONE YEAR LATER

THE FIRE HAD BURNED DOWN TO EMBERS, A STEADY ORANGE heartbeat inside the stone hearth. Maggie curled into the corner of the couch with a paperback open on her knees, reading the same sentence three times.

Upstairs, she could hear Gwen's voice: low, patient, and steady, the way it always was when bedtime stretched too long. A door shut. Water rushed briefly in the hall bath. Then a soft thump — Rosie's duck hitting carpet, probably. The twins had fought over the top bunk for a full ten minutes before deciding they hated it and wanted the bottom together. Rosie, in her "stories with feelings" era, had requested three: one funny, one brave, one with a funny and brave dragon. Gwen obliged. Of course she did.

Maggie marked her place and listened, smiling like a thief getting away with something. The book was good, but this was better.

She'd forgotten, once, how much she loved this part... the

in-between hum of their life. For a long time, the house had been brittle silence, every interaction sharp at the edges. Now it felt… whole. Different.

Gwen padded down a minute later, sweater sleeves shoved to her elbows, hair loosely falling around her face. She dropped onto the couch beside Maggie and cuddled close.

"All three down," Gwen reported, pressing her cold toes into Maggie's thigh. "Rosie's duck is fine. The twins' dignity, less so."

Maggie tilted her face for a kiss, got two. "Tragic."

They fell into quiet again, but not the old careful kind. This was the comfortable silence that came after long drives, unpacked groceries, and the chaos of discovering mittens in the wrong box. The chilly Colorado night pressed against the windows, deep and cold and full of stars. The fire popped and resettled.

Maggie traced the seam of Gwen's sleeve with her thumb and let her mind drift. Gwen hadn't touched her work computer all weekend. Maggie knew because she'd been keeping score — not to catch her out, but to marvel. A year ago, Gwen would've been tethered to her inbox even here on a family vacation in a small Colorado mountain town, frowning at deadlines while the kids begged for attention. Now, with her firm — her own firm — she chose the projects she wanted. Historic renovations, not leveled lots and boxy disgraces in their wake. No clients who treated her like a line item. No bosses reminding her she was almost but not quite enough. Gwen was finally building the work life she'd always deserved.

And Maggie was building, too. Just in smaller, messier ways. Found & Chosen gave her a paycheck and a reason to leave the house, sure, but it was more than that: Colette's chaos had a way of rubbing off on her. Between the stacks of vintage curiosities and treasures, Maggie had found herself laughing and creating art again. Little canvases smuggled onto the counter. Bowls from Tuesday night ceramics at the Y, lopsided but hers. She'd tucked some of them into Gwen's office — by the window, on the shelf behind the desk. Gwen never called them "cute." She'd once said, "This one makes the room feel less heavy." Maggie hadn't cried in front of her, but she'd come close.

Grief had a funny way of ebbing and flowing through her days, but she was learning to let the waves of it flow through her instead of pull her under. To accept that some days, the ache of missing her mom was so palpable, and other times, she went days without thinking about that heavy loss.

Gwen shifted, pulling Maggie closer. "Tomorrow's going to be chaos."

"Mm." Maggie could already see it: Pete and Danica pulling up with Gladys, who would barrel into the snow like she'd been released from a prison cell. Izzy and Kiera lugging in a tote full of board games. Eliza and Quinn racing through the house to claim their "kingdom." Their first family vacation, here in the mountains. A new place on purpose.

"I put extra blankets in the bunk room," Maggie murmured. "And sleds in the mudroom. Cocoa mix is on the counter."

"Prepared as ever," Gwen teased.

"Someone has to be. You saw the text — Eliza's in her 'more marshmallows than cocoa' era."

"What an era," Gwen repeated, amused.

Maggie snorted. "Better than her glitter glue era."

Gwen smirked. "You've taken over that one, right?"

"Ceramics is not glitter glue," Maggie said, mock-indignant, though her chest warmed at the acknowledgment. Because a year ago she hadn't believed she'd ever return to any of it — art, joy, softness. Now she had clay under her nails and paint smudges on her jeans again, and somehow Gwen didn't just accept it, she made room for it.

Maggie tipped her head against Gwen's. "You're thinking pancakes tomorrow, aren't you?"

"I may have bribed the children with them," Gwen admitted. "But yes. Pancakes."

"Chocolate chips?"

"Strawberries, if Pete doesn't eat them at midnight."

Maggie laughed softly into her shoulder. This was the good part. The part where life wasn't dramatic or fragile, just full of small things that stacked into something bigger.

She thought of Vegas and Michigan a year ago, of meddling friends and shared suites and jealousy and string lights and swans and forced laughter. Back then she hadn't trusted her face to remember how to smile. Now it was second nature.

Gwen's sleeve was pushed to her elbows, firelight catching the ink along her forearm. The window, the vines — it looked softer now somehow. Not because it had faded, but because Gwen had softened, too. The edges didn't remind Maggie of defenses anymore. They were just lines on skin, part of her.

Maggie's gaze drifted to the petals of her peony where it peeked from her sweater cuff. The colors had dulled a little, but the shape still held. Once, she'd thought Gwen's tattoo meant permanence and hers meant change. Now they looked like parts of the same story — structure and bloom, frame and color, two halves finally learning how to share the same space.

Gwen noticed her looking and smiled, small and knowing. "What?"

"I love you," Maggie said. "I love us."

"I love you," Gwen said, leaning in to kiss her.

The fire faded to glowing coals. Maggie should've gotten up to add a log, but she stayed. Gwen's weight pressed warm against her side, her hand covering Maggie's knee. Upstairs, the floors creaked once, then stilled. Outside, snow slid off the deck railing.

Maggie let the book slip shut in her lap and pressed her lips to Gwen's hair. A year ago, she'd been afraid to want this — afraid of what wanting could cost. Tonight, she wanted everything: the noise, the quiet, the people they loved tramping in tomorrow with wind-pinked cheeks, the way choosing each other had started to feel less like a gamble and more like a sure bet.

In the end, love wasn't what they'd lost. It was what they chose, again and again and again.

Pete named the conversation "Cabin Fever (Unmedicated)
".

PETE

🚗🚗🚗🚗 rolling out shortly. Gladys is
vibrating. pray for us.

DANICA

She's vibrating because you gave her half a
Pop-Tart.

PETE

she DESERVED it

MAGGIE

Is it even dawn? How are all you people
awake? Our kids aren't even awake yet.

IZZY

Cabin's gonna smell like wet pop-tart dog in
approximately 4 hours.

KIERA

Quinn just asked if Gladys is allowed in the
sled. I said no.

MAGGIE

As long as no one bleeds on the quilts.

GWEN

No bleeding when using the quilts as
sledding blankets, got it.

MAGGIE

Gwendolyn, I swear to god

PETE

GWENDOLYN?!

DANICA

NAME REVEAL ALERT.

IZZY

Gwendolyn!! A name for a queen!!

GWEN

Oh. Wow.

KIERA

Should we grab cocoa mix, your highness?

MAGGIE

Don't encourage her with that. It's on the counter waiting. Marshmallows too.

KIERA

Eliza would like me to reiterate "MORE MARSHMALLOWS THAN COCOA" so…

DANICA

My niece is a visionary.

GWEN

Maggie is pretending to drink coffee but actually keeping a mental spreadsheet of who will ruin the cabin first.

MAGGIE

Current projections: Gladys by morning, Pete by noon.

PETE

proud to accept this award 🏆

IZZY

I want everyone to remember who called it when Pete inevitably steals a sled.

KIERA

That's optimistic. She's going to steal a child's sled.

PETE

children are resilient

DANICA

That's what people say right before the ER visit.

MAGGIE

Not it.

GWEN

Definitely not it.

IZZY

Looks like Dr. Danica better be on duty.

DANICA

I hate you all.

PETE

you LOVE us, wendell

MAGGIE

Yay to officially transitioning to our getaways officially becoming family vacations

KIERA

With maybe a tiny bit of wedding planning?
While we're all together?

DANICA

YES

MAGGIE

YES

PETE

have you considered putting the entire wedding party on snowboards

IZZY

wait, I don't hate this

MAGGIE

HARD NO

GWEN

Drive safe everyone. I'm taking my wife back to bed. See you soon!

## ACKNOWLEDGMENTS

I owe endless gratitude to my wife, who read this book and side-eyed me seven thousand times to ask if I thought she worked too much. M, I love love love you (especially when I drink a little too much in Vegas and have to ask you if I'm going to die of a hangover.)

Heather, thank you for being such a kind and intelligent and thoughtful editor. This book is so much better for your touch.

Tina Maria, thank you for being the best and most patient beta reader.

Quinn, you have the voice and spirit of a perfect angel and you have brought these characters to life in a way I never thought possible. Thank you for the care and generosity you've shown this entire series.

Uncrustables, thank you for looking at the cover of this book a billion times and giving me your opinions, even when I am lazy and do not want to change it AGAIN. And also thank you for being total weirdos who make me smile every day.

And obviously thanks to the readers for joining me on this trip with this wild group of friends. I am going to miss this group so much, but I'm excited for what's to come, and I hope you stick around to see it.

ABOUT THE AUTHOR

Bryce Oakley is a Goldie-award winning author of sapphic romantic comedies and self-proclaimed pepperoni pizza connoisseur. She lives in Colorado with her wife, daughter, and a small herd of rescue animals.